NADINE LITTLE

Salvation Road

The Faction War Chronicles 2

LITTLE PUBLISHING

Sign up for my mailing list to get a free and exclusive prequel to *The Faction War Chronicles*. Discover the explosive origins of the Faction War ten years before the events of *Captivity*. Members of my mailing list get other bonus stuff and behind-the-scenes material.

Members are also the first to hear about my new books and discounts.

Join at nadinelittle.com

'What the hell we fighting for?
Just surrender and it won't hurt at all.'
Queen, *Hammer to Fall*

'Universe, do you think you can do something
about all the lonely souls?
The broken? The fallen stars?
There are so many of us.'
Rina Nath

1

Gayle from Revolutionary Front is the last person I expect to see in the ruin of Calders, even though I left her there. She was a little more animated and a lot less nibbled. The attention of the local wildlife has not improved her looks but she was no beauty queen when she was breathing. Too angular and sneery.

Torn flesh has shrivelled in the heat, flies buzzing happily in her hollowed abdomen. Old blood stains the ropes at wrist and ankle and paints her desperate struggles in the dust, the desolation of Calders a fitting backdrop.

No sign of John, the other person I left breathing when they cornered me in the mess of my former home. No gory trail of gristle and bone.

Is he still here, hunkered in the debris? Four days is a long wait in no man's land, even for revenge.

I should have avoided Calders on my way to the coast. There's nothing here but death and ghosts.

The skin prickles between my shoulder blades. I scan the rubble and squeeze the butt of the Glock 17 in my hand. Rats slink between scorched stone.

Should have also killed John instead of tying him up. Dead men can't stab me in the back.

And all the bastard does is try to kill me.

I hitch my forest-green rucksack higher, the material matching my t-shirt and combats and blending into the verdant flora of no man's land.

Not so much with the rocks and twisted metal of my faction.

My black boots kick up dirt and pulverised comrades, craters scarring the surface of the main road through the encampment, the broken asphalt melting in the sun. After fifteen minutes, grit coats my mouth, my senses dulled by the unending destruction. A distant hum teases the limit of my hearing. It throbs closer, vibrating in my chest and battling my heartbeat.

I frown at the sky.

It sounds familiar…

"You persistent son-of-a-bitch," I hiss and scramble for cover.

Stones jitter, clacking and tumbling in purls of dust. I hunker into a tunnel formed by a fractured wall and cover my ears. A vehicle glides into view, its cross-shaped shadow flitting over the encampment, four cyclone engines blazing cherry-red at the end of each arm.

The last WarCrier bought from Russia. People cowered beneath the deafening terror of its approach but the advanced warning became its downfall.

It suits John—loud, sucks up all the air.

The vehicle slows, descending into the ruins and sand-blasting the rocks in a cloud of white. I duck my head to protect my eyes, the stinging particles scouring my cheeks. Hinged supports crunch through a ribcage and settle on the barren ground. The engines power off and my ears weep in gratitude.

John, second in command of Revolutionary Front, leader in his own mind, strides down the silver ramp before it finishes extending. He's buff eye-candy if you ignore the cruel set of his mouth and the empty eyes. He fiddles with something on his throat.

"I know you're here, Anita." The voice enhancer bounces his words around the wreckage. "Took you longer than expected. I've really let my duties slide these past few days."

How the hell did he know—drone, remote camera? A sociopathic sixth sense?

"I'm glad you came back. Snatching you from Fellhill would've been harder but I was willing." He flicks his fingers and ten soldiers fan out between piles of broken stone.

He would never have captured me from the stronghold of Soldiers of the Lost. Fellhill has far greater defences than anything Revolutionary Front can counter, and that's without the ultimate weapon.

God, I miss her.

"You want to know what I've planned for you?" John strokes the knife at his hip, his glacier-blue eyes in constant motion. "I'll chain you in my room and cut you. Remove a small piece— a finger, a toe. Reckon I can keep you alive a few weeks, all slick and red."

He's always so confident in my death despite the many times I've escaped him. The deluded asshole. I didn't kill him because, technically, my original faction started the war. All the people I killed to avenge my sister and it turned out her murderer was in The People's Republic all along.

I'd felt guilty.

Well, screw that from now on. Killing keeps me safe.

"I hacked myself free in case you were wondering," John says.

"Did you say hello to Gayle? Harsh punishment, perhaps, but I like my women with more meat on their bones. And the dumb slag gave you our weapons."

She weakened herself by loving him and what did it bring her? Betrayal and death.

"Your delectable self will keep me entertained." His face twists from pleasant to snarling. "I'll show you I have no problem getting it up, you goddamn bitch."

I must learn not to insult the sexual prowess of psychopaths. When he and Gayle caught me, I goaded and disarmed him, though the bastard still cut me.

The wound on my left forearm pulses beneath the bandage. I cup my palm over it.

What a difference a few days make. Then, I was grief-stricken and distracted, returning to Calders to witness what Soldiers of the Lost had done. Now, I'm passing through on my way out of the war. Still some grief but zero distraction. No man's land is not the place to drop my guard.

There is no such place.

The soldiers disappear into the ruins. I crawl through the tunnel, away from John and his toxic self. My rucksack scrapes on concrete, chinks of light stabbing my eyes through narrow cracks in the stone. The exit blazes like a second sun. I wriggle out onto a scree slope and crouch behind a battered metal sheet at the bottom.

No crunch of footsteps, no heavy breathing apart from my own. John prattles in the background, the sound of his own voice his greatest love.

If he shut up for a second, he might get things done.

I scurry between clumps of debris, stopping at each to listen. John's voice fades. I comfort myself by picturing his fury when he finds nothing but my boot prints in the dust. It'll be the fourth time I escape him.

What a huge dent to his massive ego.

Smirking, I scoot to the next shelter of rock and nearly collide with a soldier circling around it from the other side. His rifle swings. I squeeze the bulb trigger of the electrigun strapped to my left arm. A bolt of electricity zips from the slim, grey weapon and strikes the man's chest. His eyes roll and he collapses, his heels drumming the hard ground.

I stroke the plastic casing of the gun. "Well don't you just do exactly what you say?"

First setting—stun. Check. I'll experiment with maim and kill later, especially if John sticks his annoying face anywhere near me.

I leave the soldier alive but gently smoking. The thought of John's increasing frustration buoys me through the rest of the shattered encampment. At the boundary, thick scrub spits me onto a road heading south-east. Wind-blown soil and vegetation creep in from the edges, the white line faded. Trees and overgrown fields replace the rubble and broken bodies. I hesitate at a rusted pole thrust in the ground, a tattered Saltire rippling in the hot wind and flashing the insignia of two crossed Glocks. My fingertips stroke the dog-tags beneath my t-shirt.

This is the beginning of my journey, not three days ago when I left Fellhill. Two more and I could be free.

It's what Ailsa would have wanted.

With a salute, I step out of The People's Republic and into the Borderlands.

2

The Borderlands contains no faction, only tribes of feral people pissed at everybody. They were trapped between us and the fence at the border, their desperation to escape turning to fury. It's a wild and dangerous place—another no man's land—but better than wandering to the coast through Unification Army territory.

Maybe they'll mistake me for a fellow lost soul stuck on the fringes of war.

Yeah, right. My equipment, weapons, dog-tags—hell, my personal hygiene—mark me as belonging to a faction.

It doesn't matter that it's no longer true.

The throb of the WarCrier rises from a hum to a drumbeat. The bastard has dogged me for the last four hours in widening circuits, taking advantage of the solar skin and self-perpetuating cyclone engines.

If John put this much effort into being a good second, his encampment wouldn't be a shithole on the brink of collapse.

I duck off the road into the gloom of an old spruce plantation and curl next to a trunk, sharp needles biting at my knees.

I'm a gentle forest creature. Fuck off, John.

The WarCrier glides away but other engines fill the void. I

crawl to the edge of the plantation through the rich fungus smell of soil. Four Darter FA-2 jets harry the larger WarCrier, zipping in and out like dragonflies, their double wings and bulbous cockpits glinting in the sun. Bullets scorch blackened trails across the solar skin. The WarCrier's cannons return fire, the heavy vehicle lumbering across the sky. It limps towards Revolutionary Front and the Darters gambol after.

Maybe they'll shoot it down. One can dream. I imagine John will survive, cockroach that he is. Perhaps he'll attack Fellhill, assuming I'll return there.

And they'll kill him.

Buxton isn't exactly lenient when it comes to people attacking his faction.

The peace of the next hour leaches the tension from my shoulders. I slither from an embankment onto what used to be the A7, a shattered road bombed by Soldiers of the Lost to hamper the flow of refugees. I dodge fissures and jagged mountains of rock, the route sheltered by wooded hills. Grit crunches between my teeth, my mouth coated in a paste no water can shift.

Where the hell is the other road?

I swipe at the damp hair sticking to my face and lose my footing on a hillock of stone, skidding to the bottom on my butt. Gorse clings to the sides of a deep valley, a hint of coconut filling the space. A dark shape flits through the thin veil of trees cloaking the top. I heave forward and scrabble behind a chunk of concrete. A puff of stone blooms at the peak and peppers me with shards. A woman in dappled fatigues squats in the scrub. She wrestles with an ancient rifle, darting glances in my direction.

What breed of psychopath is she? A Borderlander would

explain the crappy weapon.

Or maybe she's a Nationless survivor.

I swallow, and steady my Glock on the crumbling edge of concrete.

Better a failed refugee than a soldier from the faction I helped annihilate. Destroying their stronghold in Livingston allowed Revolutionary Front to swoop in and sack the other encampments.

I only wanted Livingston to suffer.

But in this war of lies, we all suffer.

My bullet catches the woman in the chest. She yelps and tumbles out of sight. Gun in hand, I jog away.

* * *

It turns out to be one of those days where everything with a pulse wants to rob me of mine.

My heavy rucksack barely hits the dirt in my chosen camping spot before the soil shudders under my foot. I skip back a step, the earth parting to reveal ivory burrowing spikes on a glistening pink head.

"You horrible little bastard," I say in greeting.

A semi-translucent membrane flickers across the abomination's shiny black eyes. Serrated, poison-tipped teeth flash in its elongated mouth. I stomp on its head. The squish flips my stomach, strings of tissue extending from my boot to the thing's mushed remains. I grimace at the fishy stench and wipe the mess of its skull on the ground.

Where there's one snorm, there are more. The damn things pop up everywhere. Engineering bioweapons to slaughter our enemies worked for a little while, until the escaped creatures populated no man's land.

A snake-earthworm splice—what were we thinking?

I walk an extra hour, hunger wobbling through my muscles, my tongue sticking to the roof of my mouth. The last dribble from my bottle only makes it worse.

Surely all this shit is character building?

Broadleaved trees cover the slopes of a gentle glen, the late afternoon sunlight stippling the leaves golden and dancing on the surface of a small river. I grab a water quality monitor from the rucksack and crouch on the bank among the rushes, dipping the prong in the burbling liquid, a black wire attaching it to the box. The machine beeps.

Safe to drink.

I set up camp, the novelty of the pod not worn off despite sleeping in it for the past three nights. Retracted, it's about the size and shape of a puffball mushroom, the solidness balanced in my cupped palm. I place it on the ground and slide backwards, pressing a blue button on the control pad. The pod hisses and expands to chest height. A black dome on the flattened roof shelters the laser security system. It uses motion and heat sensors, unlike the facial recognition of the laser-cameras protecting encampment boundaries that originally came from Africa. The laser doesn't activate if the control pad is outside the pod, even if I press the button by accident. A lid protects the switches from being rolled on at night and turning off the security.

I push the green button and the pod vanishes.

Amazing.

My outstretched fingers touch a cool, smooth surface almost imperceptible to my eyes. It ripples like a particle beam fence but, rather than heat, it's an effect of the flexible display transmitting a scan of the surroundings. It cloaks itself by showing only what I'd see if it wasn't there.

Technology from Soldiers of the Lost, courtesy of the Scottish Army. It was built into a stealth vehicle named the Crocodile. Buxton, their leader, and mine for a short while, was pretty damn smug about it.

Among other things.

I press a black button and the portal slides open—a magical floating doorway to the pearlescent interior. There are no discernible bulbs, only a soft opal light and a spongy floor. Pushing the black button again seals me inside. The red switch activates the laser.

It's the safest anyone can be in the no man's land of no man's land.

I cook dinner, adding rechargeable heat blocks to a pot of water, a silver bag of spaghetti bobbing in the bubbles. I eat it fast and burn my mouth, lulled by the comfort of routine.

No one to please, no orders to fulfil or assignments to complete.

The first three days were blissful. I headed south-east from Soldiers of the Lost on a familiar route through the edge of Revolutionary Front and the ruin of Nationless. It extended my journey to the coast but avoided Stirling, the stronghold of Revolutionary Front, and Saorsa to the east in the Kingdom of Fife.

Did John and I pass each other, separated by a whisper of vegetation? Him, pissed and exhausted, returning to his depressing excuse for an encampment. Me, battered and scarred, heading for salvation.

Spot the moron.

Most people would call me the crazy one, blundering

around in no man's land, even with my rucksack of precious survival goodies. But I expected more danger. Three attempts on my life seems trivial. Hell, my comrades tried to kill me more times than that and they were supposed to be on my side.

Maybe this suicidal bid for sanctuary will be the easiest thing I've ever done.

3

The air shimmers above concrete, the sky bleached white, and I actually miss the dampness of winter that brings boot-sucking mud and ice-frosted bones. Pollen powders each breath with the taste of flowers. I scrub sweat-darkened hair off my face and slug another mouthful of water, my explosive sigh scaring a herd of roe deer. They bound away in a white flash of rumps into rank agricultural fields. Oats battle the weeds for space, their seed heads drooping in the heavy heat.

Dense trees swallow the road, the shaded cool hushing the birdsong and hunching my shoulders, my hand tense on my gun.

Nothing good happens to me in the gloom of woods—abandoned, betrayed, chased by slavering abominations and baying soldiers.

I pick up my pace, the tarmac sucked into the dirt to leave a tawny scar curving deeper into the forest, dappled by sunlight and grass. Dark metal flits between the trunks of the trees ahead, trailed by the purr of an engine. My steps falter to a stop in a swirl of dust.

Who the hell is driving out here?

I rub my eyes.

Not a mirage.

Shit.

I sprint off the path, the crunch of foliage drowning everything out. I crouch in a raspberry thicket and hold my breath, slender prickles teasing my hair. The engine dies. Doors thunk. Voices.

Hide. *Hide.*

The understorey thickens but cowering in a bush doesn't seem good enough. There are no hollowed logs or caves or holes.

Bury myself in the leaf litter?

I lurch over a root and land on my knees, blinking in surprise.

For god's sake, control yourself. Do you want to be a prisoner again?

No. No, I do not.

I wobble to my feet, the trunk of an oak offering some support, and squint into the branches of green, wavering leaves.

No one ever looks up.

Men call to each other. The bastards sound excited.

I brace my boot in a knot and grab a low branch, hoisting myself clear of the ground. I reach for another, wincing at the throb in my lacerated muscle, the grip of my left hand weak and burning through my forearm. The rucksack threatens to drag me down, each metre gained more like a mile. A bough snaps with a soft crack. I drop, leaving my heart and stomach in the canopy.

I'll land at their feet, too stunned to fight. They'll beat me, rape me. Men are sex-crazed mor—

The rucksack catches and jerks my shoulders. I wedge my boots in the crook of a branch near the trunk, my legs bent at an awkward angle to hold my weight.

"Come out, come out, wherever you are," a voice sings from below.

I freeze. Someone laughs off to the side. Two men prowl through the raspberries, their guns sweeping the foliage. Long hair hangs lank over patchwork clothes.

"See her yet?"

"Nope."

"Come out now, little lady, and we promise not to hurt you."

A low snigger comes from beyond my hiding place. "Too much."

There are at least four of them, possibly more, their position marked by their snapping path through the trees.

I shift, trying to relieve my screeching joints.

The men search the forest in a grid for what feels like hours, yelling and joking, their enthusiasm for the hunt apparently undiminished despite their lack of success.

Then one of them triggers a mine.

4

The explosion shivers through the trees, close enough to hear the patter of earth on leaves.

Or body parts.

Someone screams.

Probably body parts.

The sun dips towards the horizon in rays of bronze. The grip of my hand keeps me in the tree despite my numb, useless legs. A headache sizzles down my neck and jaw.

Of course I get the persistent assholes, not your normal lazy bastards who give up after twenty minutes.

Frantic voices converge on the screams. Shrieks and the crunch of vegetation swell towards me, magnified beneath the canopy. Four men thunder into view, cradling their injured comrade, his legs missing mid-thigh. The shredded remnants of trousers cling to his lower body, red dripping in fat drops beneath belts cinched tight. He meets my eyes and chokes mid-howl. We stare at each other but his comrades spirit him away.

An engine roars. Tyres skid.

My exit from the oak is more graceless flop than controlled descent. I slump at the base, massaging my legs and hissing as blood scorches my cramped muscles. I heave myself up and limp deeper into the woods, examining each patch of ground before stepping on it.

Are the Borderlanders monitoring the roads? How far will I have to crash through the jungle to be clear of them?

Stealth and vegetation do not mix.

I stumble down a slope. My shaky legs refuse to hold and tumble me to the bottom on my face. I jar my injured arm, a bolt of pain crackling to my shoulder.

"Fuck," I gasp, cradling it to my chest and thrusting to my feet.

The rucksack crushes my ribs and makes it hard to breathe. I shove it off and pace, carving a path in the undergrowth, steadying myself and cursing under my breath.

This is what I expected from no man's land—slobbering abominations, slobbering men. I want to be free of it.

Please, god, let the rest of the world be more normal than this.

Leaves rustle above me.

I forgot to look up.

My heart gives a single, furious thud. A weight slams into my back and drives me to the ground, my air whooshing out. A knee jabs my spine and cold metal kisses the base of my skull. My electrigun and Glock are removed while I lie stunned, my mouth full of leaves.

Did one of the men stay behind?

Patient, very patient.

"Where are you from?" a voice barks. "What are you doing here?"

So much for thinking my days of being pinned and vulnerable were over.

I fight the twisting in my gut and peer at the man out of one eye, unruffled professional that I am, my cheek cradled by the dirt.

Scruffy black hair frames high cheekbones. Mud streaks his skin, cuts and grazes scabbing on his arms below the ragged line of a navy t-shirt. He hooks the chains of my dog-tags out the back of my top without waiting for an answer.

How rude.

He frowns and spears me with eyes of a startling cobalt-blue, almost violet. "Why two? Which one are you from?"

Fucking twenty-questions. I'm tired of this shit.

"Neither," I say. "I'm starting a collection."

The butt of his gun raps me on the head.

"Ow! For fuck's sake, I'm from Calders. They were destroyed, so I went to Fellhill."

He doesn't need the details. I'm not about to tell him everything while he grinds himself into my spine.

"You're The People's Republic?"

Are his eyes more violet? How does he do that? It makes me dizzy.

He leans closer, a mixture of sweat and male and forest. *Earthy*.

He yanks out his dog-tags and shoves them in my face, the embossed metal blurred through my one available eye. I blink and the words swim into focus.

Oh, *crap*.

Nationless, Livingston.

5

"Your faction destroyed my home," the man snarls, his indigo eyes shadowed by the sharp planes of his face.

"I had nothing to do with it"—stop there, for the love of god—"though you goddamn deserved it."

Whoops. I guess I still haven't learned when to shut my mouth.

The man straightens, his dog-tags settling on his chest. "How would you know what we deserved? You don't know the first thing about us."

And he doesn't know the first thing about me. I'm just a stranger in the woods, one from a faction he hates. My name means nothing to him. Wick must not have bragged about torturing Ailsa Carmichael's little sister.

"You abused the poor woman," I say. "What did you expect her to do, leave you untouched?"

Swallow, inhale.

Can the man feel my heart pounding beneath his knee?

I fist my hand in the leaf litter, slowing my breathing and willing the bile to stay in my stomach.

"No," he finally says with some reluctance.

"Then what are you pissed about? You would've done the same in her position."

"She's—the reason—my brother—is dead."

Words dry and stick to my tongue.

Say something, you idiot! Before he suspects! If he finds out who I am, he'll torture me worse than Wick.

"I—I'm sorry. Losing family—is worse than anything."

God, I know that. My sister's assassination, alongside the other party leaders', started this war and I spent the last decade slaughtering in her name. My parents retired to Kent before the independence rebellion, though they were always so proud of Ailsa.

Maybe they're dead, too.

The man's lip curls. "I don't need your pity."

"It's not pity."

"Whatever. I don't need it." The gun stays on my head. "What happened to her?"

I almost say, *"Who?"*

"She died. When Fellhill attacked Calders."

"Why did they take you in?"

"Maybe I impressed them."

"Then what're you doing way down here?"

"None of your damn business."

He smirks. "And there we were, getting all friendly. Stand up."

The suffocating weight disappears. I suck in a deep breath and roll onto my side, pushing up on one elbow.

"Why?" I say.

His navy combat trousers are torn at both knees and caked in dust, his black boots scratched and dull.

"Because I'll shoot you if you don't," he says.

Fair enough.

The electrigun is already strapped to his left arm, a Browning tucked in his waistband. I stand and he points my Glock at my head.

Heat flares in my cheeks and crackles to my fingertips. "Your gun's empty, isn't it?"

"Yup."

"You arrogant son-of-a-bitch."

My own move, come back to bite me on the ass. Did I look this smug?

"I'm surprised that mouth hasn't got you killed," he says.

"There's still time."

He snorts. "Put your hands on that tree and spread your legs."

"Why?"

"Would you just bloody do it?"

I stomp to the indicated sycamore. Maybe he'll frisk me rather than molest me. Though he could do both.

Don't throw up. Don't throw up.

I place my hands on the rough, greyish surface and stare at the orange patches where the bark has flaked away. The man kicks my foot and I widen my stance.

"Don't move."

"Yes, boss."

"Seriously, how are you not dead?"

Ridiculous dumb luck. And by being good at killing psychotic assholes.

The man runs his fingers through my hair. I flinch under the heat of his touch. His hand moves to my neck, following the collar of my t-shirt. He pats my back and I hunch.

What if he feels the scars? Maybe they won't register. Whipping is a common method to discipline unruly soldiers, not simply for torture.

He already knows I'm a mouthy bitch.

His fingers don't linger. He searches the rest of me for weapons, confiscating the SL2 and knife from my boot, plus the holster around my waist. His touch stays professional.

So one—okay, two—of Livingston's soldiers has a sliver of decency. Big whoop.

The man gestures with my Glock. "Walk."

Must not stick out my tongue. Must not be childish.

I march into the trees but the crunch of his steps doesn't follow.

Will he shoot me in the back, the fucking coward?

I whirl around fast enough to stumble and he cocks an eyebrow, settling the rucksack on his shoulders. My jaw clenches.

I'll get it back.

Grass whips my legs and carpets a small clearing, wildflowers folding their petals in the dwindling light. A wren scolds me from a branch, its little tail stuck up like a middle finger.

What a picturesque place to die.

"Stop. Sit against the tree."

I lower myself to the dirt and lean on a silver birch.

What is he going to do, shoot little bits off of me until my eyes dull? His leader would be proud.

Revulsion shivers down my spine and burrows into my gut.

"Put your arms behind you, around the trunk."

I hesitate. "I'm sorry someone from Calders destroyed Livingston but what else do you want me to say?"

"There's nothing you can say."

Great. A stubborn bastard.

Papery bark scratches my skin. The man steps behind the tree and binds my wrists. I squirm, my heels furrowing the dirt, the narrow trunk surprisingly solid against my spine. The stitches in my arm stretch in a burning line and pulse pain to my fingertips. I struggle to school my face when the man appears around the birch, showing him calm confidence instead of panting, wide-eyed panic.

He stands near my boots, the Glock at his side. "What happened to your arm?"

Like he cares.

"I'll tell you if you untie me."

"I don't think so."

"Then don't bother to fucking ask if you're going to leave me to die."

He shifts his feet, his violet eyes guarded. The flick knife from my boot hits my chest and drops into my lap.

"If you cut yourself loose, maybe you'll survive out here. If not… It's more of a chance than my brother had."

"I didn't do anything! Are you not goddamn listening?"

He turns away.

I fight not to strain against the rope. "Wait!"

"You might have enough time to get free before dark. I'd start now."

"You purple-eyed bastard! It's a war, people die."

He reaches the edge of the clearing. "You're right, people die."

I tug at the bonds. Pain sizzles up my arm, my chest squeezed tight.

"What was I—" My breath whines inward. Stupid, stupid, stupid! "What was she supposed to do? What the hell would you have done? Answer me that—what the fuck would you have done any different?"

His words drift to me, his slim body swallowed by the trees.

"Absolutely nothing."

6

Did John and Gayle feel this awful desperation? Did they curse themselves hoarse and struggle until the need for oxygen forced them to stop? I tied them up and abandoned them to the mercy of nature.

She can be a cruel bitch. As can I, it seems.

Will I be alive when the abominations eat my face? Unable to protect myself. Nothing to do but shriek.

I suppress a shudder and tilt my hips, the knife sliding off my lap. I shuffle 180 degrees on my butt, each movement pulling the wound on my arm and creaking through my shoulders. A panic attack nips at the edge of my composure, clenching my stomach and encouraging me to *scream-struggle-fight!* My sweating fingers brush the knife. I snatch it and squeeze it in my hand.

John would've had a harder time wriggling up into the wreckage to where I'd balanced his knife on some rubble. Purple-eyes practically handed it to me. John didn't even slaughter my sister. He's just a dick who keeps trying to kill me.

I press the button on the handle of the knife and the blade snicks free. I saw at the rope, the knife skittering along the coated surface to bite my wrist. Darkness bleeds into the forest, the light murkier every time I glance up from frowning at my lap. The rope yields a little under the tug of my stiffened fingers. I cut faster, the movement warming my muscles as night sucks the heat from the air. Strands ping and the rope slackens.

What the hell is this thing made of, steel?

The blade slips, slicing another fiery line across my skin. I growl at it.

An answering growl rumbles from the dark.

My head snaps up. A shape parts the gloom off to my right, its powerful forelegs whispering through the undergrowth. Nostrils flare, warm air puffing over the goose-pimpled flesh of my arms. I clamp my teeth on a whimper, my brain struggling to piece together the nightmare stalking towards me.

Tusks curl from both jaws, a wolf body sloping to a looped, quivering tail. The abomination paws the ground, mucus dribbling from its snout. Another growl vibrates deep in its chest.

I hold my breath and saw at the rope. The boar/wolf thing snarls, tiny eyes glowing in its piggy face.

Maybe I should stop staring at it.

I feign interest in my boots and peek at the beast out of the corner of my eye, trying to look submissive.

It charges.

The rope snaps.

I swing the knife around, the blade minuscule in my slippery hand. The creature tosses its head, its tusks arcing for my face. I roll and slash. The abomination thumps into the birch in a shiver of leaves. I scramble to my feet and the beast lunges with a roar. Liquid pulses, black in the dimness. The creature stumbles, its head drooping, but it wobbles another step before it flops onto its side and grunts its final breaths into the crushed grass.

I watch it until my eyes burn and night swallows the detail.

It's definitely dead. It's not going to leap to its paws/trotters and rip out my kneecap.

But its friends might if I stay here gawping.

I hustle to a decent-sized tree on the edge of the clearing and detract my blade, tucking the knife into my pocket.

"Goddamn son-of-a-bitch," I say on a sigh and start to climb.

It's no less painful without the rucksack, and harder in the dark. I bang my head on every branch, curse every twig that pokes me in the eye. One jab away from blinding myself, I settle against the trunk, my legs dangling on either side of a thick bough. A soft wind rustles the leaves and plays in my hair, stirring the grass in the clearing.

An endless night stretches ahead, straining to see shapes gathering in the black, listening for the crunch of foliage.

I hug my arms to my chest.

The man will be snuggled in my sleeping bag, sheltered by the laser security system, a smirk on his face. It's probably the first time he's relaxed his guard in the two months since I destroyed his encampment.

How has he survived this long? No food, no way to test water for toxins, no refuge. *No hope.* It suggests a level of skill beyond even my abilities and I've lived through a lot of shit. He refused to give up, no matter the odds.

Good god, he reminds me of myself. How disconcerting.

I stroke the knife through the material of my combats. Cold dread unfurls in my stomach and claws up my ribs.

What am I going to do—track him in the daylight, praying

he's not lounging in the pod with the laser on? Will I see the ripple and realise what it means before my brain cooks? Or head to the coast and hope to secure transport with only a knife? The boar/wolf abomination would feed me for a few days.

I wrinkle my nose.

The damn thing smells of spoiled milk and burnt hair. And screw climbing down to gut it in the dark, or risking a fire.

I'm crippled. Dead. What use is a knife in a world of guns and teeth?

Maybe the man isn't so lenient after all.

7

I dream.

The trunk of the birch bruises my spine, my hands curled in my lap, sunlight warm on my cheeks. The man points his gun—*my* gun—and his warrior eyes blaze violet. The black feathers in his wings flash highlights of purple and emerald, stroking the air and wafting a strangely intoxicating scent into my face.

He smells like spring.

"Time to wake up," he says and pulls the trigger.

The bullet thuds into my chest, blood spreading in a circle on my t-shirt. I touch my fingertips to the wound and raise a trembling hand.

"Wait," I choke, drowning on the taste of copper.

His feral smile steals my breath. Or maybe it's the chunk of metal in my lung. He pulls the trigger until the gun clicks empty. Liquid bubbles up my throat and spills out my mouth. My heart stutters, stops, stutters. The man walks away. I cough and gurgle and fight to form words.

Don't leave me!

He disappears in a shaft of sunlight, dancing motes flecked gold in his wake.

I struggle alone so I die alone.

* * *

I startle awake and topple to the side to be greeted by air. Vertigo swoops in my stomach. I thump onto my right arm, my head bouncing on the ground in a scatter of grass awns, the stalks swaying in front of my nose. I flop onto my back, a swirling turquoise resolving itself into leaves and sky.

"Mother-*fucker*," I say, hugging my throbbing arm. I clench and unclench my hand, rolling my shoulder to be sure it isn't broken.

"You really have a mouth on you."

Am I still dreaming?

I perform a rather impressive sit-up considering I'm disorientated from the fall. The man stands between the carcass of the boar/wolf thing and the tree he bound me to. His skin shines pale and clean in the morning light. A dark green t-shirt and trousers fit him perfectly.

How lucky for him. He can wear all the clothes in the rucksack without looking like an idiot. Apart from the underwear. And his scuffed, black boots.

My gun rides in its holster around his slim hips, the hilt of a knife sticking out of his boot. No rucksack.

The cautious bastard. Not knowing if I'd be free and pissed, or reduced to bloodied bones, he must have stashed it.

I tuck my legs and rise to my knees. "Sorry if it offends your delicate sensibilities but I can't say 'darn it' when a good 'fuck' will do."

I wobble to my feet while he seems to wrestle with his expression. My hand slides towards my pocket.

He raises the electrigun strapped to his left arm. "Take the knife out and toss it over here. If I see a hint of blade, I'll shoot you. This thing is on the highest setting."

"That *thing* is an electrigun," I say.

Am I fast enough to unsheathe the blade and toss it before he squeezes the trigger? Probably not.

Throwing knives aren't my speciality.

"Great. I will electrocute your arse if you try to pin that knife in me."

Glowering, I slide the flick-knife from my pocket and clench it in my fist.

I need my weapons. My rucksack.

I lob the handle and step towards the man, tensed to leap. The folded knife hits his chest. He flinches but doesn't grab for it and it disappears into the grass.

The bastard is good. Dammit.

He scoops the knife from the ground, his eyes never leaving me. I swallow but meet his gaze, unsettled by the colour.

It must be a mutation. No normal person has eyes that blue and violet.

"You back to finish me off?" I say as he continues to stare. My brain screams *unarmed and vulnerable, unarmed and vulnerable!* "What happened to giving me a chance?"

"You lied to me."

I fight to keep my features blank. "I don't know what you're talking about."

"I know who you are. Wick showed us video of you in the torture chamber. You—"

The buzzing in my head smothers the rest of his words. My stomach attempts to crawl out of my mouth. I sag against a tree.

"You saw—what he did?" I wheeze.

No. *No,* I can't bear it if he sneers at me, mocks me for

blubbering. For soiling myself. For being pitiable and weak.

Bile scalds my throat, white spots sparkling across my vision with each heartbeat.

"Only your arrival," he says. "Jesus, woman, take a breath."

I slump to my knees and pant into the grass. "Fuck. *You.*"

The quaver in my voice lessens the effect. I concentrate on breathing, willing my stomach to unclench and not embarrass me further by vomiting.

It's been a while since my last panic attack. I'm supposed to be escaping this shit.

Why do I have to meet the man who must surely be the last survivor of Nationless? The only person left to shove my horrific ordeal in my face, whether he witnessed it or not.

Thank god he didn't.

"What did Wick do to you?"

I claw myself upright on the bark of the nearest tree and brace my hand against the trunk.

"As if you don't know. You lived with him. Did you all watch his videos like a—like a goddamn movie?"

Huge screens graced the roofs of the buildings in Livingston. A stage for Wick to post his torture videos in colourful high definition. Maybe his soldiers picked favourites, placed bets. Who will scream, cry, lose control of their bodily functions? Who will wish for death?

Me and fucking everyone who suffered under Wick.

But I'm the only one who escaped.

My heart aches. My fingers rub my chest but I force myself to stop.

Get a grip. You've shown him too much already.

I fooled myself into believing I was getting better. But a single mention catapults me back there—terrified, broken and lost.

Worthless.

"He forced us," the man says. "Most of us. There was no choice."

The electrigun hangs at his side. His eyes are dark, drowning. I look away.

"No choice but to survive as best you could," I mutter at my boots.

"I'm sorry."

I blink at him.

"I'm sorry you were tortured."

Should I apologise for killing his brother? Or will it only remind him why he hates me? I am sorry but I couldn't have done anything else.

"Can we stop talking about it, please?"

He nods after a pause and his hand drops to the Glock. "Start walking that way."

I open my mouth.

"Nope," he says. "No questions about why or where or any sassy comments."

I release my death-grip on the tree, glad my legs no longer shake. I stand like a normal person, a soldier. No flinching or flopping at his feet, my spine straight and stiff. I pretend the last five minutes were a hallucination.

"Just one question. No sass."

He rolls his eyes. "Woman, do you never give up?"

"It's one of my best qualities. And my name is Anita, not woman."

He laughs then seems surprised, mustering his face into a frown. "Fine, *Anita*, one question."

The trace of an accent makes my name exotic.

"Are you going to kill me?"

The hint of humour leaks from his features. He watches me but says nothing and I fight not to squirm.

Why didn't I keep my mouth shut?

He sighs. "Not right now."

"Comforting."

He snorts. "Question answered. Walk."

I head into the trees, my boots crunching on foliage. He directs me with gestures and monosyllabic grunts.

Where is he taking me? Further into the wild so no one will hear the gunshot? He could use the electrigun. Or is he planning on keeping me as some kind of companion?

He's been alone a while.

I glance over my shoulder. He meets my gaze and my stomach flips. Swallowing, I turn away.

The trees thin into scrub and tangled grass, piles of broken stone and rusted corrugated metal scattered between. Farm machinery arches out of the vegetation like a prehistoric creature.

"Wait." The man kicks over a sheet of metal, exposing the rucksack covered in flecks of bronze. "Put it on."

I approach and he steps out of reach.

So very wary. *Dammit.*

At least I have my rucksack back. I could run, if it weren't so heavy.

No wonder everyone in Fellhill is a muscular giant.

I heave the bag on with my one good arm.

"Keep walking," the man says.

The land slopes downhill from the remains of the farm. An electricity pylon appears out of a clump of hawthorn, the upper portion collapsed. Ivy veils the lattice, slowly tearing it apart, broken wires snaking into the grass. We cross a dusty track and skirt the ruins of a small village, slogging through overgrown fields.

The silence itches between my shoulder blades.

If my captor is talking, he's not thinking about ways to kill me or make me suffer.

Funny, I thought the same right before Wick tortured me.

I clear my throat. "What's your name?"

"Why?"

I roll my eyes although he can't see. "I'm making conversation. You know my name."

We reach a burn obscured by trees. I slip in the mud, my boots splashing in water, and haul myself up the other side using hummocks of grass.

"It's Blake."

Weird name. Weird eyes. Who the hell is he?

I stop myself from asking his brother's name since I don't have a death wish but I struggle to form another polite line of inquiry.

"Well, Blake, I'd say it was nice to meet you but that would be a lie."

Sure, Anita, goad the guy. Much better.

"Didn't stop you before," he says.

I frown. "Didn't help me, either."

He smirks at me.

We swish through some rushes, the ground slurping beneath our boots, and discover another abandoned village plus a huge, blackened warehouse, a whiff of charred wood clinging to the remains.

"Used to be for grain storage."

I jump at Blake's voice.

"Probably one of the first places to be looted, once people realised you couldn't eat weapons."

I shrug one shoulder. "Weapons then food. We had our priorities in order."

Tall grass succeeds to elder and hawthorn. A block of trees extends to the horizon, the shade welcome in the growing heat of the day.

"Where are we going?" I say.

We, like it's a mutual decision instead of me being marched to my doom.

"Away from habitation."

Isn't he a font of information? And how does he know where the Borderlanders call home?

We seem to be heading south-west, every step taking me further from salvation. Further from the only journey I want to make. I don't want to be here, trapped in this country. I've been a prisoner enough times already. I want out. I need to get out.

I trip on a branch and fall to my knees. The weight of the rucksack crushes my chest, my heart thrashing against the pressure. I dig my fingers into the cool mulch and concentrate on the slick wetness of dead leaves, the smell of earth.

Blake steps in front of me. "What are you doing?"

"Enjoying the scenery."

He cocks his eyebrow towards my hand fisted in the dirt. I wipe my palm on my trousers.

Will he shoot me if I refuse to go with him?

Probably.

I wobble to my feet and he sweeps his arm out. I sigh and keep walking, deeper and deeper into the Borderlands.

8

We never reach the end of the trees.

Blake forces me to walk into early evening, pausing only for food and a few minutes respite.

If he plans on exhausting me to stop me from running, he's doing a pretty good job.

"Set camp here." He perches on a rock, cool and unruffled, his legs stretched out.

The river we followed for the past hour widens into a pool, forming a secluded basin circled by the forest.

A place of peace and beauty, if I weren't held captive by the last soldier of the encampment I hate most in the world.

No one will hear me scream. No one will care if they do.

I slide the rucksack off, my t-shirt sticking to me. I expand the pod on the edge of fine, white sand, the portal facing a small waterfall.

Will the view offer some comfort after whatever Blake does to me in reparation for his brother?

I shudder and toss the sleeping gear inside the pod, crouching next to the rucksack, unable to keep from glancing at him. His cobalt eyes watch me. I manage not to flinch but he aims the electrigun.

"Take your hand out of the bag."

Damn.

The control pad slips from my fingers. I straighten and wave my empty hand at him. He rolls gracefully to his feet.

"Get in the pod."

"Can I wash first?"

He smirks. "Be my guest."

I bend towards the rucksack.

"Nice try. Back up."

I raise my hands and step away.

Blake puts the control pad into his pocket and hands me a soap capsule. "The water's safe. I've drunk it before."

How far has he travelled during his months in no man's land?

He settles himself on the sand and leans against the rock, the electrigun balanced on his knee.

"You're going to watch me?" I say.

"You clearly can't be trusted, so yes. Keep your clothes on if it makes you feel better."

"How generous."

I kick off my boots and pad into the pool in my socks. I gasp but wade deeper instead of dancing out. The water is glorious once the initial shock ebbs. I halt when it reaches my chest. Keeping my back to the shore, I break the soap capsule over my head and work it down my body, clothes and all. Dirty bubbles clump on the surface. I dunk myself under to rinse my hair then slosh out.

"That's why I didn't recognise you immediately," Blake says. "You looked like this—darker hair, wet."

Wick graciously let me shower before he tortured me. Will Blake be the same?

I stub my toe on a buried stone and swallow a curse.

No. I'll kill him first.

I stalk to the pod in a trail of drips and dry myself, quickly pulling on green combats matching the pair Blake is wearing. I don't notice the t-shirt is his navy one until I see the ragged sleeves. It's washed but smells of him.

Subtle, distracting.

He ducks in the doorway before I can change.

"Wearing my clothes already?"

I cross my arms, ignoring my blush. "You're wearing my clothes."

He tosses the rucksack inside, spreading my sopping clothes over the rocks. Heat flares when he picks up my underwear. I hide my face and scoot towards the back of the pod. He climbs in. The portal slides shut. The lock thuds, enclosing us in a tiny, intimate space.

Nowhere to run. Unless I claw my way through the stiffened material.

Blake draws a length of rope from the rucksack. "Hold out your hands."

"I need to change my bandage."

He glances at my arm and passes me the plastic bag of materials. I unravel the saturated dressing, trying to keep my muscle relaxed. I pat the wound dry and clean it with an antiseptic wipe. It appears to be healing well, little redness or swelling visible. It'll leave a nice, long scar.

Neat, since John kept his blade sharp.

"What happened?" Blake says, his voice soft in the confines of the pod. "I actually wanted to know."

What the hell does he need, my tragic life story? Will it let him forgive me for killing his brother and destroying his encampment?

I concentrate on re-bandaging my forearm, confused by the intensity on his face. "John Anders tried to gut me."

The silence expands, as though Blake expects more. I smooth the gauze and secure it in place.

He sighs. "Hold out your hands, wrists together."

I frown but don't move.

"Are you going to make me do this the hard way?"

I bare my teeth. "Probably."

He lunges but I bat his hand away. His palm blocks my fist and he wraps his slim fingers around my wrist, yanking until I sprawl across his lap. He forces both arms behind my back, my heart hammering against his thigh.

"You're getting tied up, Anita. Your choice is whether your hands are behind you—which will hurt more—or in front. Keep struggling and I'll truss you up so tight, you won't be able to move."

"Goddamn you," I pant.

He relaxes, easing out from under me. I jerk one wrist from his grip and shove myself up. His body pins me to the floor. He thrusts my arms straight and sits on my shoulders, crushing my ribs.

"This is really not endearing you to me," he says through gritted teeth.

"*Good*."

"You might want to reconsider since I'm the one deciding if you deserve to live."

He binds my wrists together with quick, sure movements. I don't have enough air to berate him. He releases my arms and spins around to straddle my butt.

I tug at the rope. "You don't have to do this. We've both lost someone to the war."

Warm hands circle my ankles. I tense to kick.

"Yes, but I didn't kill your sister," he whispers.

So he does know who I am.

I wince, the guilt as solid as a punch.

No! He has no right to make me feel bad. He's never been at the mercy of Wick in his torture chamber.

He has no right.

"That's not fair." I mean for it to be a growl but it comes out a wheeze. "You have *no* idea… You can't just—"

He ties my ankles as tightly as my wrists and slides his weight off. I wriggle onto my side and sit up, my hair tousled over my face. Blake kneels, his head bowed, black hair kissing his cheekbones. He lifts his gaze and spears me with shimmering violet eyes.

So much pain.

"That's not fair," I breathe.

I pull at the ropes.

I can't move. Can't run.

My chest squeezes tight.

"I had to do… I had no… I had to. I *had* to." Snapping my mouth shut stops me from saying it over and over.

My fingers scrabble at the knots but they blur under my hands. Horrible gasping sounds shiver out my throat. I tug at the loops, claw at the knots but neither loosens. The sharp taste of metal fills my mouth.

I don't hear Blake calling my name until his hands grip my shoulders and shove my head down. I almost knee myself in the face before I open my legs, my ankles fastened together.

"Breathe, Anita. Just breathe."

One hand stays on my back, not rubbing. I focus on it, on the warmth through my t-shirt. My panting slows, the tightness eases. My faculties return enough to be embarrassed, though the shaking continues under his touch.

What the hell is wrong with me? I never fall apart in front of an enemy yet here I am, having another panic attack.

Blake will think I'm weak.

There was Gizzy, just that once in an alleyway deep in enemy territory. God, I was so grateful, so needy. I wanted to trust him because he didn't immediately hurt me.

Huge mistake.

Blake removes his hand. I stare at the floor.

"What happened to the dragon?"

Surprised, I meet his gaze without flinching.

"When she didn't bring the country to its knees, I figured something must've gone wrong." He crosses his legs, his back towards the door, his arms resting on his thighs. No outward sign of disdain.

"She"—I clear my throat—"was destroyed. A woman set fire to her interior while she was in Fellhill."

The dragon was Nationless's secret weapon. An impenetrable machine operated by a brain-computer interface. She was the only good thing to come from the horror of Wick's torture chamber in Livingston.

But the war took her from me, too.

Just what I need, a reminder of another sorrow.

"Deliberately?"

I nod. "The woman was trying to frame me."

"She was jealous."

"Easy guess."

He shrugs. "I have eyeballs."

"What—"

"Nothing. How did the dragon come to be in Fellhill? How

were The People's Republic destroyed if they had her first?"

Dammit. Details lead to more questions.

Blake continues while I consider what to say. "I just want to understand what happened to her. I helped build her."

"You built her? That's… She was… Amazing."

"Don't let these looks fool you." He flips his hair out of his face, which has fallen across his forehead to obscure one vivid blue eye. His tongue flickers across the pouty thickness of his bottom lip.

I drop my gaze and play with the rope. "I wasn't in Calders when Fellhill attacked, neither was the dragon."

Though that may not be entirely true. I suspect Buxton used the dragon to ruin them, right after I delivered it to him.

"So you lied again," Blake says.

"Simplified. I was sent to Fellhill and they captured me, had me steal her from Calders. Then they made me one of them."

He opens his mouth, probably to ask more, but I raise my arms. "Is this so I don't throttle you in your sleep?"

"Pretty much."

"You realise I could wrap my arm around your neck and squeeze with my elbow?"

He narrows his eyes.

"Okay, okay, I promise not to. Don't tie me up more."

Back to sassy, mouthy bitch instead of panting, shivering wreck. Much better.

Blake shakes his head. "You are exhausting."

I hide my grin as he prepares the bed, unzipping the sleeping bag to spread it out and inflating the pillows. A body's worth of space stretches between us. We lie quietly and breathe. The opal light darkens automatically with the setting sun, though it'll come back on at the press of another button on the control pad.

I bend my legs and ease my hands down to pick at the rope between my ankles.

"I can feel that, you know," he says.

"Did you do some fancy knot-tying course? How to ensnare one's prisoner to prevent midnight throttling?"

He sighs. "Goodnight, Anita."

"Goodnight, Blake," I smirk.

I fidget and try to relax.

I won't sleep, not properly. It's too strange lying next to him, as if we're a couple out camping instead of captive and captor. I'll get a weapon when he drifts off. My earlier vulnerability may have lulled him into lowering his guard.

All a crafty ruse.

Yeah, right.

I drop into sleep between one blink and the next.

9

I wake to the warmth of Blake and his arms hugging me to his chest. Soft breath tickles my hair. His groin presses against my butt and I remind myself to breathe.

It feels comfortable... Safe.

I roll my eyes.

Safe? The guy is deciding whether or not to kill me.

I wriggle free. Blake flops onto his back, the covers kicked off and his t-shirt twisted, exposing a flat line of stomach. I resist the ridiculous urge to trail my fingers along the smooth skin and drag my eyes to his face, his features relaxed in sleep. His lashes lie black against his cheeks, his hair tousled and falling across his forehead.

Christ, captivated by the illusion of innocence. It's at odds with the smirking, violet-eyed warrior.

And he's not unappealing to look at. More slender than most men I've been around, closer to my figure with broader shoulders, greater muscle definition and narrower hips. And those damn *eyes...*

Oh, for god's sake. Hello, libido, nice to know you're still unfazed by pretty men trying to hurt me.

Though Blake is no Gizzy, who is pampered and safe in Fellhill. Blake has struggled, like me, fighting to survive, alone and cut adrift. He's experienced real pain. *My* pain.

We have much in common.

Dammit, I respect him. I want him to respect me, too. To understand why I destroyed Livingston. Killing his brother wasn't personal; I never met him. I understand Blake's desire for revenge since it's how I functioned the past ten years.

Marshall killed my sister. Marshall had to die.

Blake can't forgive me, not for his brother. And if he can't forgive me, he'll kill me.

His body separates me from the weapons tucked to the far side of the pod. I sway over him. His eyes open, his expression serious.

A disconcerting tingle starts in the pit of my stomach. "Um, morning?"

He smirks.

Damn that smirk.

I scoot away and he sits up, strapping the weapons to himself.

Should I ask how he slept? What exactly is captor-captive etiquette?

Why do I care? The bastard is holding me prisoner and judging me.

"So how exactly will you decide if I *deserve* to live? A point-scoring system? Toss a coin?"

He cocks an eyebrow. "You could placate me rather than antagonise."

"Placate you? *Endear* myself to you?" I hug my bound arms to my chest, my fists clenched. "And how exactly does one do that—lie back and think of goddamn England?"

Blake frowns. "Jesus Christ, woman, I'm not going to rape you."

"Damn straight you're not. You touch me and I'll kill you."

Like I'd be able to stop him. I'm tied up in the middle of nowhere. He can do whatever he wants, extracting payment for his brother's death in blood and screams.

I edge towards the locked door, as if I can tunnel my way out without the control pad. Blake doesn't move, watching me with his unfathomable eyes.

His expression softens. "Did Wick…"

My throat closes.

No. I can't talk about it. I suffered everything else Wick did. The agony, the humiliation. But as soon as he tried to rape me, I broke. I surrendered to the inevitability of my death and prayed it would be over soon.

"You have no right to ask," I wheeze.

Pity fills Blake's face.

I don't need it.

"Don't look at me like that," I snap. "He didn't. He tried, but he didn't."

Blake holds up his hands. "Okay, well I won't, either. Won't even try."

Did he just make a joke? Surely not.

He unties me and we move outside. The sun crests the canopy, sparkling off the water and bathing the area in golden light.

Such a beautiful spot. And I survived the night unmolested.

It's the small victories that matter.

We potter around camp for the rest of the day. I do everything Blake says without complaint: drag logs close to the pod to sit on, set snares and gather edible vegetation. He stays out of reach, weapons ready and control pad tucked in his pocket. I scan the trees as often as I can, searching for movement, for people creeping up on us. My hand twitches at my waist, missing the grip of the Glock.

I feel naked not having weapons.

"I've been here before, remember?" Blake says during my tenth pause in the middle of repairing his ripped navy combats. He sits on the log opposite me, his elbows resting on his knees. "It's as safe as anywhere can be."

"Long way from Livingston."

"Had the time. I travelled."

"How the hell"—I clear my throat—"did you… How are you not…"

"How the hell am I not dead?" His mouth quirks.

"Well, yeah."

He shrugs. "Stayed in our bunker the first few days but John Anders found it and buried it. I was the only one outside at the time. Scavenged what I could. Moved around. Slept in trees, drank only water animals drank from. You can survive on surprisingly little when you want to live."

It sounds simple but two months alone out here… How is he not a bit crazy?

Maybe he is.

"How many people were in the bunker?" I say, tentatively, hoping it won't incite him into a, "You killed my brother, you bitch," rant.

We both seem content to skip around the subject.

"A hundred or so." His gaze pins me. "You used the dragon with chilling efficiency."

I gulp but he continues instead of shooting me. I take it as a positive sign.

"We sent a runner to get help. That's when we found out Revolutionary Front had razed the rest of our encampments.

The mood—hardly great to begin with—was pretty dismal after that."

"Was Stig there?"

Blake frowns. "How do you know Stig?"

Crap. For someone who doesn't want to discuss her past, I sure can't shut up about it.

"He, ah, helped me."

I focus on my neat stitches as if they're way more fascinating than our conversation, finishing the line and tying it off.

"You have to give me more than that," Blake growls.

I shy away from the intensity of his eyes.

Stig is the only reason I survived Livingston.

"Stig knocked Wick unconscious before… When Wick tried to rape me. He gave me a uniform and a gun. Told me where to go."

"And Wick? Did you kill him?"

I flinch at his name and stare at my lap, the trousers fisted in my good hand. I recall the metal bat going *smack, smack* in the red ruin of his face.

"Yes," I whisper.

A blackbird sings in the tree over Blake's shoulder. It spots our tense little huddle and arrows away through the branches like a feathered missile.

"Stig was a friend of my brother, his *best* friend."

My head snaps up to meet accusatory eyes. "He said the dragon was the only way to escape."

"Did he know what you planned?"

"He told me not to kill everyone." I didn't do so well at that.

"Well, he committed suicide three days after you obliterated us. Guess he couldn't live with the guilt."

I force myself not to hunch.

What I did sickens me. Knowing I deserve the blame makes it no easier to accept.

I swallow a few times before speaking. "I'm not going to apologise for destroying Livingston."

"You said you were sorry about my brother."

"That's different."

Blake straightens on the log and crosses his arms. "You can't have one without the other."

"Yes, I can. I'm sorry about… I'm sorry your… *I'm sorry I killed your brother*. But not for Livingston."

I could've taken the dragon and fled. Wick was dead. He deserved to die. Perhaps the rest suffered under his tyranny, no choice in how their leader indulged his fantasies. No choice but to survive as best they could in the nightmare created by The People's Republic.

And that was before I razed their encampment to the ground.

My heart hangs cold and heavy in my chest. I shove to my feet to pace off the horrible ache. Blake rolls backwards, sand spraying in an arc of white. He stands and points the Glock in a two-handed grip, his eyes blazing through the fall of his hair. My pulse bounds into my throat.

Maybe I should have apologised for Livingston. Too late now.

Blake releases a breath and I jump. He relaxes his stance, sliding the gun into its holster. I remind myself to inhale.

"Did you think I was going to attack you?" I say, coaxing my heart down to where it belongs.

He cocks his head. "I never know with you."

My laugh is too high. My wobbling knees want me to sit but I ignore them. Blake finally glances away and the pressure in my gut eases.

What the hell is happening? I never react properly around him. I can barely meet his eyes without feeling uncomfortable. A normal prisoner would try to kill him and escape.

But I don't want to kill him.

Incapacitate him and run away?

I've hurt him enough.

A burst of gunfire rattles, softened by distance.

"Get in the pod," Blake says.

I don't argue. He was close to shooting me. Time to try placatory, maybe bitch at him again tomorrow.

We climb into the pod and he scoops up the ropes. I clamp my lips but tug against his hold, unable to sit still. He smirks at my struggles.

"I don't like being tied up." It sounds grumpy.

I guess I don't do placatory.

"Yeah, who does?"

"Oh, some people do."

Great, Anita, make a sexual reference. Idiot.

Blake snorts, sliding away to rifle through the rucksack, gathering clothes and a soap capsule. "Stay in the pod with the door shut."

"Afraid I'll see you naked?"

What is *wrong* with you!?

"I don't care if you see me naked. It's the grabbing weapons and shooting me while I'm naked that I'm worried about."

He flashes me a disarming grin, so quick I may have imagined it. It bruises my heart, somehow, this glimpse of the normal Blake, absent of anger and sorrow.

Or maybe he's always surly. What do I know?

The portal sighs shut behind him. No bolt thuds into place.

Why doesn't he lock it? Unsealed, it can be manually opened by shoving and twisting to slide it out of the way.

Maybe he's testing me. I bet he *is* using a point-scoring system, the bastard.

There's silence for a while then splashing and a curse, muffled through the toughened material of the pod. I inch forward. My fingers hover over the portal.

Jesus Christ, control yourself.

It's tempting to see what that sleek body looks like. The talk of nakedness made me think about it. Or Stockholm syndrome.

I stretch out on my back and frown at the pearlescent ceiling. Blake returns wearing his repaired navy combats and the light green t-shirt I wore yesterday, dried in the sun. His hair is clumped in spikes, kissing his cheekbones and flopping over his forehead.

He really is quite beautiful.

I fix my gaze on the roof.

"Are you blushing?"

"No," I say through gritted teeth, refusing to look at him.

He'll be smirking at me.

10

A heart beats steadily under my ear.

It isn't my heart.

Sleep dissolves and my eyes flutter open. I'm cuddling Blake's chest, my right arm numb and trapped between our bodies. His arm curls across my shoulders, pressing me to him.

This is ridiculous. Did I crawl on him while asleep or did he pull me in? The answer seems important. Maybe being alone for two months has starved him of human contact so snuggling his brother's murderer is an improvement.

I have no excuse. I know what the longing for affection brings you.

Pain and betrayal.

Maybe it was our melancholy talk last night. It started light, safe. What we did before the rebellion, things we missed. Blake seemed baffled by my amusement at discovering he used to be a fitness instructor.

What better way to draw clientele than to look like the poster boy for sexual gratification? The warrior eyes, smirking, wicked mouth and sleek muscles. The guy is a panther—black-haired, beautiful and dangerous. Every woman's fantasy.

Except for me, of course. I am immune to such shallow charms.

I managed to make him laugh a genuine laugh quoting from classic movies. I didn't hold his preference for something more modern against him. Though our idea of modern will be outdated.

Does the outside world make movies anymore?

I hoped talking about life before the war would help him consider me as a person, instead of a slaughterer of siblings. He appeared to be giving proper thought on my right to live.

Who holds a friendly conversation with someone they plan on killing?

Sociopaths, whispers the voice in my head.

But remembering normality led to the realisation we'd not been happy in a very long time. We survived from one day to the next. Blake at least had his brother until I ruined that piece of familial bliss.

Our talk ended there.

His chest rises and falls beneath my cheek, his scent like a forest after rain.

Strangely alluring.

How can I move without waking him? He'll probably be disgusted at me for touching him. It's tempting to nestle into his warmth and drop back to sleep. Let him worry about it.

I push against his hold. My right arm tingles. His grip tightens across my shoulders and I freeze. The tingles sprout teeth. His hand slides down my back and cups my ass. I jerk upright to stare into eyes of deep cobalt-blue.

I suppress a shiver. "Would you believe I was trying to reach the weapons and fell?"

"On top of me?"

"Fine. How about you cuddle me in your sleep?"

He quirks his mouth. "Seems unlikely."

I thrust my bound hands under his nose. "Untie me. I need some air."

He grabs my wrists, his slim fingers branding my skin. I tug against his hold, unable to stop myself from squirming under his touch. He sits up, pressing my hands to his chest, his thigh a warm line next to mine. I pull harder, a feeling close to panic expanding in my stomach.

"I thought you wanted me to untie you."

I grit my teeth. "So hurry up and do it."

He smirks and picks at the knot. The rope flops to the floor with an elaborate flourish. He hooks his arm around my bent calves and yanks, straightening my legs. I yelp, slapping my good hand down to steady myself. Blake shimmies towards my feet.

"I can untie my ankles, thank you."

He pauses. "Why are you so twitchy?"

"I'm not twitchy."

"Whatever you say."

God, he's infuriating.

He raises his hands and I pull at the knot. I dig my fingernails in but still can't get it loose. Blake sniggers and I spear him with a glare.

"Would you like some assistance?" he says.

I'd hop out of the pod and to hell with it but he'll only laugh at me more.

Why the fuck do I care?

My, "*Please,*" comes out as a growl.

Blake stretches his hand towards my ankles but hesitates, changing direction to brush his fingers across my toes.

The nails are growing back but rougher and thickened. In another month or so, you'd never know they were ripped off of me.

I wait for Blake to jerk his hand away. He touches my other foot—just as ruined, just as ugly. I curl my toes.

"Stop that."

I aim for commanding instead of breathy. Fail. His stroking caress does weird things to my stomach.

He removes the rope from my ankles and I scramble for the portal.

"Anita."

I still.

"You might want to wait until I unlock it."

Why is he so damn amused? Perhaps I should remind him I crushed his brother beneath the rubble of their house.

I suck in a breath and it shakes.

A click. "You are free to go."

"Neither of us is free," I snarl and bolt outside.

I stomp into the forest, not caring if Blake thinks I'm running away or going to find a rock to bash his head in.

I don't go far. He has all the weapons, and my shoes.

My bare feet crunch on leaves and fallen branches. Startled woodpigeons clatter from the trees.

It's claustrophobia. Being stuck in the pod in one place is getting to me, making my behaviour erratic. I usually sleep in my boots, or my socks at the very least, ready to run at the first hint of trouble. I've gotten too comfortable around Blake, somehow. I want out, away from the war. I need to continue my journey before I go insane.

Or do something stupid.

The gentle constriction of the bandage on my forearm is too

much for the mounting pressure in my body. My skin feels swollen. I fist my hand and the pain helps. Concentrating on Emily's physiotherapy exercises calms me further.

She's the only person I miss from Fellhill. Their doctor, my friend.

I have to convince Blake to travel with me. He won't let me skip off by myself, blessed with his forgiveness and good wishes. He can judge my worthiness on the road. Does he know the rest of the world may be alive, if not normal? He may give me some leeway if we manage to escape.

Or he'll leave me stranded in a final, brutal punishment.

Best not tell him it was also The People's Republic who started the war and turned his leader into a torturing psychopath.

I stroll back to the pod, finding a bird nest on the way. Blake sits on a log, facing the trees.

I present the two white eggs, slightly smaller than a chicken's. "Brought breakfast."

We eat and make no comment on the events of the morning.

<h1 style="text-align:center">11</h1>

Cold water nips my bare feet, sunshine baking the top of my head. My toes sink into soft mud, the trailing stems of pondweed and water lily entwined around my ankles, the white flowers as big as my cupped palm. I wade out and stop when the water creeps above my knees, below the line of shorts from a pair of combats that unzip mid-thigh.

The rucksack really has everything.

I'm still wearing Blake's navy t-shirt, too stubborn to change since he pointed it out. He stays on the shore, his knife resting on a flat rock.

We argued about travelling to the coast. I told him someone was out there, trying to contact us, but he refused to listen, adamant we were staying until he decided what he was going to do with me. Shouting made him threaten to select the option that would shut me up quicker. The decision to fish from the pool followed our terse silence.

We can hate each other while being productive.

Of course, he elects to do the gutting since he won't give me a knife. Or a stick sharpened into a spear to harpoon the fish. He doesn't seem to realise I can knock him out with my fists if I want to. Tie him up and have him all vulnerable and—

Where are you going with this?

Settling mud tickles my calves. I unravel my improvised hook and line made from a shoelace and a hawthorn branch. Worms bait the thorns, dug from the rich loam beneath the trees. I lower them into the water and they drift among the emergent plants. A light wind flaps my t-shirt, ripples of water caressing my thighs. A dark shape approaches and I hold my breath. A tentative nibble tugs on the line. I force myself not to yank it. The shoelace tightens. I ease my right hand into the water and scoop the fish out. The good-sized grayling thrashes its muscled body of striped blue and green, showering me in droplets.

I turn to toss the fish to Blake but he smirks at the water beaded in my eyelashes and speckling my clothes. I lob the fish and it slaps his chest, leaving a wet imprint. I laugh at his startled expression.

"Goddammit, woman," he says, lifting the flapping grayling from the sand and bashing its head with the handle of the knife.

It becomes a game. For me.

I pitch the fish and Blake struggles to catch the slippery beasts. I hook four more but give up, my laughter scaring the fish away, my line jittering all over the place. I crawl out of the pool to avoid drowning and brace my hands on my knees. Blake swipes at his sodden t-shirt, ten fillets glistening on the rock beside him, blood and water dribbling to the sand.

"You look damp," I say between chuckles.

He cocks an eyebrow. "You seem to be enjoying yourself."

"Somehow, I am."

I straighten and scrub the tears from my cheeks, forgetting the fish goop on my hands. Blake laughs while I curse and dry my face on my sleeve. He pulls his wet t-shirt over his head and throws it aside.

My gaze shifts before I can stop myself.

There's a slight narrowing from sleek shoulders to slim waist, the curve of each hip disappearing into the waistband of his combats. Two pairs of dog-tags glint on his chest. I find myself fascinated with the delicate line of his collarbone and the hollow of his throat. He flicks his hair out of his startling eyes, and smirks.

But this is a different smirk. Dark and knowing and sexy.

"You're blushing," he says.

"It's a hot day."

The smirk says he doesn't believe me. I raise my chin and stalk around him.

Bastard. What the hell does he need from me? Validation he's pretty to look at? Maybe this is his punishment for my rape accusation. It would be ironic if I'm the one who begs him to sleep with me.

Not going to happen.

Blake bends to gather the fillets from the rock. My justified stomp stutters to a halt in the sand.

Scars criss-cross his back in thin, diagonal lines, like mine but less extensive. Less vicious.

He turns but I fail to control my expression.

"What?" he says. "You think Wick reserved torture for his prisoners? He was just as happy abusing his own people."

My heart clenches, a wave of fierce, baffling protectiveness making me dizzy.

"You, too? You've been in there?"

Blake nods, the emotion on his face difficult to read. A lock of hair falls across his forehead and I long to brush it away. His revelation punches straight to my gut.

It's stupid to be upset on his behalf. Soft and girly. *Embarrassing.* I can't help it. He knows—he *knows*—what it was like. He experienced the same horrible bite of the whip as it split the skin and splashed the blood.

I picture him in the torture room, stripped to the waist, his hands tied above his head to the metal hook in the wall. The muscles in his shoulders would tense, anticipating the blow, his hands clenched into fists, as mine had been.

Though Wick probably wasn't as brutal with his own soldiers.

"Twice," Blake says, his voice quiet. "The whipping was for punching one of Wick's guards. He bragged about raping a prisoner and cutting her open. I don't even remember hitting him."

Goddamn, now I do feel sorry. Sorry for Livingston, sorry for all of it.

"I'm sorry," I whisper, unable to keep my breath from hitching.

Blake shakes his head and walks past me. He places the fish in the smoker he built by digging a small ditch and crafting a box of stones over the top.

The trees should disguise the smoke from anyone who may be watching.

I trail after him. "If Wick was cruel to you guys, why did nobody stop him?"

Blake crams pieces of cut alder and ash into the smoker, his shoulders stiff. He flicks his lighter and flame licks over the branches. My fingers ache to stroke his scars, to explore the thickened ridges so similar to mine. I hug myself to avoid touching him.

It's the first time he's let me close without shoving a weapon in my face.

When he's awake, anyway.

"We were terrified of him; we'd do anything to stay on his good side." Blake pauses, his eyes haunted. "Almost anything. Funny how much you tolerate if you think you're going to win. It made everything else bearable."

He lived with that monster, defended the honour of some poor, dead woman despite his fear. And I obliterated everything. His chance of winning, his reason for enduring. His brother. Thrusting him into no man's land to die alone.

And he would have died if he hadn't met me. No bullets.

He must have been pretty desperate.

I turn towards the pod so he won't see my tears. Bricks scrape together as he seals the smoker.

"Wick had enough followers to protect him. No guarantee once he was removed someone worse wouldn't take his place. And what would that make me? A leader-assassinating traitor. This war had enough of those at the start." Blake brushes dirt from his palms, his dog-tags swinging against his smooth chest.

I scrub my face. "I killed my leader."

His eyes widen. "Which one?"

"Marshall."

"Why?"

Damn. I did it again. The past is liable to make me run screaming or start sobbing. Neither is acceptable. Maybe I'm still trying to absolve myself or talk of traitors touched a nerve.

I am not a traitor.

"Why?" Blake says, softer.

He seems curious rather than disgusted but I can't tell him

I killed Marshall for murdering my sister.

"He sent me to Fellhill to die."

Blake frowns.

I sigh. "Marshall demanded I sleep with him but I refused."

We walk back to the pod, the heat of the sun welcome after the shade of the trees, though my chill isn't anything normal warmth can cure.

"Wasn't he family?"

I shudder. "He was *not* fucking family."

Blake raises his eyebrow but I ignore it.

"Look, my point is—coming from someone who's been called a traitor more than once—assassinating your leader doesn't make you one. Some people deserve to die."

His lips curve. "So you decide who's worthy enough to live?"

I almost slap my hand to my forehead.

I'm as bad as him.

"When they're trying to kill me or demanding something that isn't theirs, I guess I do."

I flop in the hot sand and lean against the log. Blake mirrors me, his long legs stretched out. His abdominals bunch when he wriggles, hard muscle sliding under taut skin.

I wish he'd put on a t-shirt. It's humiliating how much he distracts me.

"Who called you a traitor? Soldiers of the Lost when they thought you destroyed the dragon?"

"I don't want to talk about it," I snap, angry at myself for gawping at him.

Must I repeat all past mistakes and learn nothing?

He fists his hand in the sand, letting it trickle from his palm. "You can't blame me for being interested. Wick was a sadist but he left us alone for the most part, as long as he had prisoners to keep him entertained. Sounds like your time has been pretty awful."

"Recently, it has," I say before I can tell myself to shut up.

"Oh, come on. You can't say that and give me nothing."

"Sure I can."

His eyes darken. My stomach clenches and my pulse jumps hard in my throat.

Fear or something else? Fear is wise, lust is not. I lusted after my captor once before and was reminded why you can't trust anyone.

All people want is to fuck me or kill me.

I manage to speak on my second attempt. "I tell you everything now, you'll get bored and decide to shoot me. Think I'll keep my secrets."

Feigning heat stroke, I flee to the pod.

12

"Wake up, girlie."

My heart freezes then slams my ribs hard enough to shake my whole body.

Oh no, no, *nooo*… Oh god, please, no.

My eyes snap open and my breath gasps out. Leather straps bite my wrists and ankles, cinching me to the metal chair.

I never left Livingston.

The familiar torture room assaults me: the truncheon table, the drowning tub, the whipping hook. Red smears the walls and floor.

My body is a cornucopia of bruises, my torn flesh screaming where it contacts the seat. Blisters pop and ooze fluid at my waist. Flaking blood coats my thighs, a spike of pain flaring inside from Wick's savagery as he raped me.

My skin smells of him.

I pant, unable to stop. Wick steps from behind the chair, trailing a clump of my hair through his fingers. A horrific, nose-ruffling animal odour leaches from my pores.

He smiles at me. "Oh, you are so very close to breaking. The fear and madness in your eyes are exquisite."

Broken shards of teeth fill the wreckage of his mouth. Swollen lips stretch and split with a moist rip. Red dribbles down his bare torso and stains the waistband of his briefs.

"I hoped we'd have more time." He shakes his head, flints of skull scattering to the floor. "But your fragile psyche won't survive what I'm going to do to you now, never mind your body."

He selects a tool from a shelf, the silver blades winking in the light. He squeezes the bone cutters open and shut.

Snick, snick.

"No, *please*," I whisper through cracked lips.

"The great Anita Carmichael begs!" Wick's grin turns into a snarl. "You are worthless. Weak. You are *nothing*."

A sob explodes from my chest.

"Oh, piteous creature. I've had my fun but you are tiresome and repulsive."

Wick grabs my right hand and pulls the fingers straight. I fight him, choking on my frantic heartbeat. I buck in the chair but it's bolted to the floor. Wick sneers and slips my pinkie finger between the blades, the metal icy against my feverish skin. Watching my face, he squeezes the handles, increasing the pressure and allowing me to experience the dismembering process in slow, dreadful clarity. The blades slice skin and meet resistance, steel battling bone. It shatters and my screams bounce off the walls. Lumps of meat and gristle scatter to the floor.

When I have no fingers left, Wick kneels in a grotesque proposal, removing body parts rather than asking for them.

The blades of the bone cutter dull, the bloody nubs of my toes rolling around Wick's feet. He throws the tool away, the silver shine blurred red. His black eyes sparkle, as hard and merciless as the knife he chooses. Saliva drools from my mouth, my voice broken from shrieking, each breath a whine.

Wick grips my breast in his hand and presses the blade to bulging flesh. "Once I cut these off, I'm going to get my axe and chop you into pieces."

My skin parts and a red mouth yawns open. Blood gushes over Wick's hand. He tosses my breast, the yellow fat exposed, and it slaps to the floor, the soft tissues glistening in the overhead lights. Crimson coats my belly and clumps in my pubic hair. Wick grins and licks the knife. He cuts my other breast off in slices.

The Goliath cradles a polished axe in giant hands that loved to pin me to the chair and pinch and bruise.

He'd raped me after Wick. I lost count of the others.

Wick caresses the wooden shaft, his fingers curling around to heft it in his hand. He raises the axe.

"I always win, girlie," he says.

The blade slashes down.

13

Someone calls my name. Hands shake me and I fight them off. My heart thunders, sweat slicking my skin. The hands push down but I struggle, thrash, until a body presses against mine.

They're naked.

Wick, raping me again, smearing himself in my blood and fatty tissue. He'll plunge his hands into my open wounds like a warrior daubing himself in battle paint.

A scream bubbles in my chest. I toss and squirm under the weight, my legs and fists striking out. My right fist—*stump?*—hits something soft and warm. It flinches away before pinning my arms.

"Dammit, Anita, *wake up!* You're having a nightmare."

A painful gasp snaps me to alertness, my hair stuck to my flushed cheeks. Blake is sprawled on top of me, holding my wrists to the floor of the pod. A bead of blood glistens on his swelling lip. My mouth opens and closes, fear, relief and shame stoppering my throat. The pressure builds and spills out of my eyes in a burst of scalding tears.

"Oh god, are you real?"

Blake relaxes his grip and pushes himself off me. "I'm real. It was a nightmare."

My stomach clenches. "Going to be sick."

I scramble out of the portal, squinting in the bright sunshine, and stumble to the edge of the trees. I fall to my knees and vomit into a fern, heaving until nothing comes up but stinging bile.

My dignity wants me to crawl into the plants and huddle in a ball, not face Blake.

Get up, you blubbering cow.

I shove to my feet and stagger over to the logs. I curl in the sand, my teeth chattering despite the heat.

"Are you okay?"

I search for a witty comment but can only nod. Blake perches on the opposite log, his movements tentative, as though dealing with a wounded animal.

How else can I humiliate myself in front of him? Give me a second, I'll think of something.

Little time seems to have passed since I fled to the pod and fell asleep.

"It was Wick." I suck in a shuddering breath. "In my nightmare. Haven't had one in a while."

Blake quirks his mouth. "I'm not helping, am I?"

"Not so much."

He licks the blood from his lip. I force myself up and lean against the log. No cowering.

"Sorry I hit you."

"Surprised you haven't done it before."

I manage a laugh but it dies at the sad seriousness on his face.

Christ, being with him is an emotional rollercoaster. So much sorrow, so much pain. Flashes of a teasing humour I don't deserve.

I stare at my lap. Emily's exercises clear my head and give

me something to do with my hands.

"I'm sorry. For everything." I glance at Blake then away, not waiting for his reaction. "I'm sorry for your brother, for Livingston. I was hurt. *Furious*. You broke me. I thought you deserved it. Fooled myself you were all like him. I wanted to hurt you, as I'd been hurt. But I regretted it later."

Blake shifts on the log. I keep my eyes down.

"Will you tell me what Wick did?"

I snap my head up to snarl at him.

How dare he ask me to relive it? Can't he see my suffering?

"*Please*." Anguished need bleeds from the word. "I have to know my brother's death wasn't for nothing. That you were driven to it. Please."

Dammit, I owe him. It won't bring his brother back or make him forgive me but maybe it will grant him some peace. And maybe telling someone will give me that, too.

"I've never told anyone."

Blake swallows. "I know what that's like."

"Your second time in the torture chamber?"

"First, actually. The whipping was the second time." His hand bats at the air. "That's a horror story for another day. Tell me yours first."

I bow my head.

Talking about it will make me cry. Tears already clog my throat and burn my eyes, nerves jittering in my stomach.

"What was your brother's name?"

Maybe I can work up some courage before divulging the worst, most debasing period of my life.

"Dylan. Dylan O'Riley."

I force myself to meet Blake's gaze despite the directness of his stare, his dark, drowning eyes.

"How was he in Livingston? Did he join Nationless because you were family?"

Jesus, did I kill his parents, too? No, he'd have mentioned that. Shoved it in my face.

"He was visiting." Soft regret mellows Blake's voice and strengthens his accent. "Came to convince me to return to Ireland, where our mother lived. He was stranded by the bombs."

After the debating chamber assassinations, Soldiers of the Lost targeted the travel network, hampering the flow of refugees.

No one was allowed to escape. Everyone must fight.

"The last thing I said to my mother before we were cut off was a promise to keep him safe." Blake hides his face in his hands. "But maybe she's dead, too. Maybe I'll never have to tell her I failed. I don't know which would be worse."

I hunch at his pain. He blames himself, too.

But I'm the only one he should blame.

I take a deep breath. "The worst part about the torture was Wick didn't want anything. No information, no secrets. Nothing but me begging for my life. And I don't beg. Not for anyone."

I frown at Blake, expecting him to argue, scoff. He raises his head. My eyes dart away.

"He recognised me," I say to the tree line over Blake's shoulder. "He changed. He was Daniel, the party leader, not Wick, the monster. I thought... I thought he wouldn't hurt me."

"We had no Daniel, only Wick," Blake says. "In the beginning, we thought it was the head injury. Of course he'd want vengeance. But then we realised he was a different person.

13

Darker. And he enjoyed the torture too much to stop."

"Oh, I know how much he enjoyed it. He beat me with a rubber truncheon and he *whistled*."

A lump expands in my throat.

Shit, I'm going to cry already and haven't reached the shameful bit.

I clamp my hand over my bandaged forearm to distract myself.

Don't think. Breathe. The story of someone else's life.

"I still hear the noise it made. Sounded the same as the metal bat I used to pulverise his face. But there's literally a lot of shit to get through before that part." My brittle laugh masks a gag. "The next day, I was hauled from my cell by some muscle-bound goliath—"

"Doolly," Blake growls. He shakes himself and gestures for me to continue.

"He strapped me to a chair and Wick electrocuted me. Fainted the first time. Felt everything the second."

I tell him everything—the glimpse of Daniel, how my sister's best friend made it worse. The detached flippancy lasts until I describe my loss of sphincter control. I talk through the tears, the hitching breath, the pain in my gut, remembering my despair, my longing for death.

My surrender.

I was so alone. So hurt and alone. Fleeing back to Calders, I received little solace. Branded a traitor by Hannah, which wasn't helped by me immediately shooting her in the face. Imprisoned by Marshall to become his whore. Sacrificed to Soldiers of the Lost after a week of recovery. The brief blip of happiness with Gizzy was a lie.

At some point, Blake leaves his perch to sit beside me. I end up crying into his collarbone, my face tucked in his neck. He strokes my hair and I relax under his touch, his arms holding me close.

Comfortable. *Safe.*

"Thank you," he whispers, his breath tickling the top of my head.

"Oh, my pleasure," I huff. "When you want a horror story, just ask. I have plenty."

"Always with the sass."

"Stops me from falling apart. Most of the time."

I scrub my face and force myself to ease out of his warmth. It's too tempting to cuddle against him, especially as no weapons keep me at bay. I cock my eyebrow at their position on the log.

God, if I had a portion of his wariness, I could have spared myself a lot of heartache.

He follows the direction of my gaze. "I can never tell how you'll react."

I give a watery laugh. "I don't think I'm ruthless enough to grab a gun when you're being consolatory."

"So I should go back to being an arsehole?"

"Soon. Just give me another minute."

He chuckles and it's a nice sound.

The slither of sand offers a second of warning but it's slow to register. I'm too distracted, too fragile after finally putting what happened to me into words. Sharing it with another person leaves me raw. Vulnerable.

It's a shock, then, when a low voice says, "You picked the wrong day to go camping, you faction-loving bastards."

14

"Shit-fuck-balls," Blake hisses.

Now who has the mouth?

Two men sidle around the logs, keeping them between us. The shorter man swipes the electrigun and Glock and tosses them behind him. A half-smile curves his lips, his eyes drifting across our campsite but not alighting on anything for more than a second.

"Move over there," the other man barks at Blake, gesturing with a dented Browning. Dark hair curls from the collar of his stained t-shirt. "Keep your hands where I can see 'em."

Blake and I rise together. He walks closer to the shorter man. I stay perfectly still, too dazed for fear yet.

"I see why you wanted some privacy," the other man sneers, his teeth crooked and discoloured. "Does she fuck as good as she looks? Bet she does."

A grunt finds Blake on his knees, his hands clasped on his head. The shorter man holds no weapon, nothing but a dreamy smile painting his face.

Somehow, it's worse.

The Browning touches my temple and I flinch. My reactions finally catch up, panic squeezing my heart in a fist.

We're in trouble, we're in trouble, we—

The other man grabs my hair and yanks my head back. "Bet you have to chase the men from this 'un."

The barrel of his gun caresses my cheek and runs down my neck to poke the side of my breast. I bare my teeth and he laughs.

"Bend over and spread your legs."

"Fuck you."

"Oh, honey, you're about to."

He grinds the gun into my head and twists my hair, forcing me down. He kicks my ankle to widen my stance. Keeping his grip on my hair, he moves behind me to tuck his groin against my ass.

"Hold your arms out."

I struggle to control my breathing.

Show no fear. No weakness.

He's going to rape me. I managed to avoid it up to this point. No mean feat considering the slobbering morons I always encountered.

This man will succeed where Wick failed.

I swallow bile.

I can't bear it. I *can't*.

The man folds his body over my back, his hands sliding down my outstretched arms and across my chest to fondle my breasts. My gritted teeth cage a whimper. He straightens, thrusting his hips into my butt, his fingers bruising my waist. I brace my hand on the ground to stop from landing on my face. The man pats my shorts, running out of areas to search for weapons.

"You should see her," the shorter man says. "Angel-face is pissed."

Huh. Bloodless and terrified can be mistaken for fury.

The hips thrust once more into my ass, the force swaying my hair.

"Good. I like the ones that fight."

My eyes lock on Blake's.

So did Wick.

I drop my gaze, my cheeks hot.

It's too soon since talking about my torture. I'm too open. I try to find anger, strength. *Something*.

"Let's unwrap you and see what delights we have in store." The man tugs me upright and releases my hair, stepping out of reach. "Take the top off."

I hesitate and glance at Blake. The thought of him witnessing my rape makes it more horrific.

As if it isn't horrific enough.

"Your little boyfriend can't help you," the man says. "Do what I tell you or Gavin will cut 'im."

A knife as long as my forearm appears in Gavin's hand.

Where the hell did he hide it?

"And I'll shoot you in the leg and fuck you anyway." The barrel drops to aim at my kneecap. "Top. *Off*."

I fling the t-shirt aside. Sunlight teases my shoulders. The man's lip curls, wrinkling a line of white-headed spots competing for space with a wispy moustache.

"Oh, what a pity. Just as well you have great tits. I'm a tits and ass man."

Wonderful.

Blake stares at me.

I guess it's the first time in three days he's seen me half-naked.

The only male not intent on divesting me of my clothes.

His gaze trails from the bullet scar on my shoulder to the

long line down my belly. He lingers on each, as though memorising them. When he reaches my face, his eyes are a shocking, heart-stopping violet.

"Shorts next, beautiful."

I flinch at the man's voice, distracted by Blake's expression, the ground suddenly unsteady beneath my feet.

Focus! Find a way out.

My hand drops to my waistband. The man's gaze follows the movement, his tongue darting over cracked lips.

"You're going to regret this," I say.

A lick of anger unfurls in the icy cavity of my chest. My lifelong friend chases the shakiness away.

The man grins. "I doubt it."

I shove the shorts down and kick them off. I raise my chin and scowl instead of shielding myself with my hands.

"Open your eyes, lover-boy, you get to watch." Gavin giggles, his voice girlish.

Creepy, very creepy.

He jerks Blake's head back and waves the knife in his face. Dirt turns his fingernails into black half-moons.

"Or I cut off your eyelids and force you. You choose."

Blake opens furious eyes. The other man watches them, his gun drifting from my kneecap. My pulse throbs in my temples.

No time to think.

The gun swivels. I dive. A bullet kicks a plume of sand near my feet. I grab the man's wrist with my left hand and lock my elbow, pain flaring in my forearm. I drive my fist into his nose, his blood bursting in a spray. He stumbles and I wrench the gun from his slackened grip. He trips over the log and sits hard on his butt, blinking up at me through a wash of red. I shoot him in the forehead and pivot before his back hits the ground.

Have my actions sacrificed Blake? Will I find him sprawled on the sand, Gavin rushing towards me with his dreamy smile and a blood-spattered knife?

My chest tightens, the air sucked from it.

The blade hangs at Blake's side, his slim fingers wrapped around the handle. A bead of red drips from the tip to splotch on his boot. Gavin's throat gapes like a second mouth, bone glimmering in the sun.

My muscles harden, keeping the gun raised. I stare at Blake and forget to breathe. White noise fills my skull but a hissing whisper weaves through.

Pull the trigger.

15

I have to save myself from him. He's doing something to me. Weakening me, dulling my reactions. He took me prisoner but I haven't tried hard to escape. I admire him more than I want to hurt him. He suffered and lost and struggled to survive. Like me. I want to protect him, not kill him.

Which means I should definitely kill him. To protect myself.

My finger tightens on the trigger. The knife thuds into the sand. I wait for the anger, hatred, scorn but his eyes hold resignation and sorrow.

"Do it," Blake says. "I deserve it."

How can he say that? I've hurt him too much already.

I gasp, a wave of dizziness weakening my knees. Blake shuts his eyes and bows his head. The gun drops to my side.

What the hell just happened?

I scan the trees but there's no sign of other people. I frown at the gun.

It seems a bit aggressive to keep it in my hand while I… What? Comfort Blake?

I raise my arm but hesitate.

He'll probably yell at me for touching him.

Quit dawdling, you coward.

"Blake?"

I place my palm lightly on his shoulder, my fingertips brushing the hard ridge of scars. He flinches but doesn't jerk away, a fine tremble running through his body. Pain brims in his eyes and hollows my stomach.

Does he expect me to kill him? Okay, I considered it for the space of a heartbeat but didn't really mean it.

Right?

No. No, I don't want to kill him. It would probably make things easier if I did.

"I'm"—he clears his throat—"I miss him."

The anguished whisper carves my chest, worse than if he yelled at me.

It takes me three attempts to speak. "I know. I'm sorry."

Saying it to the day I breathe my last still won't be enough.

Blake avoids my eyes, his gaze somewhere south of my chin.

I should tease him for having an excuse to ogle me but it isn't the time for jokes.

He consoled me. I can offer nothing less.

Ignoring the jitters in my stomach, I close the distance between us. He's exactly my height. I rest my head against his, my arms circling his shoulders, the gun held away. He stiffens but doesn't shove me back or snarl in my face. His shudders slow, easing the tightness in my chest. His hands slide around my waist, his fingers pressing into the small of my back and pulling me closer.

I suddenly remember I'm in my underwear.

My breath catches in my throat.

Shit. *Get a grip!* It's a hug, not an invitation or the normal reaction to almost being raped.

I seriously need some therapy.

Blake's mouth settles over my pulse.

Can he feel it pounding under my skin?

Confusion wars with something that can't possibly be arousal. Stupid hormones. He's attractive—no, fucking *gorgeous*—and consoled me while I cried. It seems to be all I need. But why is he touching me like this? Holding me tight, as if the circle of his arms can keep me safe.

He's probably lonely. I happen to be the first half-naked female he's seen in two months.

Or he *is* comforting me and I'm sullying his act of kindness.

His fingers trail up my back and glide over the scars. He explores each one, stroking from hip to shoulder beneath my hair. I shiver at the gentle contact.

I have to stop this. *Have to.* For my own sanity. The closeness, the intimacy, the bewildering attraction. It's too much.

"Blake, wait..." My voice is breathy, strangled. Jesus. "Blake, we have to go. Might be others."

There, that makes sense. A good reason to stop whatever we're doing.

And pick it up later, when we're safe?

No!

I promised never to make this mistake again after throwing myself at Gizzy, blinded by his initial compassion. Overwhelmed by the end of my self-imposed abstinence. For a brief moment, I'd felt like a woman instead of a soldier. A victim.

I wasn't enough for him. Didn't share enough, trust enough. Obey enough. He used me, deceived me and sacrificed me at the first hint of trouble. He said he loved me but the evidence pointed at something closer to hate.

The last person to love me was my sister and she's been

dead ten years.

I ease out of Blake's arms. One hand grips my hip, as if he may fight me. His eyes blaze, scorching me where his fingers can't touch. He traces the bullet scar on my shoulder, stroking down the abdominal scar. I bite my lip to stop from fidgeting.

"Wick didn't do these."

I shake my head a little too rapidly, my hair whipping my shoulders. "No. Not Wick."

Blake releases me and I stumble, my body leaning into him. He gathers the weapons, including the Browning, which I surrender without a word, and disappears into the pod.

He hates me again but it's what I want, right?

No. I don't have a clue what I want.

Liar.

I shiver and pull on my discarded clothes.

I definitely should have shot him when I had the chance.

16

A spongy log cracks under my weight. Blake doesn't turn around. He forges ahead through the undergrowth, his movements lithe and easy, the foliage parting for him. Brambles scour my legs, nettles leaping into my path to sting my knees. I sigh and hitch the rucksack higher.

We've barely spoken since breaking camp, leaving the bodies of our attackers stiffening in the sand.

Why is he pissed at me? We seemed to reach an understanding after I shared the story of my torture. He was gentle. Nice. If the two men hadn't attacked, he might have accepted what I did. Not forgiveness, that's too much to ask for, but an uneasy truce. Recognition that I was traumatised and lashed out for a brief, vengeful moment.

A release, after everything I'd suffered.

A branch slashes my face. I swipe at it and swallow a curse. Sweat nips my eyes, my hair tangled in every zip of the rucksack.

Okay, I ruined it by pointing a gun at him. A conflicted millisecond in the heat of battle. Hell, he's been waving weapons in my face the rest of the time. Tying me up. I should be the one who's pissed.

Did he think I was offering him my body as an apology?

Maybe I insulted him by pulling away. First, I accuse him of wanting to rape me then throw myself at him.

I blush, glad he isn't paying attention.

Drawing back was the only option. No more succumbing to ridiculous temptation. I don't need the heartache.

It's disappointing to discover he's like every other male in my life—one rebuff and he becomes a sneering asshole. Well, it was supposed to be a comforting hug. It's not my fault he got the wrong idea, though his touch stayed tender the entire time and never strayed below my waist.

The way he stroked my scars…

I stumble on the uneven ground and grab onto a tree.

Dammit. I should shrug off the rucksack and run for it. Taking my chances alone and unarmed in the Borderlands seems a lot safer.

I pick up the pace and concentrate on placing my feet, grassy hummocks doing their best to trip me. The trees become a mix of pine and broadleaf, my boots bouncing on needles and moss. I catch up to Blake, staying a few steps behind so he won't complain but his shoulders tense.

Great, now he acts like I'm repulsive.

A river meanders through a valley. Blake hops on stones to the other side, graceful and sure. I lurch after him, my shoes sloshing in the water. I pant upwards to the next plateau, the pines dwindling to beech and oak, their gnarled trunks thick and ancient. A large stain on one oak has dried a rusty brown.

Sap flows in sticky rivulets not a maroon ooze. Some kind of disease? The wavering leaves look healthy.

Blake walks past the botanical enigma without a glance. A sudden hush shivers up my spine.

When did the birds stop singing?

Crack. A huge shape drops from the canopy. My heart expands into my throat and my hand flies out.

Reaching, reaching but not close enough.

I see how it will happen: the heavy trunk trailing ivy and swinging like a pendulum, slamming into Blake and driving him into the oak with a wet smack and a crunch of bone. He'll die, the pain bright in his violet eyes, wondering if I noticed the danger and chose not to warn him.

The trap swings.

Blake!

17

Blake starts to turn as the trunk whooshes closer. I tackle him, my arms around his waist, a shoulder slammed into his side. We thump to the ground in a cloud of grass awns, our breaths exploding out. The trunk completes its arc with an awful whack of wood on wood. The leaves of the oak hiss. Blake rolls in a flail of arms and legs and straddles me, the rucksack propping me up at the waist. His hands grip my arms, his eyes searching my face.

Maybe he thinks I'm attacking him.

The trunk continues to bounce off the oak, each soft thud tugging at my stomach. Flakes of maroon flutter to the ground, darker rivulets staining the rough bark.

The image of Blake's broken body refuses to dissipate. Visions of his lovely corpse—tousled black hair, shards of rib tenting his t-shirt, blood bubbling on his lips.

No more smirking.

"Saved your life," I croak, hoping the words dispel the horrible picture.

He gapes at me. "Are you crying?"

"No," I say, ducking my head and hiding behind my hair. "That would be ridiculous."

He tilts my chin, his fingers trailing across my cheek. A

single tear trembles on one tip.

Well, damn.

He swallows. "Something in your eye?"

His expression is too raw to witness. I drop my gaze to his chest. His very solid, not-caved-in chest.

"Right. Makes more sense."

"And while you had this thing in your eye, you saved my life?"

The trap settles on the maroon stain, the ivy continuing to sway.

How many people has it crushed? How close did Blake come to it when he was all alone?

My breath hitches. "I don't want you to die."

"Why not?"

"What do you mean 'why not'?"

He shrugs. "I'm keeping you prisoner. Making you relive difficult parts of your life. Touching you when I said I wouldn't."

His mouth on my neck, deft fingers stroking my scars.

I lick my lips. "My fault. Forgot I was in my underwear."

"You forgot?"

"You were hurting."

"So you were more concerned with hugging me than putting your clothes on? Despite what might have happened?"

"Yes. Wait—no." I sigh. "I don't know. You confuse me."

He shakes his head, his eyes a little dazed. "You're confused? You make it very hard not to touch you."

"You *want* to touch me?"

He smirks and my heart flips. "Woman, have you not been paying attention?"

I frown harder. "But, what about—"

He presses his fingers to my lips. His skin smells of sunlight and metal.

"I forgive you."

"No you don't. You can't. You're lonely. Confused."

"You're the one crying because I almost died."

I squirm at the unwanted reminder. The movement makes me realise he's practically sitting in my lap.

Don't go there.

I jerk my face away from his hand. "Maybe you've convinced yourself you want me. You'll feel guilty after. Angry at me. I'll be the one who gets hurt. Because I killed your brother and you can't possibly forgive me for that."

He flinches, subtle but there, and the laughter fades.

"And if I still say I have?"

"Men will say, and do, anything to get what they want. I won't be manipulated this time." I curl my lip. "I'm not a goddamn conquest."

"Someone hurt you before. Someone you trusted."

Almost trusted.

"None of your business," I say. "Get off me."

Irritation finally replaces the bewildering jitters in my stomach. Blake sits back but doesn't stand up. My legs tingle.

"Not until you tell me about it."

"I can make you move."

He smirks. "You can try."

God, he's infuriating. I should have let the booby trap reduce him to tenderised meat.

I shudder and he tenses, probably anticipating an attack. A feeling like nausea tightens my throat.

Maybe I'm ill. Some toxin in the pool not recognised by the water quality monitor has insinuated its way to my brain and turned me into a blubbering moron.

There's no other explanation.

Blake's unflinching eyes bore into mine. I want to look away.

I'll be steadier when I'm in control.

I bend my leg and trap his calf with my foot, tilting my hips and grabbing his arm to stop him from bracing himself on the ground. He topples but instead of switching our positions, he uses my momentum and extra weight to keep the roll going and slam me onto my side. He wriggles clear and shoves me onto my chest. I wince and yank my bandaged arm free. Kneeling between my legs, he leans his slim body over the rucksack, pressing my uninjured arm to the ground.

Pinned. *Again.*

"Goddammit, Blake," I say.

He chuckles. I thrash, incensed, and try to kick him. His knees force my legs wider. I end up panting, sweaty and helpless.

"If it makes you feel any better, you'd kick my arse if your arm were healed. And you didn't have the rucksack on."

I whip my head to clear the hair from my face and glare at him over my shoulder. "I saved your life, quit being a dick."

"Tell me about the person who hurt you."

"Why?"

He isn't even out of breath. I grit my teeth.

"Perhaps I want to know what's turned you into the fascinating woman you are today."

He's smirking at me, dammit.

I buck, my hips and elbows pushing against the ground. He jerks my arm and I thud down with a wheeze.

"You're going to exhaust yourself."

"Fuck you."

"Feeling better, are we?"

I suck air into my abused chest. "The person who set the trap could come by at any moment. We don't have time for this."

Yes, appeal to his sense of danger.

"The quicker you tell me, the quicker we can leave."

"And then what?"

"Then you get to walk in front until you've calmed down and promise not to beat me up."

"That is a promise you will not be getting."

He laughs and leans closer. I can't inhale but it's probably for the best.

I have nothing complimentary to say.

His lips brush my ear, his breath tickling my cheekbone. "I like fighting with you."

The soft and intimate voice tightens places low in my body.

"His name was Gizzy," I blurt.

Better to remind myself of a lapse in judgement before making another spectacular one.

Blake stills for a heartbeat then eases his weight off and retreats to the nearest tree, one graceful shoulder propped against it, his arms crossed. I scramble to my feet, losing the rucksack and cracking my spine. I pace instead of smacking him in the face as he deserves. Nervous energy fizzes to the tips of my fingers and toes.

The next time he tries to manipulate my ridiculous desire for him, I vow to start singing, "I killed your brother, la-la-la," over and over.

Bet his forgiveness disappears.

I stride in a tight circle, refusing to look at him, his gaze heavy on my skin.

"He captured me in Fellhill, treated me like a person instead of an enemy. Seemed kind, compassionate. Held me while I cried. Sound familiar?" I glance at Blake and start to pivot away but stop mid-motion. "Can I get a gun?"

He raises his eyebrows.

"I think it's obvious I'm not going to kill you. I need one. I hate being unarmed and…"

"Vulnerable."

I scowl. "Yes, fine—vulnerable."

He unbuckles the holster from around his waist and holds it out. I sidle over to him, my muscles tensed for any sudden moves.

"You think I'm going to attack you?"

I swipe the holster from his grip and skip out of reach. "I never know with you."

His smirk—dark and knowing and sexy—punches straight to my gut. I fasten the holster around my hips without any adjustment.

So slim. So dangerous.

I remove the Glock and squeeze it in my hand instead of hugging it to my chest. The familiar weight of it steadies me.

"You were saying?"

I sigh and resume my circuit. "Gizzy promised he wouldn't hurt me, said I could tell him about my torture when I was ready. I believed him. He was the first person I let myself get close to since this whole mess started."

God, I sound naive. Or think a promise, once made, is meant to be kept. Though, as Blake has learned, some promises can be broken no matter how hard you try.

"Are you saying he was the only person you've had sex with

this entire time, and recently?"

I frown at his incredulous expression. "What? Yes, he was the only one. Were you humping like rabbits in Livingston?"

Blake opens and closes his mouth, his eyes sparkling. "No, not like rabbits, no. Normal human beings."

Delight suffuses his face and softens it. His grin is as devastating as his usual sultry expression.

"No wonder you believed everything he said."

I glare at him. "Fine, so I fucked him and lost all my senses. Happy?"

"I'm sure that's not true. I can't imagine you ever let your guard down completely. Not even during an orgasm."

I hug myself.

Just get to the end.

"The woman who torched the dragon, he dumped her for me. Pretty much immediately, even when I was an enemy. That's why she framed me for it. Almost worked, too."

Blake's face sobers, a slight flush still pinking his cheekbones.

"Gizzy followed his leader in believing I'd done it. Destroyed the only thing I loved in the whole damn war. When I was sentenced to death, he was ordered to join the firing squad—"

"He wouldn't."

"—and would've blasted me to pieces if the stupid bitch hadn't stashed the petrol cans in her house. I was released. She was executed. Gizzy stayed in the line. I think he was the one who shot off half her face." My voice rasps, my hand aching where it fists around the Glock. I will myself to relax, taking deep breaths. The words keep coming. "That's why I left Soldiers of the Lost. Couldn't live in Fellhill with Gizzy, who'd promised not to hurt me then pointed a fucking shotgun at me because his leader told him to."

Blake places a hand on my shoulder. "Ease up on the gun, Anita, before your knuckles explode."

I slam the Glock into its holster and my fingers cramp. "Ow. *Dammit.*"

My eyes burn.

No, no more crying. That traitorous bastard doesn't deserve my tears. I'm over it, over him. I didn't even love him.

Pity I wanted to.

Blake lifts my hand and massages his thumb into my palm. I hiss but don't yank away.

"My own fault," I say. "Got what I deserved, believing in him. I won't make that mistake again."

Blake's fingers wrap around my wrist, his other hand continuing to knead. "You can't let one arsehole stop you from trusting and finding someone who makes you happy."

Christ, he's a romantic. How is it possible? After everything I've put him through, he should be more cynical than me.

"You think I should trust you?"

"Who better to trust than the guy pointing guns at you from the start?"

"At least you're honest about hating me."

"I don't hate you."

"You should."

I try to ignore his touch, keep it platonic, but tingles dance up my arm and swoop to my stomach and lower places.

Definitely lower.

A pulse throbs between my legs at each press of his fingers. I tug against his grip. His hands tighten, his eyes dark, hungry. My breath catches.

Goddammit. Why can I never hide my reaction to him?

So *needy*.

"How about you believe I've forgiven you and I'll believe you trust me not to hurt you?" His hand slides up my arm, his thumb rubbing firm circles.

"Fine, okay, whatever," I gasp, fighting not to squirm. "Can we go now?"

He brushes the sensitive skin at the bend of my elbow. I shiver and he presses harder.

"Your pulse is racing."

I lick my lips. "I'm upset."

"Liar."

I jerk my arm out of his grip and cuddle it to my chest. "Lying is the only thing keeping me safe right now."

"From what, me?"

"No, from fucking aliens."

A slow grin curves his mouth. "You like me."

"Don't be ridiculous. You are unbelievably annoying."

"Baby, that's the truth."

Warmth blooms in my chest.

Crap.

I don't want to snap at him for calling me baby. I like it.

Double crap.

"Are we done here? You got what you wanted."

"Not quite." Blake steps closer. "Admit it."

My laugh wobbles. "Admit what? You're delusional. Being alone out here has ruined your social skills."

"Always have to do things the hard way. Admit it and we can go."

"You said that already. Fine—I respect you, all right?"

"Try again."

He stalks towards me. I back-pedal and my spine hits a tree, halting my retreat.

"What are you doing?" I yelp, flinging my arm up to ward him off. "I-I don't detest you."

"Getting warmer."

My hand touches his chest. The shock tingles up my arm. Before I can pull away, he traps my hand with his, his heartbeat fluttering under my palm. An answering pulse quivers in my stomach.

"Admit it."

"Why?"

"It's important to me."

"I admit nothing."

He rolls his eyes. "God, you're stubborn."

"Damn right. Now let go or I'll hurt you."

"Oh, you won't hurt me."

The smug bastard.

I swing my free hand at him. He grabs my wrist below the bandage and presses both of my hands to his chest. I struggle to think past the heat of him. The smell of him.

What would it be like to kiss him?

"Okay, you win!" I squeak. "I like you. Stupidly attracted. It's Stockholm syndrome. Or I'm a masochist. Pick your favourite."

He chuckles. "I knew I could make you talk."

"I hate you," I say through gritted teeth.

"No you don't."

Also true. Dammit.

He releases me and scoops up the discarded rucksack, shrugging it on.

I sag against the tree. "Why was that so important? What

the hell do you want from me?"

"Confirmation."

I force myself to meet his heavy gaze. "Why?"

"Guess we'll find out."

Run. Run right now.

He walks away and my traitorous legs stumble along after.

18

The familiar warmth of Blake curls into my back. His arm and leg flop over mine, hugging me to his chest, his heart beating steadily against my spine.

This is *not* fair. It's hard to resist his touch during the day when he's awake and teasing me. How can I endure it if he keeps cuddling me in his sleep?

You can't, whispers a little voice. *You don't even want to. You want to surrender. You want him to fuck—*

I stomp on the little voice and ease out of Blake's arms.

We didn't go far from the booby trap. It took a while of careful manoeuvring to avoid other tripwires, snares and spike-filled pits. We left the trees for old agricultural fields overgrown with scrub and rank hummocks of grass, setting the pod in the ruins of a farmhouse, the thick stone walls and roof cloaked in ivy and honeysuckle. Collapsed stairs prevented access to the upper level.

I distracted myself by making camp, collecting water, cooking dinner. But then it was time to climb into the pod and I shied away from the intimate, shimmering space. Blake laughed at me, apparently pleased with his effect, but promised to keep his hands to himself.

Sleep seems to render it invalid.

I wriggle further, his fingers sliding up my arm. He murmurs and I freeze but his breathing stays even.

He left me untied, the Glock in my possession. A show of faith.

Why does he want me to trust him? How has he gone from loathing me for killing his brother and destroying his home to wanting to touch me? Loneliness isn't enough to overcome what I did. I can understand grudging acceptance, a mutual parting of ways and never seeing each other again. Nothing more than that.

Would I have forgiven him for Ailsa if our positions were reversed?

But I want him to touch me. Imagining it twists through my stomach and does crazy things to my pulse. And how in the hell have I let that happen? I need to avoid the emotional entrapment. I can't risk sleeping with him. It will make me— *love him, love him*—like him more and he'll leave, having never felt anything for me. Used and discarded. Gizzy on repeat.

Perhaps Blake's beauty hides the blackest heart of all.

He tenses. My heart leaps into my throat, thundering in the confines of the pod.

Crap, he's awake. I'm not ready.

I pretend to sleep. He rolls away from me, the movement pulling me onto my back, and props himself on his elbow.

"Morning," he says and smiles, his hair flopping into his eyes.

Man, they're even more beautiful close up.

Stop staring at him, you dumb bitch! This is why terrible things always happen to you.

I scoot further from him and jerk into a sitting position. "Morning. We should get moving."

I stuff the covers into the rucksack while they're still wrapped around him.

The less time I spend with him in small, intimate spaces, the better. Remove the temptation.

I spy my Glock and fasten the holster around my hips.

Better than a chastity belt.

"We should talk about what happened yesterday," Blake says.

I glance at him. "Nothing happened yesterday."

"You said you liked me."

"I was coerced."

I tug the sleeping bag from under him and cuddle it.

For the comfort, not because it's warm and smells like him.

"Okay, I'll give you that. How about we discuss what we're going to do now, then?"

"What are you, some kind of girl?"

My stupid heart flutters.

Does he want to know where this is going, where we're going?

I swipe a pillow and punch it instead of myself, cramming it into the rucksack. Blake's pillow can stay right where it is.

"I know you're just lashing out because you're embarrassed, but that really hurts my feelings," he says.

A laugh expands in my chest. I squash it and frown at him.

"I have nothing to be embarrassed about."

"You're right. You don't have to be embarrassed about liking me, Anita. I like you, too."

My fingers shake. I lunge for the cleaned pot and forks from last night's dinner.

"Fine," I say, tossing them into the rucksack, "now we've established we're BFFs, are you ready to go?"

"Do you trust me not to hurt you?"

Yes.

No! I don't trust anyone.

I swallow hard. "There are lots of ways to hurt someone."

"There are and it sounds like you've experienced pretty much all of them. But I made you a promise."

Yes, he promised to never do anything I didn't want him to. The problem is, I want him to do everything.

I have to get out of here.

"Great," I say with as much sarcasm as I can muster, "because I don't want you to continue this conversation."

"I only want you to feel comfortable around me."

"I don't think that's ever going to be possible."

For Christ's sake, the guy's presence tingles in my skin and does crazy things to my stomach. Though I probably shouldn't let him know that.

"I mean, I think I'm as comfortable as I'm going to get," I say quickly. "Good talk. Let's go."

I sidle towards the portal, the sleeping bag clenched in my fist.

It isn't much of a shield, and I have no idea what I'll do with it once I get outside, but I'm not about to let it go.

"Do you always run away from things you don't like?"

"I'm not running away," I say, forcing myself to sit still.

He cocks an eyebrow.

The arrogant bastard. If he's so desperate to have a meaningful conversation then I'll choose the subject. It's his turn to be badgered into spilling his secrets.

"Okay, you want to talk?" I snap. "Tell me about your first time in Wick's torture chamber."

He flinches as if I've slapped him. "What if I don't want to talk about that?"

The sudden vulnerability is unexpected.

"I'm sorry, forget I said it. You don't have to tell me anything. Some things are too terrible to share with anyone."

He peeks through the hair fallen over his forehead and framing his eyes. "You shared your thing with me."

"Again—I was coerced."

"Yeah, I really should stop doing that." He sighs. "Guess it's only fair to tell you. I'll look bad if you're brave enough to talk about your thing but I'm not."

"Competitive, are we?"

His eyes lock onto mine. "Oh, yeah. I like to win."

I drop my gaze and slide the sleeping bag into my lap, playing the material through my fingers. We sit in silence for a few minutes, birds flitting in and out of the glassless windows outside the pod.

What did that sick son-of-a-bitch do to him? Do I want to know? Blake is too similar to me. Better than me. How much closer will I feel to him if his experience is as awful as mine?

I'm already too close.

"The first time Wick ordered me into the torture chamber it wasn't to be punished." Blake scrubs his hands through his hair so it falls in messier layers around his face. "He had a girl tied to the table. Naked. Terrified. She was just a kid."

I don't want to hear it. I want to return to him asking me annoying, unanswerable questions, not listen to the torture performed on a poor girl's fragile body.

By Blake.

I spent five days with Wick. Blake lived with him the whole of the war. *For ten years.*

I don't know the half of suffering.

"It's not your fault," I say. "Whatever he made you do, it's not your fault."

"Christ, I didn't think it'd be this hard. It was ages ago."

"But you've never told anyone?"

"Not even Dylan. I was embarrassed and just wanted to forget." Blake shivers.

It's cool in the pod, the building shielding us from direct sunlight, though bright enough due to its indeterminate opalness. I wriggle onto my back and kick the sleeping bag over me. I hold the other side open. Blake eyes me warily but lies down next to me, careful not to touch. We stare at the ceiling.

He clears his throat. "I'm worried you'll think less of me."

"Oh, come on. You heard my story—I turned into a shit-stained, quivering wreck. Plus, I already think you're an asshole, how much worse can it get?"

"True. It's easier knowing you've been in there. You know how terrifying it was. Nobody talked about it. We pretended it didn't happen. But you know."

"I know," I whisper.

I find his hand beneath the covers and wrap his icy fingers in mine.

19

"He wanted me to rape her," Blake says in a rush. "He thought it might be more damaging to be raped by someone who looked like me."

Too beautiful for his own good.

And mine.

"I refused, obviously. Wick had three guards at that point: Selena, Christine"—the Guard-bitches who dragged me to the torture chamber, no doubt—"and Doolly. They grabbed me. I fought them but you saw Doolly. They stripped me and dropped me on the girl. She screamed while they held me there, laughing, goading me on."

How could Wick be so cruel to his own soldiers? The people he needed alive and strong to defend his faction. Marshall was a cuddly puppy in comparison to Wick's savagery. How is Blake not a corrupted shadow of a human being? How can he treat me with forgiveness and compassion and more?

"*I killed them,*" I say, before deciding whether it's a good idea to remind him I destroyed his encampment. "Doolly and one of the Guard-bitches."

He turns his head, close enough for his breath to brush my lips.

"Guard-bitches?"

"My name for Christine and Selena."

"We called them the Hell-twins. I would've killed them if they survived you but none of them did."

Neither did the person he needed the most.

I swallow and shut my eyes but Blake tugs on my hand, forcing me to look at him.

"You're thinking about Dylan."

"I'm sorry. I really am sorry."

"Wick is the reason my brother is dead. Of course you razed us after he brutalised you. He dragged us all down." Blake sucks in a breath. "So I'm just going to say this next bit really fast to get it out of the way—they held me on top of the girl but I couldn't get an erection."

No bloody wonder. Forced onto an unwilling woman, ordered to rape her... Not the ideal conditions for sexual arousal.

"Wick was disappointed. Beat me with his rubber truncheon, but you can't make a guy get excited about raping someone."

Most of the guys I knew wouldn't have needed the order.

"He injected me with a stimulant. Wasn't a normal needle. Went directly into the urethra."

I wince.

Sweet lord.

"After twenty minutes, it had the desired effect, despite me never wanting to have sex again in my life."

How did he find the desire to be intimate again? One man betrayed my trust during sex and I became a nun.

"They tried to push me inside her but I struggled. The girl was hysterical. Wick acted as if it was hilarious but he told them to stop. I thought he'd kill me. Part of me didn't care.

It'd hurt less."

I know what that's like.

"The girl saw the goddamn erection and screamed some more. Wick handed me a knife. He said if I wouldn't rape her, I had two options: watch him with her or kill her myself."

"Jesus," I breathe.

How did he carry this inside him for so long without it hollowing him out?

He is stronger than I can ever be.

"She was just a kid, Anita. She looked at me and her face filled with hope. She wanted to live but she didn't understand what it meant. She had no idea what Wick would do to her."

Blake's eyes glitter. I stare, entranced.

"So I slid the knife into her heart. She didn't even flinch. I killed her because I couldn't stand to watch what Wick would do to her. I don't even regret it. I only wish I'd done it sooner. Not for her sake, but mine."

I roll onto my side, hesitate, then curl against him. He moves his arm and I slot into his shoulder. His heart beats thickly under my ear.

"She was dead as soon as Wick captured her," I say. "You let her go with minimal agony."

"Maybe. But what if she was like you? What if I'd left her alive and she managed to escape?"

"No one's like me."

Blake snorts. "Truth."

I resist pinching his ribs but can't stop from playing with his dog-tags through his t-shirt, my fingertips running over the beaded chains.

"What about your brother? Did Wick do the same to him?"

"Don't know. Thought about it, but I didn't want to know.

He noticed I was distant. Never said anything. Wick either didn't approach him or he did and it didn't bother Dylan as much." Blake's hand strokes my arm. "I tried to forget and Wick left me alone. Apart from when I punched his guard in the face. God, I was petrified of what he'd do. When all he did was whip me, relief almost made it a reward. But it took me a while to let anyone close."

"How did you? Let anyone close, I mean."

He shrugs the shoulder I'm not lying on. "I got lonely."

The thought of a sad and lonely Blake clenches my throat and makes me want to do anything to chase the sorrow away. But I can't cuddle him any tighter without losing myself.

"I imagine it didn't take long to find someone. I'm sure you had your pick of the ladies."

His lips quirk, a shadow of his usual smirk but it gladdens my heart to see it.

"You're not one for coddling, are you?"

"I'd rather get you to laugh again than pat you on the head and say 'there, there.'"

I mean for it to be flippant but it sounds too intimate. Too close to the truth. I want to make him laugh, smile, whisper my name as he touches me.

I want him to touch me.

"Are you not horrified, appalled, shocked?"

"All of those things. But for you, not by you."

He props himself up, my head cradled in the crook of his arm. His fingertips skim my cheekbone and trace my mouth. I stop breathing.

"I'm glad I told you," he says while I stare at him.

I manage a nod and a breathless, "Me too."

God, he's so close.

He smiles, a proper, tender smile that stuns me. His hand slides into my hair. I tilt my face, my lips half-parted.

Oh crap, oh god, what am I doing?

He lowers his head, his eyes fixed on me and really not helping the drowning sensation or the frantic thudding of my pulse.

He promised never to do anything I didn't want him to. All I have to do is say no.

"Do you trust me not to hurt you?" he says.

I should say no. It's the only way to protect myself.

"Yes," I whisper.

And he kisses me.

20

The kiss starts as a gentle caress of lips, so soft and warm. Blake kisses me like he thinks I'm delicate. The tentative pressure rips my defences away, scattering them as if they never existed. I moan into his mouth, my hand fisted in his hair. I arch my back and he shivers above me.

What's one more lapse in judgement if I get to taste that perfect body?

The kiss develops into tongues and teeth and panting breath. Blake thrusts his hips into mine, thick and straining against the material of his combats.

My reasons for resisting vanish.

I tear my mouth from his on a gasp. "Please, Blake. Please."

He props himself up. "Tell me to stop, if that's what you want."

"God, no. Don't stop."

He chuckles a delighted, masculine sound and presses his lips to mine. Gentle again. It isn't enough. I try to deepen the kiss but his grip on my face controls me while the teasing glide of his mouth undoes me. I writhe underneath him, small begging noises in my throat. My heart thunders hard enough to shake my body.

"Please, please, please," I whisper, my voice choked. "We

need to be naked."

He collapses with a groan and devours my mouth. "Baby, you're killing me."

We yank at our clothes. His hands are amazing, stroking my skin until it burns. I'm naked and don't remember how I got there. He pushes himself onto one elbow and watches my face as he slides his fingers inside me. I cry out, bucking underneath him. The orgasm explodes in a rush of heat and leaves me dazed.

Jesus, he barely touched me.

I blink at him through half-lidded eyes.

He grins. "So eager."

"Oh, you bastard. Why did you have to be good?"

"You want me to be rubbish?"

He trails kisses along my jaw and down my neck, his hand skimming my breast.

"No," I sob.

He smirks against my collarbone. I fumble at his combats, frustrated by the weakness in my grip. My fingers curl around the muscled length of him and he shudders, his breath catching in his throat. The trousers disappear. He holds himself off me, his eyes blazing violet.

"Blake, please. I need you. Inside me."

"Finally," he whispers against my lips, "she speaks the truth."

We move together, the slide of his skin almost too much to bear. A glorious weight builds.

God, he knows what he's doing. No jack-rabbit sex from him.

He fills me, surrounds me. Captures me. He guides me to that delicious edge, and jumps. I may scream, blind and deaf to everything but sensation.

Minutes, hours—*days?*—later, he buries his face in my neck, his heart hammering against my chest.

Is he trembling?

I hug him, my fingertips exploring his scars. Ridged and firmer than the untouched skin, they run from his shoulders to the middle of his back, the lumbar area and the curve of his ass perfect and smooth.

He shivers under my touch. It tingles through me. He lifts his head and I catch my breath.

He brushes my hair out of my face and places a delicate kiss on swollen lips. "What have you done to me, you wicked temptress?"

I laugh and it tightens me around him. The sound dies at the heat in his gaze. My slowing pulse bounds into my throat.

I manage to cock an eyebrow when all my other muscles are aquiver. "Already?"

A slow smile curves his lips. "I like to win."

He rotates his hips and my eyes flutter shut, my breath escaping on a moan.

"What have you won?"

He stops moving. I open my eyes after three attempts. The tenderness on his face stuns me.

"You," he says.

My hips rise to meet him, and I lose myself.

21

There's no awkwardness, no tingling rush of embarrassment. Blake cuddles me afterwards, his hands stroking my skin as if he can't stop touching me. His arms feel like home, a refuge, a place I can be myself. No pretending, no running.

Terrifying.

I experienced similar with Gizzy. Damn endorphins. It's stupid to trust them.

Maybe this time it will be different.

Blake has already pointed a gun at my face.

His voice tugs me from worrying about his intentions. "Do you still want to escape the country?"

"Yes..." It sounds suspicious, even to me.

He hoists the rucksack onto his back. "Then I have a better location, one with guaranteed boats rather than relying on what's left in Eyemouth harbour."

I fight to keep my expression neutral and swallow before speaking. "You want to escape with me now?"

"Were you thinking I'd sleep with you and leave? Mock your gullibility and demand a share of the rucksack?"

"No. I don't know. You didn't like my plan earlier."

He crosses to me and I force myself to stay still, meeting his gaze instead of staring at my feet.

"You caught me at a bad moment. You'd got under my skin, somehow. It made me feel disloyal to Dylan."

Blake quirks his mouth, his hands encircling my waist and pulling me against him. I place my palm on his chest, unable to resist touching him.

"I'm pretty sure he'd forgive me. So, yes, I'm coming with you."

He closes the tiny space between us. The warmth and smell of him scramble my brain. I fist my hand in his t-shirt, an eager sound in my throat. His answering growl speeds my pulse, desire curling in my stomach. His fingers tighten and I grind my hips against him. I remind myself I am an intelligent woman—a soldier—not some panting nymphomaniac but he slips his talented hands under my t-shirt and strokes up my ribs. My spine bows, tearing my mouth from his. He nibbles along my jaw, his teeth grazing my throat over my thundering pulse.

"God, you can't control yourself around me, can you?" he whispers with something like awe.

I open my mouth but don't have the strength to lie. "No. It's not goddamn fair."

"I like it. It's endearing."

I've never been called that before.

Releasing him, I reboot my brain cells. "You said you had a better location in mind?"

"Yeah. Would you get the map?"

I pull the flexible screen from a side pocket of the rucksack and programme it to show the eastern coast.

"Here." His finger taps. The image magnifies to an area called Scoughall Bay, half-way between North Berwick and Dunbar. "North Berwick no longer exists. Dunbar, stronghold of Unification Army, controls the majority of coast, right up to Embra. They moor their warships in this bay when on patrol. What about that for an escape vehicle?"

The screen creaks under my clenched fingers. "How the hell do you know that?"

"Wick. He pushed us deep into no man's land to capture prisoners from different factions, people who might have the knowledge he needed to create the dragon. When she was capable enough, he took her on test flights at night, dropping into encampments and spiriting people away."

I shudder in the heat.

I never heard rumours of a beast swooping from the dark without warning. There were no unexplained disappearances from Calders. Perhaps Wick only harvested from distant encampments to avoid alerting his neighbours.

If we knew what he'd built, we would have attacked before he slaughtered us all.

"He captured a man from Dunbar. The man begged for mercy and Wick said he'd grant it, if the man shared his faction's secrets. He talked about the warships. Wick tortured him until he died." Blake grimaces. "Watched the whole video of that one."

I tuck the screen into the rucksack, banishing thoughts of Wick before they spoil the day. We leave the ruins of the farmhouse and plunge into tangled fields stretching to the horizon.

Blake has the electrigun strapped to his left arm, the Browning tucked into the waistband of his combats. I've no idea where he stashed dreamy Gavin's knife. The Glock sits around my waist, the SL2 and flick-knife in my boot.

Back on the road after a confusing hiatus with something

unexpected—a companion. One who went from wanting me dead to making me beg, so eager and breathless.

I mean, Christ, how many times did I say, "Please?"

My cheeks flush.

Finally with the embarrassment. But no regret.

Not yet, whispers the voice.

Blake leads me through choking scrub and hummocks of grass, angling towards our destination.

It's unlikely we'll reach it in one day, having a late start from being somewhat distracted but tomorrow… Tomorrow I could be looking at these famous warships.

If I'm not *distracted* a few more times.

God, he's good. Smirking mouth, clever fingers. Excellent stamina.

I wobble and grab onto an elder bush. A sharp smell rises from the leaves crushed in my fist.

"You okay?"

"I'm having a flashback," I gasp before I can think of lying.

"To…" Blake stops and laughs a very satisfied laugh. "A sex flashback?"

"Shut up."

He chuckles, so immensely pleased with himself. I release my grip and crumpled leaves drop to the parched ground. Blake steps towards me.

"No, don't touch me, it'll make it worse. I turn into a slavering idiot when you touch me."

"An endearing, slavering idiot."

I bare my teeth. "Keep walking."

He pivots on his heel, still grinning, and crunches on through the foliage. I berate myself and trail after him.

Who knew that slender body could be wielded with such

skill? He's a warrior—tough, unflinching—but gentle enough to make my eyes roll back.

I trip over a root, thumping to the grass on hands and knees.

"Shit," I mutter at the dirt.

"Do you need me to carry you? I never knew you were this clumsy."

Has he drugged me? Or hypnotism, yes. But not with his eyes. No, with another part of his anatomy.

Stop picturing him naked!

I shove to my feet. "I'm fine. Dehydrated, or coming down with something. Distract me. Talk."

"About what?"

"I don't know. Your first pet's name. Your favourite ice cream. What subjects you took in high school. Indulge me."

He arrows through a patch of broom, scattering the yellow flowers in a waft of coconut. "Sylvester—my gerbil. Best pet ever. I like cherry vanilla but have forgotten what it tastes like. Paid little attention in high school. Didn't care for anything but P.E. Bit of a rebel."

A bad boy. How is a woman supposed to resist?

"Grew up at sixteen when my dad died. Cancer. My mum waited until I finished school then moved back to Ireland. Dylan went with her. Two years after that, the rebellion began."

We stop in a circle of hawthorn to rest and eat. I frown at my fingers, gathering courage. I peek at Blake through my hair.

"What was your brother like?"

"Blond. Bulkier than me. Competitive arse." Pride tinges his voice. "He would've liked you."

It's difficult to say much after that.

22

The heat eases, the fields continuing in an endless patchwork bordered by trees and tangled hedgerows. We follow the remains of roads, every village deserted and crumbling into the dirt.

Where are the Borderlanders hiding?

The ground undulates beneath our feet in ankle-twisting mounds. I claw myself out of a trench flanking the next field, copying Blake in snarling at the sting of nettles, though my words are slightly more profane.

"What was your role in Livingston or did you just work on the dragon?"

My confidence grows with each question. He hasn't snapped at me to shut the hell up or mind my own business.

Like I would have.

"The dragon took up a chunk of time but I managed the jets when not working on her. Advanced to team leader."

Course he did. He likes to win.

"Dylan was jealous of that one. I officially got to boss him around, though didn't do it for that. I was making myself invaluable so Wick wouldn't drag me back into the torture chamber."

I bark a laugh. "I thought I was pretty invaluable. Respected.

Turns out Marshall just viewed me as another Carmichael to fuck and be conquered."

Blake jumps over a ditch on the other side of the field and pauses to catch his breath.

"Don't take this the wrong way, I absolutely hate the guy—he's a vile sexual predator—but a tiny bit of me understands his obsession."

I roll my eyes. "What, I lure men with my aura of charm and mystery?"

"I'm here, aren't I?"

"I have no idea why you're here. With me."

"You think I should've killed you? Hurt you and abandoned you with nothing?"

"It's what I did to you. What I deserve."

He shakes his head. "Everything you said when we first met was true—it's a war, people die; I'd have done the same—but I didn't want to listen."

"I killed your brother."

His sad smile bruises my heart. "You didn't personally look him in the eye and bash his head in. You had no clue who or where he was. You were a force of nature. A vengeful bitch of one but a force of nature nonetheless."

"The bitch part is right."

"Seems like you've been punishing yourself better than I have." Dark, serious eyes meet mine. "Maybe we deserve a little happiness. You've lost someone, too."

"But you didn't kill my sister."

"That was unfair of me to say."

"No, it wasn't."

"Do you always argue, even when it's in your favour?"

I open my mouth to disagree then shut it again instead of

proving his point.

The smart-ass.

We enter the shade of trees. A river burbles, golden beams of sunlight dappling the ground.

Blake glances over his shoulder. "Anyway, what's with the background check? You deciding if I'm trustworthy?"

I blush. "Sorry."

Damn. Too obvious. I want to know more about him. I want to know *everything*. What was a typical day like in Livingston? Why were they so certain Revolutionary Front were to blame for Daniel Wick's near-assassination? How many battles has Blake fought in? How many people has he killed? Is it anywhere near my level of rampage?

He cups my face. "You're sexier when you blush."

I blush harder, the cool air under the trees too thick to breathe. Blake purrs low in his throat and kisses me.

Oh, the addictive taste of his lips.

My arms wrap around his waist, my hips pushed into his. The slide of his tongue tingles to my toes and shivers through my stomach. I moan into his mouth, my fingers gripping his ass to avoid crumpling at his feet.

That would be undignified.

He pulls away on a shaky laugh. "God, woman. You make it easy to forget where we are. But this does seem as good a place as any to set up camp."

Crap. Camp means getting naked, and sex. More glorious sex. Every time I sleep with him, I forfeit another piece of myself.

Nervous anticipation jitters in my stomach but it fails to dampen the arousal. I suspect death will be the only thing that can.

Mine, or his.

My throat tightens.

Jesus, when did I become so emotional?

A grassy hollow opens beside the gurgling river, sheltered by an overhang of earth, trees and dangling roots. The water, tested clean, has carved a trench, swirling into a lazy pool beneath a rock face.

The routine of making camp settles me. I smooth the sleeping bag and inflate the pillows.

Touch my weapons for reassurance.

Blake appears and presses me to the covers, his slender body fitting so perfectly.

I'm not so settled anymore.

His mouth captures mine, his hands slipping under my t-shirt and skimming my nipples, separated by fabric. He pulls my top off and trails his lips down my neck to the bullet scar in the hollow of my shoulder. He licks it, his tongue burning and wet. I jump, my breath shuddering out. He wriggles lower, his mouth tracing the abdominal scar. He raises his head and I whimper.

So needy, so eager.

"When did you get this?"

My power of speech appears to be lost. It takes three attempts to form words. "In Calders. Before I stole the dragon."

"What did you lose?"

I clear my throat. "Spleen and part of my liver."

The gentle caress returns. "You don't have knife scars. Well, not recent ones."

His fingertips tickle across an indiscernible silvery line near my hip.

Evidence of John's first knife attack.

"I was beaten. After I was shot."

God, the desire in my voice couldn't be more obvious. I crave Blake's touch too much for the subject to divert me.

"And you flew to Fellhill in the dragon like that?"

"I'm a stubborn bitch."

"Yeah you are." His fierce expression punches into my gut. "I won't let anyone hurt you again."

I close my eyes.

It's too much. I don't deserve it. Don't deserve his attention, his forgiveness…

Him. I don't deserve him.

How can he want me?

"You don't believe me?" he says. "That's okay, I'll prove it to you."

His breath scorches my stomach. He kisses the sensitive skin between my hip bones, his fingers curled in the waistband of my combats, so very close to the aching centre of me.

"What's the opposite of pain? Oh, yes."

He licks my stomach and my eyes snap open. He smirks, his slim fingers unfastening the trousers and sliding them down my hips.

"Wait!"

"Why?"

I have a reason, right? A good, sensible reason?

"I don't know."

"God, you're still fighting your attraction to me." His voice holds heat but it's not anger. "That is so fucking sexy."

He pulls my combats and underwear off. I fist my hand in the covers, struggling to ground myself. He spreads my legs with a wicked smile and everything south of my waist pulses.

My eyelids flutter, my breath rushing out.

Oh god, that mouth. That smirking, knowing mouth. I'll beg and tell him everything, anything he wants to know, as long as he touches me.

He nibbles my inner thigh and it bows my spine.

"Blake, please," I moan, blinking at him.

He raises his head, his eyes violet fire. "What's your biggest fear?"

That I'm good enough to fuck but not to love.

"Spiders," I gasp. "I'm deathly afraid of spiders."

He chuckles, placing a soft kiss on the most intimate part of me. My body spasms.

"Liar. Try again."

How does he sound calm? I'm fighting to hold myself together.

He lowers his head and I tense but his mouth teases my other thigh. His fingers caress behind my knees, each stroke tingling between my legs.

I squirm, my voice shaking. "That's not fair. I can't think… Blake."

His hands tighten. "Tell me."

"Being alone." *Shut up, shut up!* "And you."

Oh, Jesus.

"You're afraid of me?" The emotion in his voice hurts my chest. "You weren't afraid when I was marching you around at gunpoint but now you're scared?"

"Yes."

"Why?"

I shake my head, my hair whipping across my face. His tongue trails a scorching path between my legs. I jerk upwards with a strangled cry. He pulls away and I collapse into the pillows.

"You bastard," I say, my eyes half-lidded.

"Tell me something I don't know."

Frustrated arousal threatens to burst me into a thousand pieces. My skin stretches, thick and swollen.

"Marching me around at gunpoint made sense. But this—this I don't understand."

"What's to understand? When we met in the woods, I was close to giving up. Exhausted, starving. I had nothing but grief. You had what I needed and I took it. Felt justified knowing you were The People's Republic. Discovering you were the one—Wick's last prisoner—I wanted to hurt you. But you were not what I expected. You've been hurt worse by so many people. What right did I have to punish you for something you couldn't control?"

I fail to relax with his hands gripping my thighs, his hot breath caressing fevered skin.

"I could've flown away. Killed Wick and left the rest of you."

"Really? Thinking we were sadists like him? Wondering if we'd watch the video of your ordeal? Knowing we would attack Calders to take back what was ours?"

I shudder and my breath hitches. "No, okay? I had to. I had to destroy you so I could live. Heal. Forget. I'm sorry."

"You don't need to apologise anymore. I'm the one who's sorry. But I'll make it up to you."

His fingers skim higher over my hipbones to tickle the sensitive skin of my stomach. My heels dig into the covers. His weight on my thighs traps me at his mercy.

He lowers his head. "You still scared?"

"Terrified," I pant.

"Baby, I guess you'll have to trust me."

Finally—*finally*—his mouth is between my legs. He hums a deep sound of satisfaction, the vibration thrumming through me. I squirm, his hands pressing my body to him. He explores me with lips and tongue and nibbling teeth.

"Oh god, oh god, oh god," I whisper.

It's impossible to stop.

That *mouth*.

My world explodes.

I may faint.

Blake chuckles against me and I yelp. He scoops my limp body into his arms and cuddles me to his chest.

"Not alone anymore," he murmurs into my hair.

23

Chilly water caresses my bare ass and sensitive, swollen places. I curl tighter in Blake's arms as he wades into the river.

I can't protest since I'm having trouble forming words like a coherent human being.

I still don't understand. How can Blake treat me with tenderness? He should be angry. Slaughter me to avenge his sibling, like I did with Marshall, not treasure and tease me.

Maybe he will, in the end.

I shiver and his arms tighten. "Don't worry, I'll warm you up soon."

Oh god, he isn't finished.

Water swirls over his waist and into my lap. I hiss, climbing higher up his body. He chuckles and shifts me in his arms. I wrap my legs around his waist, suddenly staring into his disconcerting eyes.

He presses me to the rock face. "Now, I'm going to fuck you. Hard."

My body pulses, my skin flushing despite the coolness of the river.

"Yes, please," I gasp.

Dammit, already with the begging.

His fingers grip my thighs, angling my hips. He thrusts into me and I writhe against the stone. He draws himself only far enough out to slam back in. The water eddies, a cold caress, but his skin burns me anyway. The rock digs into my spine. His lips crush down and I moan into his mouth.

Our weapons are in the pod. We're unarmed and naked. Anyone—anything—could discover us but dying with Blake inside me doesn't seem like such a bad way to go.

He grabs my hands and presses them above my head.

There's no flutter of panic at being pinned.

His fingers entwine in mine. I arch against him and he pulls away.

"God, Anita, you are freaking amazing," he groans.

My name on his lips drives me crazy. I tighten around him. He shudders and his breath rushes out. The pleasure builds, spilling my soft cries. My head flops to the side, my eyes half-lidded. Blake freezes and my eyes snap open.

"Look at me," he growls. "I want to see your face when I make you come."

"Blake, oh god, don't stop. Please don't stop."

He drives himself into me and I squirm, so deliciously close. I stare into the eyes that disarmed and confused me from the start.

They are violet and cobalt-blue light, filled with need and wonder and possession.

One final thrust undoes me. His gaze darkens and he cries out.

The vulnerability of release is too much. Too intimate.

I shut my eyes and buck against the stone. We collapse into each other but Blake keeps us upright, the swirling river swallowing our heat. His heart thunders in harmony to mine, the fading sunlight gilding his slick skin. I curl around him, craving the feel of him, the taste of him, the smell of him.

It's intoxicating.

I want to climb inside him. To never let go. I want more of him. All of him. Everything.

Oh, shit…

I love him.

24

Nope, not possible. I've known Blake for four days, most of which I've been his prisoner. The orgasm euphoria is confusing my hormones.

I repeat it to myself, stumbling from the river and climbing into the pod.

Blake doesn't love me. Sex is a basic human need and I am the only willing female. Maybe he pretties it up in his head with forgiveness and mutual, bewildering attraction but he'll never love the person who murdered his brother. How can he without picturing Dylan's dust-smeared, blood-spattered face after digging him free of the rubble I buried him in?

He can't. So I'm not in love with him.

Simple.

If we reach the rest of the world and it's safe, our paths will separate. He'll forget me as soon as a flock of other women surround him.

Soft, feminine women who didn't destroy his home and family with a war machine.

I dismiss the ache in my stomach as a result of our exertions in the river. I'm not upset at the thought of him leaving me.

That would be ridiculous.

He sighs and cuddles into me, spooning his nakedness

against mine. "Goodnight, Anita."

He kisses my bare shoulder and the ache expands into my chest.

Stop this foolishness. You like him. He's amazing in bed. Don't be tricked into thinking it means something. You're being a girl.

I clear my throat. "Goodnight, Blake."

He wiggles closer, his groin pressed to my butt. I bite my lip but his breathing steadies, his body relaxing into mine. I fall asleep berating myself.

* * *

I wake sprawled across his chest.

What else is new?

Pearlescent light shimmers, the burble of the river a pleasant backdrop. Birds twitter in the trees outside.

I push myself up with my good arm.

Black lashes caress Blake's cheekbones, his head turned to the side. The curve of his neck begs me to kiss it. I drop my gaze to his chest, to the line of his collarbone and the rise and fall of his ribs.

Screw it. At least I'll make myself difficult to forget. It's time for him to be the one squirming and begging and breathless.

I straddle him and kiss the corner of his mouth. His lips lift in a smile.

"Morning," I whisper.

I kiss him as though I want to climb inside and roll around. Kiss him until his heart pounds as fast as my own and his hips flex, his hands pressing me to the hard length of him.

It's too easy to get distracted. I want to be the one in charge.

His body responding to me, writhing for me.

Moaning my name.

I break the kiss on a gasp. Blake blinks at me, his expression dazed.

I surrender to my fascination, to the thing I wanted to do since he first took off his t-shirt and fried my brain cells.

I trail my mouth down his neck and lick along his collarbone to the hollow of his throat. He shudders and I slide lower. My tongue teases each nipple. He squirms, a whine in his throat.

Oh, god. Adorable.

Focus!

I suck the bunch of each abdominal muscle. Blake watches me, his lips half-parted, his eyes frantic.

"Anita, wait."

Desperate, as I was under the promise of his mouth. My body pulses at the loss of control in his voice.

"I haven't—I won't—"

I lick him. His breath shakes. I bend my head and slide him into my mouth. He cries out, his hips bucking. His reaction tingles through my gut and between my legs. I swallow him as deep as he'll go, my throat spasming around him. Already, he's overcome.

I am a sex *goddess*.

It takes him a few minutes to stop writhing. I grin at his half-lidded eyes and the pulse fluttering in the hollow of his throat.

"Now who's the eager one?" I say.

His gaze narrows.

Great, Anita, insult his sexual prowess.

I open my mouth to apologise or make a joke. He clamps his legs around my waist and rolls me over. His body presses me to the floor. Naked, scorching.

"You're going to regret that," he whispers, his mouth nuzzling my throat.

A tightness in my chest eases.

He isn't mad at me.

Jesus. How far have I fallen?

"I regret nothing," I say. "About time you lost control. I can't be the only slavering idiot around here."

His lips tickle my collarbone, heat pooling between my legs and shivering in my stomach. One hand skims my ribs, his fingertips brushing my breast. The moan slips out before I can clamp my teeth on it.

Blake smiles, his hot breath branding my skin. "No deal. It's more fun when it's you. And it's not my fault—you caught me off-guard."

"Off-guard? I barely had to touch you."

He flexes his hips and I lose the ability to breathe. The weight of him on top speeds my pulse, the feel of him so very close. Anticipation tingles to my toes. My hips rise, aching for him.

"Oh no, you're not getting that yet, you wanton little hussy," he chuckles, lifting himself off me to balance on his elbows.

I try not to pout. "That's not fair. At least I didn't demand to hear your secrets."

He shifts onto his back, pulling me against him. His arm pins me to his side. I slide my hand down his stomach but he captures it and places it over his heart.

"You want secrets? Okay then. I haven't been touched like that in a while."

I pause in my attempt to tug my hand free, and raise my head. "I guess two months would seem like an eternity for someone like you."

"What's that supposed to mean?"

"Oh, come on. You scream sex. Your eyes, your body. It all says, 'I am awesome in bed. You will beg for me.'"

He bites his lip, a strangled noise in his throat. "Awesome, am I?"

"I… Shut up."

"And you're what, sexless? Have you looked in a mirror?"

"Fine, fine. I'm easy on the eyes. Most men just see the blonde hair."

He releases my hand, his fingers weaving through it, tugging gently. "While I'll admit it is a distraction, it's not what I see."

"You also a tits and ass man?"

He laughs and his fingers tighten. "Don't remind me. I'm glad you shot the sneering twat. I wanted to kill him for touching you."

"You hadn't touched me then."

Blake's face sobers. "The scars finally made me notice how often you've been hurt. I wanted to protect you."

"That's not all you wanted."

To my surprise, a slight flush pinks his cheeks. "God, I was pissed at myself. Pawing at you. After what the guy might have done."

"My reaction was hardly revulsion."

"I can never tell with you." His fingers slide through my hair to cup my head. "You're not like any other enemy I've met."

"And that's why you wanted confirmation?"

"Confirmation it definitely wouldn't be rape."

God, he is too perfect.

I kiss him and lose myself in the taste of his mouth. I trail my hand downward and stroke the swell of each abdominal muscle. With a soft noise in his throat, he catches my hand again and presses it to his chest.

"Now you're the one who can't keep her hands to herself."

My cheeks heat. I dodge his sparkling eyes and frown at his collarbone.

"Well, that wasn't much of a secret. Of course you haven't met another woman out here. None you'd touch without gloves and some strong bleach, anyway."

"I wasn't finished. You diverted me by saying how awesome I am."

The blush spreads, prickling my neck and burrowing between my shoulders.

I really need to think before I open my mouth. Talking gets me into trouble. Talking to Blake, telling him my secrets, is dangerous.

Especially now.

I swallow. "Go on then. Finish it."

"It was longer than two months."

"You said you were all having lots of sex in Livingston."

"Sex, yes, but…" He shrugs. "I focused on them having a great time. Didn't force them to reciprocate. I still got intercourse."

I stare at him and he avoids my gaze.

He's embarrassed. How cute.

"The women of Nationless are idiots. How could they not touch you like that?"

After Wick, he must have wanted to know anyone in his bed was willing to be there. Begging him to fuck them.

To drown out the person who begged him not to.

The expression on his face hurts my heart. So strong, so honourable.

So vulnerable.

"Most people are selfish. But not you." He squeezes my hand. "You look at me like…"

I gulp. Crap. Don't ask—"Like what?"

Dammit.

"Like you see me. Know me. Like… I don't know. Something deeper."

Change the subject!

"Oh, I see you all right." I let a slow smile curve my lips. "I'm going to have such fun with you."

His eyes widen. My mouth hovers over his.

"I'm due some payback."

"Payback for what?"

"For turning me into a slavering idiot."

I give him a version of his own knowing, sexy smirk and kiss him, a soft glide of lips. I pull away and his heart pounds under our linked hands.

God, I love—

Nope. I'm having fun teasing him. That's all.

He tenses beneath me, an eager sound in his throat, and my hard-won control vanishes. I mould my body to his and eat at his mouth. Desperate, throbbing, needing to be closer, to have his skin, hot and slick, against mine.

He rolls, breaking the kiss with a gasp. "Dammit, woman. I was the one getting payback. How do you do that?"

I blink at him, too dazed to speak.

He chuckles. "Okay, the expression on your face is worth it. If you behave yourself, maybe I'll get you to moan my name later."

"Blake…"

"Mmm. Like that but a bit *breathier*."

I choke. He grins and climbs off me, dragging clothes from the rucksack.

"What are you doing?"

"Come on, get dressed. Let's go hunting."

"Hunting?" I goggle, my brain bereft of blood.

"God, woman, do you only think of one thing? We're low on food. If you want to keep humping like rabbits, we need sustenance."

I close my stupid mouth and blindly tug on combats and a top, my blush strong enough to warm the pod. Blake continues to smirk at me and I drop my gaze.

"Oh, goddammit," I sigh at the navy combats and t-shirt.

"Always wearing my clothes. If you want to be my girlfriend, you just have to ask."

Is that all it takes? Ask him, *ask him!*

"Shut up," I growl.

His laughter chases me out of the pod.

25

"Venison for lunch?" Blake whispers, the electrigun steadied against bark.

I shift to peek around his shoulder, trying not to breathe loudly. "That's presumptuous. You've not fired this thing before."

The roe deer lowers her head, nibbling oak leaves from a sapling and flicking her velvet ears.

"This *thing* is an electrigun," he says with an exaggerated eyebrow raise. "Can't believe you doubt my skills."

I swallow a laugh. The deer paws at the ground, the white flash of her rump bright in the gloom of the trees.

"Forgive me, oh Master. You are mighty. You are wise. I am but a humble—"

"Stop it," he snorts. "You're ruining my aim."

"Hurry up then, before the storm gets here."

Swollen clouds hulk over us, close enough to touch. The air presses in, weighted by static. Blake's fingers tighten on the bulb of the electrigun. Thunder grumbles. A blaze of electricity zaps from the weapon. The deer bounds away and the bolt strikes a silver birch, crisping the papery bark.

"Shit," Blake sighs.

I clap a hand over my mouth to smother a giggle.

"You better not be laughing at me, woman."

I shake my head, my fingers clamped to my face, my breath whistling through my nose. Blake steps towards me, his dark hair falling into dark eyes.

"You—set fire to—a tree." I hiccup, my voice wobbling. "Such skill."

"What did I say about behaving?"

"You're right, you're right. A feast of charred bark awaits."

My laughter bursts out. A predatory smile curves Blake's lips. He lunges for me and I dodge with a yelp. He chases me through the trees. I struggle to breathe, laugh and run, a wild excitement curled in my belly, a feeling close to fear gripping my throat. He almost corners me in a maze of bramble. I squeal—*squeal*—and dart away. Blinded by tears and winded from laughing so hard, I don't get far. Blake tackles me to the ground, pins my wrists above my head and straddles my hips.

"You're not perfect," I pant. "Hallelujah!"

"You think I'm perfect?"

"Not anymore," I snicker, wriggling under his touch. "Oh, god. Stomach hurts. Not laughed—so much—in ages."

"It's only been a few days. Lobbing fish at me amused you."

"Don't remind me. Hilarious. Your *face*."

His expression softens. "God, you're beautiful."

He kisses me and sucks the last of my oxygen away. My heart thrashes against my ribs. Thunder rumbles, raising every hair on my body. Blake pushes himself up and leaves me woozy.

"I like hearing you laugh," he says.

"Not had much to laugh about before now."

Lightning flickers, caged within the lavender-tinted clouds. I can't meet his gaze. It's too piercing, too perceptive. He sees inside me.

"Me neither," he says. "Even with Dylan, Livingston wasn't a happy place. Wick's damn torture videos."

I shudder. Thunder provides an ominous backdrop, the clouds forcing a premature twilight over the landscape. A fat raindrop strikes my face and trickles down my cheek.

Blake climbs to his feet and holds out a hand. "Come on. Before we get soaked."

I let him help me up, my legs a little shaky. Rain hisses through the woods, quaking the leaves and darkening the soil. We jog, hand in hand, to a shallow overhang of rock. Trees and roots sprawl at the top, dangling to obscure the entrance. I tug on Blake's hand, jerking him back a step, and beat him into the coolness of the shelter. He follows half a second behind, grinning at me, rain speckling his green t-shirt and combats.

How can he look at me without seeing his dead brother? How can he be playful and affectionate? He deserves to be happy. I'll do whatever it takes to keep him that way.

I like hearing him laugh, too.

Love it.

Lightning bursts from the clouds, gilding the forest silver. Rain drums on the ground and batters the undergrowth.

Blake fists his hand in my hair and pulls me against him. "Just because I've decided you can live doesn't mean you get to stop being placatory."

"At least you're not a hard man to please."

"That mouth of yours. It must have gotten you into so much trouble."

"You have no idea."

Chuckling, he kisses me. The soft and gentle exploration plays havoc with my pulse. His hold on my hair controls me, his other hand cradling my face, his thumb brushing my cheek. Eager sounds build in my throat, my fingers gripping his slim hips. I grind myself against him and his hands ease me away. He smirks while I blink and tremble.

"Could you ever refuse me?"

I raise my chin. "Yes. If I wanted to."

"Liar."

I bat at his hands. "You don't have to be so smug."

"Sure I do. This definitely means I win."

"We'll see. I'm not finished with you yet."

He slings his arm around my shoulders. "I hope not."

The storm drenches the forest, water cascading from the overhang above us to form a shimmering veil. The shushing roar isolates, soothes, Blake and I the only two people left in the world.

"You want to hear another secret?"

I jump at his quiet voice, mesmerised by the tinkling splash of water.

"What?"

"Wick was attracted to me."

I drag my gaze from the rain to meet Blake's serious eyes. "He what?"

"After he whipped me—when I was stripped to the waist, my hands bound above my head, bleeding—he said if he liked guys, he'd spend every day buried inside me."

I shudder. "Sweet-fucking-Jesus. Why does that make me think of him ripping you open rather than something tender and intimate?"

"Because you met him."

Bruised clouds roil, lightning chasing the thunder without pause. It highlights Blake's face and dances shadows through his eyes.

"I'm sorry you had to live with him. I barely managed five days but you survived *years*. He tortured you in his own way. Did Dylan know?"

"Couldn't tell him. You're the only one who knows all my secrets."

"Thank you."

The simple words swell with everything I can't say. One day, I hope to deserve his trust.

"It gets worse," he says.

"Of course it does."

"He forced me to watch while he called in one of his women to service him. Janine. I don't know how she stomached it. Everything he did and she worshipped him."

I jolt. "I knew Janine—dark hair, pixie features?"

"Yeah. How?"

"From before. We worked together. We were friends." I recall her snarling face and the way she spat my name when I bumped into her during my escape from Livingston. "She was nothing like I remember."

"Are you saying you haven't changed? You've always been this warrior-woman who can't form more than two sentences without using the f-word?" Half his mouth curls in a pale imitation of his teasing smile.

The sadness hurts my heart. I want a proper smile, delight flashing in his eyes. Or the dazed look he gets when I turn into a panting nympho.

He's had enough pain.

"Okay, so there may have been less swearing. And some girlish softness."

He snorts. "Can't picture it."

"Don't you mock me."

"Or what? You'll hurt me with your girlish softness?"

I flash him a wicked grin.

He tenses. "Don't—"

I duck under his arm and shove him. He lurches into the deluge, his clothes moulded to him in seconds.

"How's that for soft?" I shout over the rain, my laughter bubbling at his startled expression.

Black hair drips in spikes to frame the planes of his face. Water beads in his eyelashes and slicks his skin. Taking advantage of my open-mouthed adoration, he lunges through the waterfall separating us. Slender fingers curl around my wrist.

"Wait!" I squeak.

"Oh, I don't think so."

He jerks me out of the shelter and into the warm torrent. It pounds the top of my head, soaking me instantly. I stumble and he catches me, his arms around my waist, my hands on his shoulders.

"It's actually quite refreshing," he says.

I cup his face, my thumb tracing the water from his pouty bottom lip. "You're beautiful, too."

He swallows, droplets ringing his violet eyes. "Beautiful, awesome and nearly perfect? You're going to turn me into a narcissist."

I trail my fingers along his collarbone, dipping into the hollow of his throat. His pulse flutters against my fingertips and an answering throb starts low.

"God, I love the way you look at me," he growls.

He lifts me up. My legs wrap around his waist.

He tastes of rain and earth. *Life.*

Peeling me from sodden clothes, he drives me to the edge of madness with his body, my heartbeat rivalling the thunder. I scream his name and triumph blazes in his eyes, dazzling me more than the lightning.

We stagger back to the pod half-drowned, Blake managing to shoot a bedraggled pheasant in a puff of feathers. The storm peters out in the evening, too late for us to cover any ground. We spend the extra rest time cuddled in the sleeping bag, skin to skin, drying off and talking.

He tells me what Livingston and Nationless were like, about the battles he fought, the people he knew. He talks about his family and the early chaotic years of the war.

I tell him how I was captured by Revolutionary Front and taken to Lowkirk, John's encampment. I tell him everything. Nearly everything. He already knows my most shameful memory, has been victim to the worst I can do, and still holds me in his arms, his warm mouth kissing my bare shoulder.

No man's land *has* made him crazy. Crazy enough to forgive me.

But I guard the last, tiny piece of myself. I can't share it. It's too ludicrous. Too dangerous. Blake has enough power over my body.

I can't tell him he has my heart as well.

26

Fields spit us onto the remains of a motorway swathed in windblown soil and sand. Rust flakes from the braided wire of the central reservation and speckles the grass below.

"Christ, look at that," I say, walking further up the carriage-way. "I guess the rest of the world tried to respond after all."

Battered vehicles rust on the concrete in a convoy of black and twisted metal. United Nations, Red Cross, some kind of media van. Bullet holes pock the trucks, the road beneath them fractured.

Probably Soldiers of the fucking Lost. Some of our blame was misguided but they still did a lot of shit.

We climb across the central reservation, scrambling up a low embankment through gorse and willow. It slopes to the remains of a railway line, wires drooping between masts, the rails and sleepers removed or rotted away. We crunch over a collapsed wooden fence past a pile of pink-bricked rubble and reach our penultimate road.

A dirt track stretches uphill between towering trees and tangled vegetation. The crumbling skeleton of a village wavers in the heat. Ash trees grow in the broken stone and soil, the dusty ground swirling in the strengthening wind.

Each breath tastes of the sea and fires excitement to my

fingertips.

The road continues past the shattered buildings, flanked by a low wall thick with dying moss. Pine trees sway above us, framing a slice of shimmering blue.

"Stay and rest a minute," I pant. "Christ, it's hot."

Blake smirks. "Never would have pegged you as unfit."

"I can see you gasping and sweating from here. You're not even wearing the rucksack."

He pauses in the act of wiping his forehead on his sleeve. "I'm not sweating, I'm glowing."

"Of course. My bad."

He opens his mouth but stops and cocks his head. The purr of engines drifts somewhere from the other side of the woodland. Our eyes meet.

"Well, that can't be good."

I slug tepid water from our bottle and pass it to him. "Hide or keep moving?"

The engines sputter and die.

"Hide. Less noisy."

We hop over the wall and hustle into the ruins, hunkering down in a building with three sides left standing. I press my shoulder to filthy stone and peer through a shattered window facing the road, sunlight winking off the shards of glass left in the frame. Nothing moves in the needle-carpeted space of the forest. No crunch of branches or whisper of voices.

"Reminds me of the day I met you," I say, glancing at Blake and squeezing the Glock in my hand.

He leans against the wall on the other side of the window. "How so?"

"I heard an engine that time, too. Hid in a tree while four guys searched for me. Borderlanders, I think. One of them stepped on a mine."

"I heard it from my own hideout in a tree." He flashes a grin. "You escaped them to get jumped by me."

"Not a great day but not one of my worst. Seeing where it actually led, I guess it became one of my best."

His grin softens. The gap between us suddenly seems too wide. I want to wrap myself around him, bathe in the heat of his body and taste—

"This is hardly the time, woman," he says.

I swallow hard and drag my gaze from his mouth. He chuckles while I frown into the emptiness between the trunks.

The damn guy can read my mind. Or my face. Or both.

We wait half an hour but nothing stirs in the woods. We stretch our cramped legs and creep from our hiding place, sticking to the forest for two hundred metres then re-joining the road. The trees hiss in the wind, the drum of a woodpecker mirroring my pulse. The path heads uninterrupted in both directions.

I keep my gun in my hand and start walking. "Maybe they weren't looking for us."

"Maybe," Blake says, matching my pace. "Seems like too much of a coincidence, though. In my experience, people don't wander around in no man's land without a compelling reason."

"That's what I thought, too, but it's getting pretty crowded out here."

We scan the trees on either side of the road, our weapons ready, shoulders tense. A chaffinch alarm-calls from a twist of bramble and flits away in a streak of orange.

I can almost imagine the pounding of surf and the salt spray on my face.

We're so close.

The crack of a gunshot fractures the delicate peace, a bullet puffing into the dirt near my boot.

"Move, and the next goes into someone's skull," a voice says.

27

Four men materialise from the forest to block the path. Four pairs of eyes glitter from skin darkened by combat paint. Four SA80 rifles level, the stocks tight against camouflage-covered shoulders. The men form a wall of solid muscle, broad through the shoulders and chest, narrowing to the hips.

Welcome to Unification Army.

"Ladykiller, get their weapons," the soldier on the right barks, flicking his rifle. "Both of you drop your guns or things get messy."

My Glock and Blake's Browning thud into the ground next to our feet. The man at the opposite end of the line steps forward, his combat paint too thick to determine skin colour. I must make some small movement because he grins, sidling towards Blake with his gun steady on me.

It's probably stupid to ask but… "Ladykiller?"

The grin widens and wrinkles the paint on his cheeks. "You'll find out why soon enough."

Wonderful. If the next one is Flesheater, I'm making a break for it.

Ladykiller stops level to Blake's shoulder, keeping out of his comrades' line of fire. He watches me as he presses the barrel to Blake's temple and shoves his head to the side. The muscles in Blake's jaw clench but he stays silent.

"Remove that contraption from your arm. Toss it over there."

Blake complies, his movements stiff. Ladykiller walks behind him and lowers his rifle. He uses one hand to pat Blake down, transferring the two knives to his belt, whistling at the length of dreamy Gavin's blade. He scoops the Browning from the dirt. His face is entirely bald—no hair, no brows, no lashes. Just watery blue eyes framed by bright pink lids.

"On your knees, hands on your head."

"Please," I whisper, "don't hurt him. We'll do what you want."

Blake flashes me a puzzled glance and drops to his knees, lacing his fingers on top of his head. The position stretches the t-shirt across his shoulders and, somehow, in the midst of disaster, my fingertips ache to follow the curves of his body.

I don't want this morning to be the last time he trembles under my touch.

I widen my eyes at the man who seems to be in charge. His oily gaze lingers on my chest.

"Don't worry, it's you we're after. We don't have many women in our encampment." He drags his eyes from my breasts. "None that look like you, anyhow."

Ladykiller wrenches the rucksack from my back. I stagger but force myself not to struggle despite the increasing pressure in my gut. He pats me down to find the knife and SL2, collecting my Glock from the ground. He returns to Blake and places the rucksack at his feet, cradling his rifle in both hands.

My dry throat clicks.

I have to get them away from Blake, no matter what it takes. Beg. Bargain.

He deserves to live.

Even if I'm not there to see it.

"What now, Bossman?" Ladykiller's gaze flicks between us.

"Kill him."

"No!"

I throw myself at Blake and slam us both to the ground, my body curled around him. Hands tug at me. I hunch against them, my fingers clawing at the dirt. Blake is warm and solid and alive underneath me, his breath scorching my collarbone. A boot crushes my bandaged forearm. I hiss and raise my head, shaking the hair from my eyes. Ladykiller aims his gun at my hand. Bossman crouches, his elbows on his knees, his rifle loose on its sling.

"We want you alive but we don't need you whole," he says. "Move or we will hurt you and kill him slowly."

"Please," I gasp. "I'll come with you. I won't fight. Just don't kill him. *Please.*"

Bossman jerks his chin. The remaining two soldiers dig their fingers into my biceps and yank, ripping me off Blake. I thrash against their hold, my heels furrowing the soil, a whine trapped in my throat. Blake pushes to his knees, his violet eyes locked on mine. His cheeks are flushed, his lips parted, dirt smudged over his face.

He's never looked more beautiful.

Ladykiller presses the SA80 to his temple.

28

"Please. Please don't kill him."

I sag between my captors, my vision drowned in tears, Blake soft-edged and wavering where he kneels in the dirt.

If this is his final moment, I want to memorise every detail—the tousled black hair, the curve of his neck and the line of his jaw. His throat works, his eyes dark and filled with too much I can't read.

He flashes a lopsided smile. "It's okay, Anita."

How can he say that? They're going to kill him.

A signal passes between Bossman and Ladykiller. My knees buckle. The men tighten their grip to keep me vertical. I stare at Blake, unwilling to look away, even if it means watching him die.

His blood splattering, eyes glazing. The sigh of his last breath.

My stomach heaves.

Ladykiller reverses his rifle with a smooth flip and slams it into Blake's temple. The thud reverberates in my chest and blooms as an ache behind my sternum. Blake slumps to the ground, a red trickle weaving past his eyebrows and soaking into the earth. I jerk towards him but the soldiers fastened to my arms hold me in place, their hands crushing muscle against bone.

Bossman snaps his fingers. "Let's go."

Is Blake breathing?

"We're not going to shoot him?"

"Nah, don't have to. Something will come along and eat him."

The men laugh and shove me forward. My numb legs stumble. My captors drag me into the trees but I twist to stare at Blake crumpled on his side in the middle of the track.

Alone, vulnerable.

Unmoving.

The forest thickens and steals him from me, the loss scooping out my heart and grinding it to mulch. My feet shuffle mechanically, adjusting to the pace of the soldiers, the scent of crayons wafting from their combat paint. Bossman and Ladykiller bring up the rear, joking with each other in a blur of masculine grunts, like pigs snuffling in the mud. Time skips. I blink, my eyes unfocused, my body limp, passive.

Blake will die if you do nothing.

I twitch and suck in a breath. Another. Tears dry in a tickling line on my cheeks.

If he's not already dead.

I twist my left forearm and the pain clears my head. What the hell is wrong with me? Uninjured. No fear. Why am I in shock? I've suffered worse than this.

I glance at my captors from beneath my lashes, keeping my posture hunched. They hoist me over deadfall and around tangles of bramble. The man on my left is similar in height, showing a flash of skin on the back of his neck where he's missed a patch with the combat paint. His SA80 hangs on its sling. Beads of sweat ooze from the shorn scalp of the man on my right and drip off his hooked nose. His moist palm clings to my arm, his other hand clasping his rifle.

I drop my head further, a picture of defeat, and peek under my armpit. Bossman carries the rucksack on one brawny shoulder a few paces behind next to Ladykiller, who's gawping at my ass. I focus on the gait of the man on my left and feign a trip to match it, my right foot crunching in synchrony on the carpet of pine cones.

"You're going to have to wait your turn, you do too much damage," Bossman says. "Plus, Minister will want her first."

Ladykiller, Bossman and Minister. Who are these people?

"Come on, B-man, I always—"

I lash out, kicking the man on my left in the side of the knee. The joint pops, all of his weight on his foot. He shrieks and topples towards me. I pivot in front of the second man, sweeping his right arm out and ramming my knee between his legs. His body softens and I drive him backwards, connecting with Ladykiller. They sprawl in a yelling tangle of limbs. Bossman's mouth gapes, his barrel swinging too slowly. My fist hammers his temple and he collapses with a grunt.

Ladykiller shoves at the man on top of him. "Get the fuck off me!"

His comrade cradles his balls. I dive at Bossman and grab the gun from his slack grip, yanking it to its full extent on the sling and emptying the magazine into the other three men. I scrabble to Ladykiller and his entangled friend, their torn flesh bright against their camouflage. I point the man's rifle at Bossman. Dazed eyes reel, his hands flapping for his SA80. Thirty bullets reduce his head to a smear of gore and shards of bone. I shove to my feet, my ears ringing, and roll the man off of Ladykiller. His one remaining eye fixes on the canopy, the rest of his face minced. The tang of copper drowns the pine and combat paint.

How long ago did I vow to stop killing, afraid of turning into a sociopath? Seems stupid now.

No one hurts Blake and lives.

I tug Ladykiller's rifle free, adjusting the strap until it sits tight against my body. I reclaim our weapons and the rucksack and take the SA80 from the man with the ruined knee. I sprint through unfamiliar terrain ignored in my pathetic haze, bursting onto the track and startling a rabbit munching on a tuft of grass.

No Blake.

I spin around twice but the road stays empty.

"Calm the fuck down," I growl between wheezes.

Trees pass in a whir of green, my boots kicking dust. He lies where they left him, blood staining the ground around his head. I throw myself next to him and shrug off the rucksack.

He's dead or in a coma. Brain swelling, bleeding. Severe trauma.

The world sways. I bow my head, shivering despite the sun on my back. Deep, even breaths soothe the sickness roiling in my stomach. My fingers fumble at Blake's throat.

Nothing.

I whimper and press harder, digging my fingers beneath his jaw.

Broken neck, fractured skull, mental impairment…

His pulse throbs against my hand.

I curl over his body and sob a little.

29

An antiseptic wipe cleans the clotted blood from Blake's face, my touch tracing the curve of his cheekbone and the gentle arch of his brow.

He'll be able to open his eyes without ripping out his lashes.

If he ever opens his eyes.

Shut up.

Fresh blood oozes from the wound. I dry it with a piece of gauze and seal the rent with butterfly sutures. There's no indentation or softness to indicate a skull fracture. Both his pupils react to light. I concentrate on applying a pad and self-adhesive dressing, darting glances into the trees when another upwelling of tears threatens at the sight of him lying there. I scrub my cheeks and ease back on my heels. He breathes quietly, arms tucked against his chest, his face serene, stunning.

My shaking fingers stroke his hair. "Goddamn you, Blake."

The bastard has made me love him.

How is it possible?

I shake my head, unable to form a harsh enough word to berate myself with. It doesn't matter. I'm already being punished. What better way to ensure unrequited love than by murdering his brother?

I'm my own worst enemy.

Huffing, I raise my gaze to the forest.

We have to move. Other soldiers could head our way, searching for their muscled comrades. Perhaps they monitor the roads or Bossman's group stumbled across us by chance.

Blake has to wake up.

I need to see his eyes like I need my heart to beat.

My fist raps my forehead. "Moron. Moron, moron, *moron*."

Begging for his life showed him I love him. He'll torment me with it as soon as he wakes up. Pass it off as female hysteria? A ruse to fool our attackers?

"Are you—talking to me? Seems unfair."

I jump at the croak of his voice. He blinks dazed eyes at me and I struggle not to sob all over him. *Again.*

His face pales. "Going to be sick."

I scuttle backwards. He rolls, propping himself on quivering arms, and vomits into the dirt, his shoulders tensing on each heave. I crawl around him and cradle his trembling body to stop him from flopping in the mess. We end with his head in my lap after he drinks some water, spitting out the first few mouthfuls.

"Oh god," he says on a groan, "what happened?"

Amnesia! Amnesia will save me!

Though it doesn't bode well for his recovery.

I clear my throat. "What do you remember?"

"The soldiers. Taking our weapons. You."

The word resonates. Me, pleading for his life, crying, desperate. I avoid his gaze but my traitorous hands continue to pet him.

"Are they dead?"

I nod, unsure of my vocal capacity. Blake grips my hand,

stilling it over the steady beat of his heart. It pulls my eyes to his face.

"When do I get to rescue you? This is very hard on the ego." He smiles the same lopsided smile he had when they were going to kill him. "And why does no one want to kidnap me for nefarious sexual purposes? Aren't I pretty?"

He is pretty and amazing and too perfect to be real.

My breath hitches.

Oh shit, I'm going to cry.

I tug on my hand. His hold tightens. He brushes my cheek and a tear wobbles on his fingertip.

Is this going to happen every time he almost dies? I don't think I'm strong enough to take much more.

"You really care about me," he says, softly.

Love him. I love him. I love him. I love—

I shake my head in a swirl of hair.

Am I denying it or having a seizure?

"I need you," I say, "for the warships."

"Is that all?"

"And the sex. Definitely the sex."

His smirk leaves me breathless. "Still fighting me, my beautiful, stubborn warrior."

His. I am his.

But he will never be mine.

"We should get out of here," I say, attempting to regain my equilibrium. This is a partnership. We're using each other. *Sure.* "Can you stand?"

I help him to his feet and he sways, blinking rapidly. I dig ibuprofen out of the rucksack and practically shove it down his throat.

He flaps at my hands. "Jesus, woman, I can take a pill. I'm

not an invalid."

I back off.

May as well have 'I am desperately in love with you' branded on my forehead.

I concentrate on giving him his weapons, including one of the SA80 rifles from our attackers. He inspects it and adjusts the sling.

"Well, look at you, breaking hearts and kicking ass."

His grin eases a pressure in my chest. I want to hug him and cry on his shoulder. I pull the rucksack on and pretend to be a hardened veteran instead of a wimpy little girl.

"You're babbling. The head injury must be worse than I thought."

"Ouch. Belittle the wounded guy."

We walk down the track. I stay close to his side, ready to catch him if he stumbles.

He seems fine but I'm no neurosurgeon. His brain could be bleeding and I won't know it until he drops into a coma. Or I wake next to his stiffened corpse.

I trip and sprawl in the dirt, the grit crunching between my teeth.

"Did they hit you on the head, too?"

"No," I say, scrambling to my feet in a cloud of dust, lacking a witty rejoinder to salvage my dignity.

The stupid feelings will fade if I ignore them. They'll die when we're free and he abandons me with a cheery wave, never looking back. It'll hurt but I'll get over it. Right? Better to have loved and lost than never loved at all?

I curl my lip.

Bull. Fucking. *Shit.*

<h1 style="text-align:center">30</h1>

We don't go far. Blake needs to rest.

A river meanders away from the track and deeper into the forest. Steep, slippery rock borders crisp, clean water. I stop on the other side of a rise where the banks lower, and expand the pod between the crowded trees. Blake props himself against a trunk, his legs stretched out.

I unpack the rucksack instead of rushing to his side to check his pupils and demand if he feels drowsy.

"Thought you weren't an invalid," I say.

"Don't want to stretch myself. Head injuries are serious, you know."

If he is bleeding in his brain, when will he show signs—a few hours, a day? More? How long should I worry about him keeling over? Will I ever stop worrying?

Jesus.

"Come on, sick boy, get in the pod," I say, my voice light.

He holds out his hands. I roll my eyes but ease him to his feet. He bumps his hips against mine and wraps his arms around my shoulders.

"I like this caring side of you," he whispers. "Makes me feel all warm and fluffy."

He kisses me, soft and insistent. I melt into his arms on a

moan, opening my mouth to the slide of his tongue. It weakens my knees and shocks my heart into a canter.

Sex would be bad. It's too strenuous for someone battered unconscious by a rifle butt.

Sex won't help my delicate condition, either.

I pull away and swallow hard. "You won't think that when I wake you every few hours."

He stills in his attempt to kiss me again. "You're kidding."

"Am I? Get in the pod."

He mutters but does as he's told, his movements slow, eyes dull. Tucked into the covers, he immediately falls asleep. The opal light fades with the setting sun. I memorise the way his lashes caress his cheekbones, the fullness of his lips, the silken fall of hair across his forehead. I count his breaths. Darkness fills the pod and I curl my body around him, my fingertips resting over the beat of his heart.

He takes the first couple of times I wake him in his stride, uncomplaining while I shine a light at his pupils and ask him questions.

"Blake O'Riley. Twenty-second of June two thousand and five. Two thousand and forty." He throws me a cheeky salute almost lost in the black.

"Happy birthday a week ago."

He yawns and winces. "Not my best. Two months in no man's land. No cake or presents…"

The third occasion—some unholy hour—he growls, "Baby, if you wake me again, you will regret it."

I chuckle against his shoulder. "Irritability is often a sign of worsening head trauma. Maybe I should wake you every hour to be safe."

He shifts and pins me before I can stop him. Like I could

ever stop him. His eyes glitter in the dark, the weight of him speeding my pulse. He lowers his head and nibbles along my jaw. I bite my lip.

"Wake me and I will show no mercy." His hot breath caresses my neck. "I wonder what else I can get you to tell me."

Oh god, that mouth.

He wriggles lower, placing soft kisses on my collarbone. I squirm underneath him.

I'll probably tell him I love him.

"Okay, I won't wake you again," I say, my voice wobbling. "No sex until you've recovered. Too strenuous."

His lips curve against my skin, his tongue licking the hollow of my throat. "Like you would refuse me."

I bare my teeth but he kisses me and I forget to breathe. His laugh drifts from the blackness.

"God, the way you react to me is just awesome."

"Yeah, yeah, you're beautiful and irresistible." I slap his chest. "Now get off me and go back to sleep."

He rolls away but pulls me across, his arm around my shoulders. His body relaxes under mine, his heartbeat lulling me. I fight to stay awake.

"Are you in pain?"

"Not anymore," he whispers.

* * *

I wake to a horrible panic clawing at my throat and battle against the tangle of covers, scraping the hair from my face and whirling to where Blake lies on his back. The violet eyes blinking at me contrast with the glazed and slack expression I expect.

"Christ, woman, I'm still alive. Calm down."

I hunch and attempt to re-swallow my heart.

Why am I so weak in front of him?

He sits up, the sheets settling at his waist, a slow smile stretching his face.

I narrow my eyes. "What are you grinning at?"

"You're being cute."

The purple bloom of a bruise trails from underneath the dressing at his temple towards his eye. A small patch of blood has dried through the white.

"This is not cute. It's ridiculous."

"Don't be so hard on yourself. You've already told me how great and beautiful I am."

"Stop laughing at me! This is all your damn fault."

"How is it my fault?"

I shut my mouth.

"Why did you beg for my life yesterday? Why does the thought of me dying make you cry?" He pauses. "Why are you scared of me?"

What the hell does he want, to destroy me? He had the ability from the first moment he was inside me. The bastard. He's turned me into a blubbering, heartsick *girl*.

"You already know. You don't have to fucking ask."

"I want to hear you say it."

"Fuck you."

He grins. "Soon. Tell me why first."

"You're a close friend."

"Nope. Try again."

"You're like a brother to me."

"Gross."

A snort slips out. I clap my hand over my mouth and mumble into my palm, "Fine. I care about you, you insufferable asshole."

"Does calling me names make you feel better?"

"Yes, it does"—I suck in a breath—"you dick."

He laughs and seems satisfied but the pressure in my chest doesn't ease. Nerves jitter in my stomach.

He's going to find out. I can't shut up around him. The thought of telling him terrifies me.

Blake, member of a faction I hate, who tried to kill me and took me prisoner—the love of my life.

Pathetic.

Happy endings are for fairy tales, I've learned that already. He'll be horrified and run at the first opportunity. Or he'll stay out of misplaced honour until we complete our journey. Stilted conversations, everything that was easy and fun, awkward.

No more intimacy.

Or he'll laugh, his cobalt-blue eyes hardening to steel, a sneer twisting his face, feral and mocking but still beautiful. His forgiveness a lie.

It isn't worth the risk. Stupid to even consider it. I'll bury it deep and ignore it. I've done it before with the painful memories of my torture so they didn't tear me apart, I can do it again.

Blake winces, his fingers massaging his forehead. I give him another ibuprofen, managing not to cram it down his throat.

"I need to change your bandage."

He nods. I peel the dressing from his temple and he grimaces. I clean the swollen skin of his wound with an antiseptic wipe. His hair flops over and I brush it away, my fingers stroking through the softness. He watches me. I duck my head and fumble open a self-adhesive dressing. I smooth it on, my traitorous fingers continuing to his cheek, drawn by the warmth of his skin. He grips my hand and traps it against him.

"Still can't keep your hands to yourself. You going to take advantage of me while I'm injured?"

I force a smile. "You wish."

"Oh, I do."

"You need to rest."

"I'll rest when I'm dead."

I try not to flinch.

Get a grip!

We breakfast on the last of our dried food, supplemented by fresh raspberries and strawberries. Blake lets me check his pupillary response with a long-suffering sigh before he drops into a deep sleep.

I press my hand to his chest to feel his heart beating but force myself away when my own expands against my ribs and threatens to spill out my eyes.

31

Blake complains throughout his enforced rest. I relent on the afternoon of the second day. I wanted to wait a minimum of three but he badgers me about continuing our journey.

The possibility of escape means he can finally find out if his mother is alive.

I haven't thought about seeing my parents again. What a terrible daughter I am. Ailsa was their favourite—ambitious, driven. Destined to be the next First Minister, which suited my dad's love of politics and my mum's obsession with status. I always felt like a distant relative who came to visit—welcomed but never quite at home.

I can't think about what will happen. My energy is focused on the present—Blake, surviving this war-torn cesspit—not what I'll do if we succeed in escaping and the world isn't another, larger war-torn cesspit.

If we make it to safety, our cosy bubble of intimacy will burst. He'll leave. At least the distance will help me get over him.

But I don't want to get over him! I want to be with him and—

Not possible. Shut up.

We pack camp quickly, excited by how close we are to the

coast. A couple of hours and we'll be looking at the sea.

And hopefully, some warships.

***

"Oh, fuck, is that a weapon?" I say, a gap in the hedgerow allowing a glimpse into an abandoned field and a black post towering out of the vegetation like some alien monolith.

"If it was, we'd be dead already. There are tyre tracks leading up to it."

We edge closer. A border of trampled grass surrounds the base. The slick surface vibrates under my palm. I shiver and rub my hand on my trousers.

"Whatever it is, it's goddamn creepy."

Moss-covered tiles top deserted buildings beyond the field, windows gaping into blackness and framed by rotten wood. Our steps echo in a farmyard, a dusty track continuing between more derelict fields in an area of wild land bordering the sea, miles from any encampment in Unification Army territory. Blake stops where the path curves past a shed surrounded by pine. The air holds the hint of pig shit despite the passage of years.

My hands tighten on my SA80. "What—"

"Listen."

I cock my head, as if it will help. The trees sigh. Loose boards creak in the wall of the shed. Waves hiss and break on the shore.

"Is that—"

"The edge of our world, baby."

Potential freedom is an expanse of water away, whether we head straight for Europe or loop around the border fence where it hovers out to sea for a mile, supported by solar-powered airlifts and deadly to approach within 200 metres.

I pick at the bandage on my arm. "What if their world is no more normal than ours? What if it's worse? The radio broadcast my friend heard was two years ago and said something about New London. What if we get there and it's the same crap in a different country?"

What if I lead Blake into another hellhole and get him killed?

He draws me close and brushes a strand of hair off my face, his fingers trailing across my cheek. "It's not going to be worse. We would've heard something. Seen something."

"What if they're all dead?"

"There's no global catastrophe that would kill everyone else and leave us untouched. Someone's alive out there. We just need to find them."

My palms stroke his chest and the dog-tags beneath his t-shirt. The bandage on his head flashes brilliant white in the sunshine, his hair flopping over.

I swallow and drop my gaze. "How can you be an optimist *and* a romantic *and* have the forgiveness of a saint?"

"Hey, you make me sound like a wimp. I can be wicked." He grips my hips and presses me into him. "I can be bad."

He kisses me and my hands fist in his t-shirt. I barely resist climbing his body and riding him to the ground.

He breaks the kiss with a laugh. "Dammit, woman. We shouldn't lower our guard now, this close to the end."

"I do believe you kissed me."

His smile softens. "Come on. Let's go find out the state of the rest of the world."

He ignores the curving path and heads down an indiscernible track consumed by greenery. The vegetation blocks our view of the sea, though the rush of it draws nearer.

"If they are normal, or at least civilised, what do you think they'll do to us?"

"Technically, we're still UK citizens," Blake says with his back to me, placing his feet carefully as he stalks through nodding grass, the branches of a hawthorn tugging at his t-shirt. "If we don't reach England, we'll be shipped there as soon as possible. I imagine there'll be a lot of questions and waiting around but if we both have living relatives, that's where they'll send us."

Separated. Him to Ireland, me to Kent. Would I ever see him again? Would he even want to?

I stop myself from asking—too pathetic—and blurt out another worry slicing at my brain. "You don't think they'll arrest us as war criminals?"

The path dips to a bowl of land terminating at a field of reeds on the far side. Blake places his hands on my shoulders and forces me to halt. The tenderness on his face hurts too much to look at.

"We're not war criminals. *You're* not a war criminal."

"Wilful killing, wanton destruction. Seems pretty criminal."

"Justified and proportional to what we deserved."

"You didn't deserve this," I whisper, raising my eyes. "If it wasn't for me, you'd be in Livingston right now."

"Yeah, hiding from Wick and watching him enslave the world. Sounds great."

"You would've had Dylan." I duck my head.

Warm fingers tilt my chin to meet serious violet eyes. "But not my humanity. And not you."

"I'm no great prize, not over family."

He hugs me and I stiffen, a baffling urge to cry stoppering

my throat.

It feels like goodbye.

Every step brings us closer to the end.

I slide my arms around him and bury my face in his neck, his pulse fluttering against my cheek.

I need to savour this and each moment until the last. The heat of his skin, the smell of him—sunshine and grass.

I'll gather the memories to console myself when the loneliness gets too much.

"Then you don't see yourself," he says, his soft voice almost lost in the wind hissing through the reeds behind him.

How can he see anything other than his dead brother when he looks at me? How does he not blame my stubborn ignorance for believing in The People's Republic and perpetuating the war that trapped him in a faction led by a psychopath?

Hell if I know. He really is a saint.

He eases away as if embarrassed and I let him.

There's no point delaying. Best get the painful part over and try to move on. At least I'll be free. Hopefully. Free and alone.

One of those is new.

We walk to the edge of the field of reeds, our last barrier to the sea probably no more than a hundred metres wide.

But what horrors skulk in the whispering gloom?

Purple panicles bob to the music of the wind above our heads, their stalks thick enough to grab in one fist. Leaves spike in all directions and form a solid screen. I trail after Blake, my hands gripping my SA80, my boots crunching in brittle mud. Yellowing stems tug at the rucksack, dragging me back, the air sticky and hard to breathe. I pant, swallowing dust and decayed plants. The rustle of our movement drowns everything out. I pause to listen while Blake continues further into the reeds, his navy t-shirt clinging to his shoulders and daubed with powder. The plants settle into place behind him as if he never existed. I move to follow but turn my head at a curious scraping.

An unblinking, orange-gold eye stares back at me from the shadows.

32

A low hiss shivers through the reeds and down my spine. I stare at the terrible orange-gold eye, my fingers frozen on my rifle. A wedge-shaped head rises almost to the height of the panicles, the scales blending with the vegetation. I slide one foot backwards. A bee drones overhead; muffled gunfire rattles to the west. The snake's mouth opens, straightening hinged fangs as long as my arm. A yellow droplet trembles from one tip and sizzles on the parched ground.

"Blake," I wheeze, my voice drowned by the rustling plants.

The glistening maw closes on a flicking grey tongue. The snake and I watch each other for the space of two heartbeats, its heavy head swaying to the dance of the reeds. It dips its nose and lunges. My brittle finger squeezes the trigger, a line of bullets strafing the beast's lower body. It shrieks, the noise frosting my bones and tingling to my fingertips. It barrels towards me, its wounds flashing pink. I whirl and drop to my knees in the crackling mud, curling into the dirt and presenting the rucksack to the furious reptile. The force of its strike slams my face into the ground. I yelp and swallow a mouthful of dust.

I hope my hot, coppery flesh distracts it long enough for Blake to escape.

The snake rears and hoists me into the air. My boots thrash the reeds, my weight pinning my arms against the straps of the rucksack. The snake's jaw works. It shakes its head, jerking me from side to side, leaves slashing my face. Blake crunches through the reeds and stumbles to a halt, rifle tucked to his shoulder, his eyes wide.

"Blake—shoot—it!"

The straps wrench my arms at each shake of the snake's head. I tuck my knees into my stomach. Blake shoots at the snake's creamy belly, the bullets thunking into flesh. The creature twitches with another bowel-clenching shriek and tosses its head, hurling me through the reeds. I crash to the ground, crumpled stems scouring my skin. I suck another earthy breath and scramble to my feet, lurching towards the enraged hissing.

The snake attacks. Blake rolls, standing in a cloud of dust and rustling leaves. His eyes narrow, his expression fierce, black hair falling across his forehead. He nocks the SA80 to his shoulder.

A mangled band of exposed tissue and broken scales stretches across the snake's belly. Blood splotches the ground and reeds but the beast advances, its mouth wide, orange-gold eyes glittering.

What kind of immortal abomination is this thing?

Blake's rifle clicks empty. The snake strikes, ruby drops scattering in its wake and twinkling in the sun. Blake straightens his left arm and flicks his wrist. My bullets slap wetly into the snake's body as a burst of electricity ripples over its scales. Blake glances at me, a second of meeting his eyes, before the creature swoops. Another bolt shimmers over its body but the thing keeps going, its head thudding into Blake's chest. He sails backwards through the reeds on an explosive exhale. Stillness settles in a pattering cloud of dust. Flattened reeds mark the battle zone, a circle of light in the shaded green. I pant on the scorching air and bound over to the snake. One glistening eye stares at me, its tongue lolling, mouth propped open by the fangs buried in the dirt.

It looks dead, but I'm no veterinarian.

I empty my magazine into its head.

I scrabble to Blake and fall to my knees, my hands fluttering over his chest. He lies sprawled on his back, his bunched t-shirt exposing his smooth stomach and the thrust of his hip bones. A small graze oozes red on his cheek, his face smudged with dirt.

Oh god, has he been knocked unconscious again? How much battering can one brain take and remain viable?

I bow my head and swallow a sob. Words bubble up my throat.

Don't. Don't say it, don't say—

"I love you," I whisper to his bellybutton. "Please don't die."

Well, crap.

I squeeze my eyes shut and grope for his pulse with shaking fingers. A hand captures mine. I gasp and jerk my arm to my chest, toppling backwards. Startled blue eyes blink at me.

"What did you say?"

"I… Don't die?"

The heat of his gaze steals my breath. I duck my head, hiding behind my hair.

"Before that."

"Nothing. You must have hallucinated."

He tries to sit up but groans and flops back down. I frown at my knees instead of soothing him and rummaging for painkillers.

My desperate need to be loved has ruined everything. How could I have been so stupid? I deserve this. This awful, sucking sadness clenching my stomach as I wait for him to make his excuses and dash for a warship, leaving me crying in the dust.

This is justice. Justice for killing his brother and destroying his home. Justice for believing the lies of my faction and murdering in Ailsa's name. Justice for forcing Blake into no man's land, grief-stricken and hurting. Justice for daring to touch him, believing I could make him happy. *Me*, the person who caused him the pain.

I am worse than Wick.

"Anita, tell me what you said."

I shake my head and refuse to look at him. "Nothing. Babbling, as usual. Ignore me."

Yes, brush past it. Forget it happened. I'd rather have him with me, knowing he doesn't love me, than lose him.

And that is a new low.

"*Coward.*"

My head snaps up, a snarl on my lips. Blake smirks at me and I flush, starting to drop my eyes. He fists his hand in my hair.

"Look at me! Look at me and tell me what you said."

Why is he being cruel? Does he want my complete mortification, to hear me say it aloud so he can spit in my face?

I glare at him. "No. Let go of me or, I swear to god, I will punch you right in the chest."

He laughs then winces. "You won't hurt me. You can't."

"Can. Already have." I hold my fist over him, ignoring how much it trembles. "Let me go. *Now.*"

His hand curls around mine, lowering it ever-so-softly to

his chest.

"What are you doing?"

His heart jumps against my fingers. I squirm at his gentle smile, panic gripping my throat.

"I love you, too, you idiot."

"That's not what I said," I yelp.

He's trying to trick me.

"I love you."

I can't get enough air. I want to run, hide, escape but his light touch on my hand paralyses me.

"Stop it. You don't. You can't."

He rolls his eyes. "Why? Because you killed my brother?"

"Why the hell else? I murdered what might be the last of your family."

"It wasn't murder, Anita. We've spent years slaughtering each other. Fight or die, you know that."

"Fine. Confuse me with logic. What if we escape and your mother's alive? You going to introduce me? Tell her how Dylan died?"

"Yes."

"Don't be ridiculous. She'd hate me and be upset with you."

"She'd forgive you, like I have. You've suffered enough. It was my fault. Our fault—Nationless. This is our punishment and we deserve it."

I shake my head. Blake drags me closer. I growl at him but he grins.

"You really are scared."

"I'm not scared."

He reels me in.

I can't struggle. I don't want to hurt him.

I brace my left hand on the ground, my other hand still

trapped to his chest, the beating of his heart disarming me faster than any threat or weapon ever did.

"This is why you cry every time I get hurt. Why you begged for my life. Why you can't control yourself around me." He releases my hair and cups my head. "You love me."

"I don't," I whisper against his lips.

"Liar."

He raises himself a tiny fraction. My self-control evaporates. I whimper and climb into his lap, kissing him as if I can inhale the air from his lungs. He chuckles, his hands dropping to my butt beneath the rucksack. I fist my fingers in the dirt, trying to keep my weight off his chest. He thrusts his hips and rational thought disappears. I collapse into him on a moan. He grimaces and I jerk upright.

"Shit! I'm sorry. Wait, no. It's your fault."

"Sure, blame the injured guy," he groans. "I think my ribs are pulverised."

I swallow the fear and grab at the change of topic. Away from feelings. Too dangerous.

"You got to rescue me for once and already with the complaints."

I crawl off and help him sit up, swiping the dust from his t-shirt. He winces but seems to have no trouble breathing.

"Turns out it's not as fun as I imagined."

"Did you lose consciousness? Do you feel dizzy? Nauseated?" I squint at his pupils.

He kisses my quivering fingers. "I'm fine—winded. No need to quiz me on what year it is."

I ease out a breath. The quivering travels from my hand to my chest.

This love crap is hard on the heart.

"And you know I didn't lose consciousness. I heard what you said."

Shit. Back to that.

He tucks my hair behind my ear, his fingers trailing along my jaw. "I love you, Anita."

"No, you don't."

He grips my upper arms and gives me a shake. "I love you, you stubborn, mouthy, pain in the arse."

My lips twitch.

Huh. A declaration I can believe.

33

The torn corpse of the snake shrivels behind us, attracting flies.

I don't care.

We sit in no man's land, unguarded, distracted.

I can't care less.

Blake's lips glide over mine, teasing and soft and scrambling my brain. His hands press me to his slim body. I tug his t-shirt and rifle off, breaking the kiss. He raises his arms to assist and smirks at me.

"Need to assess—your ribs for damage," I manage to pant.

The smirk grows and darkens his eyes. I stroke my fingers down the beaded chains of his dog-tags to the red mark blooming across his chest.

"No fair," he says, flicking one strap of the rucksack. "I can't undress you."

"Safer that way."

He growls and everything south of my waist pulses. I scrabble at the button of his combats and yank the zip, spilling the warm length of him into my hand. I squeeze and his head falls back on a groan, his eyes dazed. His reaction throbs through my body.

God, I love him. Need him inside me.

I tense to rise, eager to shimmy out of my clothes. A hiss ripples over my shoulder. I leap to my feet and spin around, almost falling back to my knees. I sweep my Glock over the reeds, dreading the glimmer of an orange-gold eye. The wind sighs through the stalks, the sun baking the corpse of the snake.

"Jesus-fucking-Christ," I gasp, holstering my gun, my legs shaking. "We should get out of here."

Blake nods, climbing to his feet. He stumbles and I dart to his side. He pivots into me, one hand in my hair, the other gripping my hip. Trapped.

"Clumsy me," he says and grins.

My fingers trail up his spine before I can stop myself, electrified by the warmth of his skin.

He nibbles at my mouth. "Let's set up the pod."

"The pod? But the warships—"

"Will wait." His hand tightens in my hair and pulls my head back. He draws his lips down my throat, hovering over my pulse. "If I'm going to make love to you, I want to do it right. To tease you, oh so slowly, until you tell me what I want to hear."

"Blake…" It's more plea than warning.

If I don't say it, it isn't true. I'm not weak and stupid and hopelessly in love with him.

His lips curve against my neck. He bites me over my stuttering pulse and I moan, my spine bowing.

"Such a wanton little hussy," he chuckles.

He releases me and I stagger. I catch myself before crumpling at his feet and scowl at his pleased expression, lobbing his t-shirt at him. He snares it with a laugh and slips it on. My intelligence immediately increases. He leaves his empty rifle in the dirt and I dump mine next to it.

He glances at his left arm. "Damn. I liked this thing."

Jagged cracks split the casing of the electrigun. Blake shakes his arm and something tinkles inside the weapon.

"I think it took the brunt of the impact."

I unstrap the gun and cradle it in my hands.

It could've been his ribs, shattered bone piercing his lungs and embedding in his heart.

I swallow and drop the weapon in the dust.

"Promise me you won't die." The words slip out, my gaze fixed on the broken electrigun.

His fingers trace my cheekbone. "Baby, you know I can't promise you that."

"No. *No.* You can't make me—feel this much and then—die."

"Still can't say it? That's okay. You will."

"You arrogant bas—"

He kisses me, hard, desperate, burying his fingers in my hair. I sob into his mouth and arch against him.

He pulls away, his eyes wild. "I promise I'll try my fucking hardest *not* to die."

At last, a promise I trust.

* * *

Blake shows me he keeps his promises.

He undresses me with excruciating tenderness, kissing each uncovered part as if it's the most precious thing he's ever seen. He strips my defences as easily as he removes my clothes, leaving me naked.

Vulnerable.

He stops me from touching him by pressing my hands to

the covers.

"Let me prove how I feel."

And he does. I have no choice but to believe him.

Loved. I am loved.

Finally.

He kisses my tears and cups my face with trembling fingers. "I love you, Anita."

"I love you, Blake," I whisper, "you bastard."

Delight fills his face. He circles his hips and I writhe beneath him.

"Oh, woman, what you do to me. You and that mouth."

His lips taste of salt. Mine? His? I wrap myself around him. It's impossible to get closer unless I eat him.

He tangles his fingers in my hair. "Say it again."

I try to scowl but the lazy thrust of his hips rolls my eyes back. He purrs, so immensely pleased with himself.

With my downfall.

"Blake—"

"Say it."

"I love you, dammit."

"Without the cursing."

His lips nibble my throat, his body continuing to ease in and out of mine. A slow, punishing, glorious rhythm. I struggle to hold myself together. He's already made me scream his name twice and I've lost count of the number of times I said please.

It still isn't enough. I want all of him. Always.

I am so screwed.

He raises himself up, brushing fresh tears from my cheeks. His eyes capture me and I can't look away, my heartbeat thundering in the confines of the pod.

I can't lie to him. Not for long, anyway. He sees me, sees

everything.

"I love you," I say.

He smirks, dark and knowing and sexy. "Damn right you do."

<h1 style="text-align:center">34</h1>

Three warships absorb the light of the crescent moon, their bristling weapons and antennae darker than the night. A fire crackles on the beach and sends shadows carousing across the sand.

"They can operate with a full crew of twenty or a minimum of three," Blake says, stretched beside me in the marram grass at the crest of a sand dune, the rucksack a black hump on his back.

"So we have no idea how many soldiers are on each. One could even be empty and that's the whole crew drunk down there."

Three men sprawl beside the fire, sucking on bottles, their loud voices echoing in the bay. The oars of their small rowing boat point at the stars, the keel licked by gentle waves.

"Not knowing's part of the fun, isn't it?"

The rocks on our edge of the bay glow white and disappear into the sea. A burst of laughter scares something in the gorse behind us, branches rustling as it skitters away. I peer into the blackness, the field of reeds less than a hundred metres north of our position.

Just a mouse. A teeny, tiny mouse, not a man-eating snake.

I inch closer to Blake. "Okay, since I can't see people on any of the decks and we have no idea what we'll find on board, why don't we aim for the nearest one? The less time in the water, the better."

"You don't like the sea?"

"Not in the dark. How am I supposed to know if something's about to bite my ankle?"

"It's your optimism that first attracted me to you." His teeth flash, the moonlight carving shadows under his cheekbones and filling his eyes with silver.

He made love to me all evening. The guy has amazing stamina. In the end, he didn't have to demand those three little words. I whispered them, over and over, while he held me in his arms. The luckiest woman in the world.

And the most terrified.

"Anita?"

"Hmm?"

"You're staring at me again."

I jump. "Shit."

You'd think admitting we love each other would make things easier, more equal, but I still want to blurt out how awesome and gorgeous and perfect he is whenever he looks at me. And ask if he is truly, definitely sure he loves me.

Anita Carmichael—vengeful sibling, war veteran, mouthy bitch—reduced to this. An insecure, lovesick moron.

I don't deserve it but I never want it to stop.

Blake wriggles closer on his elbows, the heat of his body pressing against me from shoulder to hip. A healing scab covers the wound on his temple, the dressing removed to avoid it gleaming in the darkness, along with the bandage on my arm.

"God, woman, you have fallen hard. You don't do anything

by halves do you?"

I muster a laugh but it sounds more like a wheeze. "All or nothing, that's me."

"Good, because I want all of you."

His soft lips meet mine, insistent, the taste of him intoxicating. I balance on one elbow to fist my hand in his hair, my heart bounding into my throat, chased by a small, eager noise. The tips of marram grass poke into my bicep, sand shifting as I try to shimmy underneath Blake.

He chuckles and pulls away, his thumb skimming my bottom lip. "Even now—here—you wouldn't say no."

Hell, I've been abstinent for fifteen years and cultivated my frigid bitch protective shield to perfection. Gizzy managed to sneak through a crack but Blake blasted it to pieces.

If I don't have sex with him two, three times a day I feel starved. Achy.

"I'm great at saying no. Just not to you."

"Do you want to say it?"

"God, no."

He growls and kisses me. The world spirals away at the electrifying slide of his tongue.

Once more won't hurt. Who knows how long it'll be before I get him naked again? Maybe never. What if he di—

Shut up, *shut up!*

A cackle from the beach forces us apart, the movement disguising my shiver.

"Tempting as it is to take you right here," Blake says, tucking my hair behind my ear, "quiet sex is beyond you, apparently."

My cheeks heat, the night not enough to hide it if his smirk is any indication. My attempt at an eloquent protest dissolves into a splutter.

"Don't get me wrong—it's fucking hot."

I squirm in the sand. "Oh god, don't say that."

"What?"

"You hardly ever swear and, when you do, it makes me want to rip off your clothes."

Great, Anita. Why don't you tell him everything? Like he hasn't got enough ammunition to tease you with.

The delight on his face makes it worth the embarrassment.

"You mean every time I swear you want to rip off my clothes and"—wicked, wicked smile—"*fuck* me?"

I groan, ducking my head to hide my blazing cheeks and the no doubt slack-jawed expression of arousal.

Jesus, I have it bad when screaming, glorious sex a few hundred metres from enemy soldiers and their hulking warships seems like a wonderful idea.

"Stop it. Or we'll never get off this beach."

"Sorry," he says, muffling a snort. "You're just so damn cute."

I bare my teeth at him.

"And there's my arse-kicking warrior."

His. His and only his.

He kisses me again, a quick, teasing glide. I lean into him and he shoos me away.

"Woman, you are a nightmare for my self-control. Let's go steal us a warship."

He starts to crawl to the edge of the sand dune. My hand shoots out and grabs his wrist, my skin suddenly cold.

"We don't have to do this," I say to his cocked eyebrow. "We could find a nice cave on an empty bit of coast and be safe there."

"And when it gets freezing and food is short?"

"We'll cuddle and eat gulls. No shortage of those squawky

rats."

"And when our ammo runs out?"

I open my mouth. Close it. The tenderness on his face doesn't help my fragile equilibrium. Tears burn my eyes.

"Still trying to protect me," he breathes. He rolls onto his side and pulls me into a tight hug, my face buried in his neck.

"I can't lose you," I mumble to his pulse, voicing the words that petrify me the most.

It'd be pathetic if it wasn't completely sincere.

"I know, baby, but I haven't forgotten my promise. You have to promise, too."

I suck in a shaking breath. "I promise I will try my fucking hardest not to die."

"And that's true even if the worst happens. Even if I—"

"No! Don't even say it or think it or... *No.*"

His lips curve against my hair, his hand smoothing my back. "I love you, too. And I don't just want to live in a cold, damp cave with you. I want a house, and a bed. Hot running water. Fewer arseholes trying to abduct you. Isn't that worth fighting a few more hours?"

"Yes," I huff. "I want all that, too."

God, please let the rest of the world be better than here.

Blake eases away to cup my face. "I love that you worry about me."

"I'm not so psyched about it myself."

He grins and guides me to the edge of the dune. We crawl down to the beach on hands and knees, cool sand hissing between the grass. We skirt patches of crunchy seaweed and keep our distance from the fire, hoping the light of the flames ruins the soldiers' night vision. They seem more intent on drinking and telling tales of debauchery than monitoring the beach.

They are either supremely confident in the protection from their comrade ships or supremely stupid.

Stupid people can still kill you.

The sand solidifies, glistening silver and lapped by the waves teasing the toes of my boots. On a promontory of land along the darkened coastline, the amber lights of Dunbar reflect off the water. Spotlights sweep out to sea, quickly swallowed by the dark. To my left, the coast stretches black and empty.

Nothing there but ghosts.

I won't miss it. It might be my country but it stopped being my home a long time ago. There's too much pain and horror leached into the soil. Maybe I'll return if the war ends to marvel at the remains or maybe I'll never see Scotland again. It doesn't matter. My future lies in a land a stretch of water away. My sanctuary is a life without battle and bloodshed, my home wherever Blake is.

A weak, yellow light tinges the deck of the furthest warship, no movement from the others. The soldiers around the fire remain oblivious, engrossed in a story about a threesome.

And a goat.

I turn to Blake. "How much would it bruise your ego if I beat you to the warship?"

"Oh, woman, there's no way that's happening."

"So cocky."

He smirks. "I like to win."

I shake my head and step into the sea.

35

What sharp-spined abominations lurk in the watery dark?

The sea swirls around my thighs, tightening my skin and raising goosebumps.

There'll be no warning, only a burst of pain as teeth sink into flesh or a stinging tentacle wraps around my ankle. A primitive instinct bids me to claw my way out of the water and back onto the land where I belong.

My throat clicks, loud in the stillness. Blake has spent the last few minutes cursing under his breath. His sanitised version of cursing, anyway. I focus on the warship and ignore my thudding pulse. Blake's teeth chatter, the water tinkling at chest-level as we ease ourselves deeper, slow and steady to avoid any splashes.

"This—is colder—than I expected," he hisses.

My mouth twitches into a rigid smile. "Wh-where's that winning attitude now?"

"I'd rather—curl up—by the fire."

"I'm sure the soldiers—would be very accommodating."

"Maybe they'll share—their beer."

Icy liquid caresses my neck and my air whooshes out. I lift my feet, buoyant and heavy in the grip of the sea. My graceful breast-stroke resembles the flailing throes of a dying beetle. Blake mirrors me, the rucksack breaking the surface and leaving its own wake.

We sealed the smaller equipment in a dry-bag: control pad and pod, weapons, ammo, med kit. The sunshine of another country will dry everything else.

We are so close to freedom.

I try not to think of every moment in my life where it all went to shit right at the end. Snatching our right to independence for it to be drowned in a massacre, my sister dying in my arms. Almost escaping from Lowkirk to be captured and tortured by Nationless. Marshall. Fellhill and Gizzy.

This time will be different.

Ah, my eternal optimism.

Laughter rolls from the beach.

The assholes. Warm, drunk and relaxed despite lounging in no man's land, secure in sight of their warships. There must be more people on at least one of the vessels. An empty warship, no matter how renowned, will offer no help if they're attacked.

Are we being watched? Is the reticle of a scope settling over one of Blake's beautiful eyes?

I jerk, splashing, and grit my teeth.

Stop being a fucking baby.

The warship bobs, no closer than when I stood on the beach. The cold weaves strength-sapping tendrils through my muscles. Blake breathes easily, his lithe body cutting through the water. My fingers and toes tingle, the temperature dropping the further we go. Something brushes my leg and I gulp a scream.

A fish. A tiny, cuddly fish.

I clench my jaw and surge forward, drawing level with Blake. I slow my panting and force my thrashing limbs to sweep through the water. The sigh of the waves on the beach and the slap of liquid at the base of the ships hopefully masks our approach.

Our warship looms, a black iceberg more welcoming than the sea. A metal ladder stretches down the port beam, the bow aimed for open water. No pale faces leer over the side. Blake reaches the ladder and hoists himself out, droplets plinking all around. He hooks his arm on a rung and tugs me free of the icy grasp of the sea. I wrap my trembling arms around the ladder, my boots on the bottom rung, and he curls his shivering body over mine, not a whisper of heat between us.

He opens his mouth and I flap my hand. "Yeah, yeah. You—like to win. G-good for you."

"Such a sore loser."

"The rucksack—gave extra buoyancy."

His cold nose brushes my ear. "I like a competitive woman."

Our spasms increase, the soft breeze a howling storm through our sopping clothes. Blake eases away and I climb the ladder, the metal warm in my wrinkled fingers, my knuckles a startling white. I place each boot, careful not to clang and announce our arrival to any soldiers on deck.

At least our unprotected backs face the coastline and not the other warships.

A soft light glows in the pilothouse towards the bow, off when we started out. A figure crosses the open doorway and prods buttons on a large console, a sheaf of papers in his hand. The moon illuminates a second soldier walking towards the forecastle, a chain of bullets clinking on his shoulder. A third person crouches beside an unfamiliar double-barrelled machine gun at the stern, her back to me.

I duck down. Blake trembles against my legs, his long-sleeved t-shirt moulded to him. The tips of his hair stick to his face, the rest mostly dry. Mine clings to my back and dribbles water in shiver-inducing rivulets.

"Three soldiers—one at the helm console, the other at the bow and the last at the stern, both with machine guns. I'll go forward, you go aft."

"Check you out with your boat terminology. But how do you get two and I only get one?"

"I'm better than you."

Blake cocks an eyebrow. "That has yet to be established."

God, I love him.

I drag his smirking mouth to mine, tasting salt and ice. My knees weaken, threatening to tumble us back into the sea.

How can he do that with only a kiss?

He strokes the bedraggled hair from my face, his expression serious. "I know we're going to try and take them alive but—"

"Don't risk myself. I know. You either."

My ridiculous idea. I guess I *am* worried about saving my tattered morality. We are the unprovoked attackers stealing their warship. It seems a bad omen for our last act in the war to involve slaughtering the crew. They can join us on our journey to the rest of the world (bound and gagged, of course).

Maybe they'll thank us.

"Keeping prisoners isn't easy." Blake smiles softly, his fingers skimming my cheek. "Look at all the trouble you caused me."

"But you didn't kill me, though I deserved it."

"You made it very difficult to hate you."

"So we don't kill them, if possible. And if not—don't hesitate. If I have to kill twenty more people to keep you safe, I will."

"That's the sweetest thing anyone's ever said to me."

Buoyed by his chuckle, I haul myself up the ladder and pray my ethical enlightenment won't lead to the death of the only man I've ever loved.

36

Blake lopes through the moon-brushed night towards the stern. I stop myself from following him, fear and doubt a frozen lump in my stomach, colder than the wet clothes sticking to me.

Who knew love would be the toughest thing to endure?

I wrench my gaze from Blake's shadow gliding between long-barrelled guns, coils of chain and cylinders I have no name for sticking out of the deck.

He can take care of himself. He lived under Wick's rule without turning into a sociopath and survived two months alone in no man's land.

Commandeering a warship is nothing.

Maybe I should check he's okay—

Quit stalling, moron.

I run in a crouch to the pilothouse, darting behind pallets of ammo covered in tarp, my boots squelching softly. Windows circle the structure on three sides, the rear wall containing the doorway. The tinted panes cast no reflection of the interior, white letters and symbols scrolling on the central window. Through it, the blurred shape of the soldier on the forecastle loads the bow machine gun, facing away from the pilothouse.

The man at the helm console mumbles to himself, jabbing

buttons and flicking switches, his head constantly twitching towards the papers clutched in his hand. A maroon birthmark on the back of his neck creeps under the collar of his crisp, black shirt.

The closest warship off the starboard side sits dark and silent, blocking my view of the final vessel.

I hope its full complement of crew are the ones lounging on the beach leaving only their sister ship to respond. The fewer potential casualties, the better.

What a time to be crippled by my conscience. Okay, so I regretted destroying Livingston pretty soon afterwards, more from the monstrous body count than anything else. And when I learned the truth of the war, I felt guilty for every person I killed in Ailsa's name. Though it was the only thing that kept me safe.

Meeting Blake was the paradigm shift. Killing is easy when I don't have to stare into the wounded eyes of the victims I leave behind. The sorrow of his brother's death shadows him and always will, despite his forgiveness.

And I'll always be the person who murdered him.

How can Blake love me?

Would you focus, for god's sake!

I scrub my face with wrinkled hands, salt nipping my eyes and clumped in my lashes. I grip my flick-knife in my fist, the blade sheathed.

Maybe I won't need it.

I slink into the pilothouse, keeping the man between me and the window, his frame shorter but broader than mine. Instinct takes over, silencing my overactive brain.

Fight or die.

I look forward to a life where the choices aren't so stark.

I wrap my arm around the man's throat and jerk backwards, taking us both to the ground, my legs clamped to his sides, my heels hooked on the inside of his thighs. The sheaf of paper scatters to the shiny black floor. I flex my arm and force the man's head forward with my free hand still clenched over the knife. His pulse beats against my skin like tiny wings. He sags in my arms, a faint gurgle the only sound he makes in the five seconds it takes him to lose consciousness. I bind him at wrist and ankle with the last of our rope, tying the fancy knots Blake used on me, practised in the pod when we planned the theft of our warship.

Blake also proved I was too hasty in declaring I don't like being tied up. Under the right circumstances…

I shake my head, my cheeks hot, and slice a strip from the bottom of the man's shirt to gag him. His eyelids flicker but he'll be groggy for a while. I leave him on the floor and scuttle down the port side of the pilothouse, unable to resist a glance towards the stern.

No sign of Blake.

He's hurt, dying. I'll never touch him again. Never—

Shut up!

The man at the bow pulls the cocking handle of the machine gun, muscles bulging under his black t-shirt, his bald head covered in tribal tattoos. Space yawns between us but my time is running out. He could turn around any second, his job done.

My fist tightens on the slippery handle of my knife and I step onto the forecastle, dashing across the metal deck on rigid legs.

My skin itches with drying salt and the expectation of discovery.

The man tenses. I throw myself at him, my arm snaking around his throat, his chin nocked in my elbow. I struggle to squeeze his thick neck. The heat of him bakes my dripping clothes, my cold hair slapping his shoulders. I try to wrench us backwards but he bends at the waist, lifting my boots clear of the deck. My heart pounds against his spine.

One twist and he'll toss me to the floor, the perfect position to stomp on my head.

I punch my blade into the side of his throat. He jerks, choking, and shrugs me off. I thud to the deck, the soldier looming over me and framed by the moon, the gentle light shadowing his face. He whirls towards the pilothouse, spraying blood, the burning droplets speckling my cheeks. He falls to his knees, his trembling fingers clasping at the dark liquid boiling from his neck. Wide, white eyes meet mine. He slumps and lies still.

I pant at the stars, my skin both chilled and hot. I swipe at the stickiness on my face and hand, the knife smeared red. The coppery stench burrows into my nose and coats my tongue. I roll to my feet, forcing myself to grab the ankles of the dead soldier and drag his bulk off the forecastle, telling myself I don't notice the smear he leaves behind. I tuck him into the narrow space on the port side of the pilothouse, crossing his arms over his chest and smoothing his clothes into place.

The black material disguises the worst of the blood.

My hand rubs the dog-tags beneath my long-sleeved t-shirt. "I'm sorry," I tell him.

He did nothing to me, nothing to my sister. Sure, he was loading a weapon that would turn numerous people into sushi but he hadn't attacked me.

I abandon his body to stiffen and cool on the deck of his

warship and press my shoulder to the corner of the pilothouse, peering towards the stern, my hand on the Glock at my waist. The deck stretches empty.

Clamped lips keep me from shouting Blake's name.

The man in the pilothouse struggles weakly, his eyes half-lidded and dazed. I hook my hands in his armpits and tug him out of the doorway to the hatch amidships, my gaze flitting between the silent warships and the darkness cloaking ours.

Where is Blake?

He's fine. Don't give away your position. Don't call his name. Don't—

"Blake?"

Dammit.

A footstep. A black shape moves, too broad, too bulky to be—

"I'm here."

My air whooshes out, my knees collapsing and tumbling me to the deck with the man in my arms. I pretend to lower him to the ground but no doubt the obvious relief paints my face.

"Worried about me?"

Blake grins and places the woman he carries next to my prisoner. She blinks at me, her shiny hair in disarray and caught in the strip of material gagging her mouth. Her eyes fasten on Blake as he kneels beside me and she whines.

Is this the first time she's seen him properly? Gazed into those glorious eyes? I know exactly what she's feeling—stunned, awed, unbearably confused.

Horny.

She wriggles closer and arches her back, another whine trapped behind the gag.

"I think she likes me."

"Of course she does. She's not dead."

Blake cups my face, his thumb brushing my cheek. He shows it to me, daubed red. "The third solder?"

"I tried not to," I say, ducking my head. "But he—"

Blake's lips swallow my words.

Words? What are words? The taste of his mouth and the slide of his skin are my whole world.

"You did what you had to."

I shake my head. "I attacked him. That makes me the monster."

"Monsters don't care this much." Blake tilts my chin and forces me to look at him. "I love you, Anita. *All* of you."

How can he?

Tears burn despite the woman now glaring at me from her position on the deck. My chest swells, threatening to force them out.

Christ. I cry when he almost dies, cry when he's fine and telling me he loves me. This is ridiculous.

I suck in a shaky breath and scrub my face. "Okay, we have to stop this. Before you make me cry again."

"But it's—"

"If you say endearing, I will hit you."

He smirks. "So violent, you monster."

We grin at each other, crouched on the deck of an enemy warship, two prisoners bound at our feet. One shout away from capture and death.

And the happiest I've ever been in my life.

37

No soldiers lurk below-decks to slaughter us in a hail of bullets before they pitch our tangled bodies into the sea. We sweep the rooms, shoulder to shoulder, our guns out. Cabins, mess hall, storage, engine room, offices. We lock our prisoners in a cabin, laid out on the bunk-beds so they're at least comfortable for the few hours we hold them hostage. The guy growls, saliva dampening his gag. The woman keeps trying to rub herself on Blake and it takes all my willpower not to slap her.

Possessive, who me? It'll only get worse when the women of the rest of the world see him. They'll love him. How can they not?

He dumps the rucksack in a corner of the pilothouse and wiggles his fingers over the helm console, the multitude of flashing lights, buttons, handles and dials apparently a delight rather than a confusing jumble.

If I were on my own, I'd never get the damn ship to move.

"I can't believe you know how to sail this thing."

"This *thing* is a faction-renowned warship. Unfortunately, the credit lies with Wick. The man from Dunbar was pretty talkative in the end. Wick thought about stealing one for himself."

"Not a lot of sea in Livingston."

"No, but it would've made a glorious monument. And the weapons would've worked."

The text stops scrolling on the central window, replaced by a 3D display showing the position of our warship, the depth and the sandy bottom of the sea. Twisting a dial changes the orientation. The coastline and other warships glow green, black water stretching ahead. A kilometre further out, something large slithers over a cluster of rocks, a nightmare of tentacles and barbs.

"What the hell is that?" I say, my spine attempting to accordion into my pelvis.

"Best not to think about it. At least we don't have to go back in the water."

The view zooms in, banishing the abomination but the image of it stays imprinted on my retinas. Blake presses a button and the engine purrs, the floor vibrating under my boots. He pushes a t-shaped lever and the warship eases towards the dark, open sea.

My heart skips. "Holy shit, we're actually doing it."

"Seriously, your optimism, so sexy."

"Hey, I used to be an optimist but it got battered out of me. When I left Fellhill, I expected to die in no man's land. This is unbelievable."

Blake's arm slides around my waist, tucking me into his side, hip to hip. "Dying in no man's land was a better prospect than staying with Soldiers of the Lost?"

"Sure. But I had no intention of going quietly."

"That's my girl."

Before my stupid hormones get all weepy at the endearment, static crackles from a speaker panel on the edge of the helm console.

"Ramsay, why must you test me?" barks a female voice. "It's not enough North rushed his checks to get shit-faced on the beach, you have to make an unscheduled manoeuvre?"

Our warship slices through the water, picking up speed. Moonlight transforms the sea into silvered glass.

Are we above the abomination yet? Is it watching the shape of our vessel pass overhead with a thousand glistening eyes?

"Ramsay, you're not due to sail for another hour. Cut your damn engine. I'm sick of this macho bullshit. Do what I say or I'm reporting you to Black Agnes and she'll rip your balls off through your throat."

Blake raises his eyebrows. "Black Agnes? She sounds lovely."

"Oh, Jesus, I bet it's their leader. Lady Agnes Randolph was countess of Moray in the thirteen hundreds. She defended Dunbar Castle against the Earl of Salisbury."

"And you remember that how?"

"I know my Scottish history. Okay, Ailsa knew her history and wouldn't shut up about it. But naming yourself after a heroic figure seems like the kind of thing a leader would do. I'd rather not meet her. Women can be crueller than men."

Our warship pulls away from the empty vessel beside us, exposing us to the final warship and the owner of the pissed-off voice.

"Ramsay, are you there? Where the fuck are you going? *Ramsay!*"

A spotlight flickers on the multi-jointed mast of the furthest warship. The bright circle banishes the night and sweeps towards our vessel.

"Stop or you will be fired upon!"

Crap. I guess she's hardly going to wave us off.

"Can we disable her with one of our weapons?"

Blake flips a few switches on the console. Words scroll to one side of the screen.

"The main weapons are still booting. It'll have to be one of the manual guns. The stern one is good to go."

I sigh. "So I have to kill more people."

"I can do it."

"No, you're better at driving this thing than I'll ever be."

I head for the doorway but he grabs my wrist and pulls me against him. He kisses me, his fingers buried in my hair and, as usual, I forget to breathe. The chill of my sodden clothes fades, the shrill tone of the woman becomes muted. There is only the heat of Blake's mouth and the press of his skin. His grip prevents me from climbing his body and I make a frustrated noise. He chuckles, breaking the kiss.

"Did you just say I was better than you?"

I manage to blink at him. "No. You must have hallucinated."

"I do that a lot, it seems."

Blinding light halos the pilothouse, spilling through the doorway as we continue to pull ahead of the other warships moored in the bay.

Blake releases me. "Go. Wreak havoc. But be careful."

"You worried about me now? You're right, it is cute."

I sprint for the stern, keeping to the darkness thrown by the equipment on the deck and crawling the last few metres to the mounted weapon.

The woman will shoot at us soon enough, I don't need to offer myself as a target.

I lunge for the dual spade grips of the machine gun, swinging it round to angle at the blazing spotlight. The black coating of our warship sparkles with rainbow colours under the light.

Breath-taking.

37

I jab the thumb triggers, my eyes narrowed to slits. The gun roars and kicks hard enough to rattle my teeth. The spotlight explodes in a shower of orange sparks that bounce off the deck and dance on the water. I squint against the afterimages seared on my eyeballs and strafe their pilothouse, aiming low to damage the helm console. Glass shatters, metal buckles and shrieks. Spent casings tinkle at my feet. The cannon on their bow disintegrates and my machine gun whines to a stop, cordite burning my nose.

For a legendary warship, it didn't offer much resistance.

It lolls in the water, smoke billowing from the pilothouse, no movement on deck. The last warship remains dark and still. The fire on the beach is a dwindling spark in the gloom. The three drunken soldiers wrestle with the oars of their tiny wooden boat and paddle into the bay, preceded by their panicked voices.

Bet their beer sits sour in their stomachs.

Black Agnes will not be happy.

I crouch to pick up one of the bullet casings, the metal warm in my palm. It's thicker than anything I've seen before.

A special ingredient? Maybe normal ammo does little damage.

Maybe they didn't expect their own weapon to be turned against them.

I lope into the pilothouse and Blake grins at me. "You're better with guns, I'll give you that."

"Damn right I am."

The green contours of the coastline recede on the central screen, the other warships stationary. The speck of the soldiers' boat is nowhere near their vessel. They can chase us but we'll be far ahead.

Home free.

We decided to go straight east instead of skirting around the border fence and risk triggering it. No matter what country we land in, we'll be shipped back to England if their population has survived and retains some order.

I want as much time as possible with Blake before they split us up for questioning. Or arrest me for war crimes.

"How long until we reach land?"

Blake types a projection on the screen. "Less than eight hours."

Eight hours and we'll learn if the rest of the world really is a sanctuary or another prison.

Have I led us to salvation or a death worse than anything I can imagine?

Stop it. It'll be fine. The rest of the world will welcome us, protect us.

Optimism—it's a curse and a gift.

I rub my belly, giddiness and nerves wrestling for supremacy. "Do we have enough fuel?"

"Biodiesel and electrolysis." Blake pats the helm console. "As long as there's water, she'll take us anywhere—"

A light flashes on the console accompanied by the sharp beep of an alarm. Blake silences it with the press of a button. My stomach clenches at the frown on his face.

"What is it? Has the other warship fired at us?"

He shakes his head, twisting dials until the screen zooms out. The undulating coast appears, our warship bordered in red and pointing east, to the right of the screen. Two stationary warships sit in the bay.

And to the south, at the bottom of the screen, the unmistakable shape of a jet glows green and streaks towards us.

38

"Now this is more my style," I wheeze. "You think you've made it and it all goes to hell."

My hands shake, the giddiness crumpled to ashes in my belly.

I can't take another battle. Another failure. Not when it means Blake dies. That is too high a price to pay. Too cruel.

He squeezes my fingers. "We knew Unification Army would respond. If the guy from Dunbar told the truth about the weapons on this thing, we have nothing to worry about."

Blake jabs buttons on the helm console, the rigidness of his shoulders belying his calm words. Code scrolls on the central window, ending in the message 'Systems Ready'.

Yes, yes—blast the fucking jet out of the sky. Screw justification. I want Blake safe.

A blinking cursor replaces the text. The jet zooms closer. The alarm chirrups a proximity warning. Blake slams his palm against the suite of controls and I jump.

"The arsehole held something back after all," he says, awe and despair warring in his voice.

"What?"

"The larger weapons—missiles, laser turrets—and the defence shield, they're password protected." He raises beautiful,

203

bleak eyes to me. "I can't unlock them."

My heart lurches into my stomach, trapped there by the tightness of my ribs. Paper crinkles under my boot.

"Wait! Ramsay was looking at these while he was in here."

I drop to my knees, my trembling fingers scrunching the sheets in my haste. Lists of procedures, system checks, routes to patrol.

No password. That would be too goddamn easy.

I tilt my face to Blake, the paper crumpled in my fist. "Ramsay. The woman. They'll know it."

We run onto the deck, stuttering to a stop at the hatch. Dunbar shimmers on the coast surrounded by darkness. The two warships in the bay are difficult to make out, black on black, moonlight hinting at angles and glass. A roar increases from the direction of Dunbar. White lights twinkle.

Not stars.

I fumble at the handle of the hatch, the noise of the jet battering my senses.

"Anita, it's too late."

I whip my head up, my wet hair heavy and sticking to my cheeks. Ready to argue, deny, lie.

Blake's sad smile hurts my chest. "Why would they tell us? They can hear rescue coming. They have nothing to lose."

But we do. *I* do.

Our warship continues to sail placidly for the unseen horizon, the wind of its passage chilling my damp clothes.

"The gun at the bow. We could shoot it down."

"Tricky, even for you."

"Better than jumping in the sea."

He shivers. "Go for it. I'll get the rucksack just in case."

His hand clutches mine, fingers tight against bone, his skin icy. We step towards the bow and the pilothouse explodes, the force of the blast knocking me off my feet. I sail backwards and hit a stack of pallets, the edge bruising my spine. I thud to the deck on hands and knees, my ears ringing, Blake sprawled beside me. The jet screams overhead, one wing stirring a column of smoke billowing from the pilothouse in a waft of hot metal.

Our warship glides to a halt.

How stupid to think I deserve to be free. My arrogance has sacrificed us both.

"I'm sorry," I say, my head bowed. "For dragging you into this. This is all my—"

Slim fingers grip mine, painfully strong. "Stop that. You didn't drag me anywhere."

The pilothouse crackles, flames brightening the deck. The roar of the jet shudders over the water.

Blake climbs to his feet. "Look at me, Anita."

I stare at the floor wavering in front of my eyes.

"Woman, look at me."

I raise my head. He steps in front of me, framed by fire, and holds out his hand. I blink at it.

"I'll drag you off this boat if I have to but you are coming with me. What's it going to be—on your arse or on your feet?"

I bare my teeth. "You drag me and I'll knock you on *your* ass."

He smirks, moonlight kissing the curve of his lips. "You can try."

Caught between a snarl and a laugh, I clasp his hand and he pulls me to my feet, jerking me off balance so I slam into him, his hands fisting in my hair, his mouth claiming mine. He demands, takes.

I give him everything.

"We are not quitting," he says, shaking me a little. "So we find that nice cave you mentioned and regroup. Make another plan."

"It'll be hard without the rucksack."

"I managed. Just. And when has living ever been easy?"

"Since I met you."

He tugs my head back, his eyes drowning and dark. His mouth hovers over mine and I struggle to breathe, to think.

Shouldn't we be running now?

"Baby, you have a funny definition of easy."

He captures me with a kiss and, somehow, the death streaking towards us doesn't seem so scary anymore.

39

The scream of engines increases off the port side. Winking lights carve a graceful arc in the night sky.

"It's coming around."

"Swim to the beach," I say. "Lose it in the dunes."

Blake's thumb skims my cheek. "Fancy a trip to Eyemouth? A rotting fishing boat will be a disappointment after this but I'll cope."

The roar of the jet swells, less important than the man in front of me.

"Thank you."

"I'll drag you back any time." He hugs me, hard and quick, trembling in my arms. "You dragged me back."

What does he mean?

It's too late to ask.

We sprint for the stern of the warship, Blake's hand in mine, our boots slapping the deck.

Are more missiles whispering towards us in the dark?

We reach the transom without slowing, hopping on it in tandem and propelling ourselves over the water. Vertigo plummets in my stomach quicker than I drop towards the sea.

"Anita!" Blake yells. "Don't let go."

The wind snatches my words away but there is only one that matters.

Never.

A detonation shatters the world behind us. The warship groans. A blistering gale slaps my back and tumbles me in mid-air. My head hits the water, the cold ripping the breath from my body in a roil of bubbles. I twist and roll, confused in the dark.

Everything is black. An icy, numbing black. My hair fans around my body and tickles my face, a pressure expanding in my chest. White spots flash in my eyes at each frantic beat of my pulse, a welcome break from the nothingness.

What am I missing?

I float in shadows, a rushing in my ears like waves breaking on the shore.

Have I drifted that far?

The pressure in my chest increases.

Don't let go.

I gape at my pale, empty hand.

Shrieking Blake's name expels the last of my oxygen. Bubbles explode from my lips and dance towards my toes.

What the fuck? Which way is up?

The blackness burrows into my open mouth and fills my belly with slush.

I can't breathe.

My wide eyes see nothing but darkness. No up or down. No surface.

I need to breathe.

I thrash, panic hollowing my stomach.

Stop flapping and follow the bubbles, you moron.

I paddle my arms and kick hard. The pressure rises to

unbearable, forcing me to inhale. I suck in a breath, waiting for the gush of water into my lungs, and break the surface, gulping sweet, night air. Thick smoke billows from our stricken warship, obscuring the stars and tunnelling into my throat. The ship lists to port, the sea boiling into exposed compartments in a huff of air and sizzling metal.

Are our prisoners still alive, trapped in their cabin as it slowly fills with water?

What an awful way to die.

I kick to stay afloat, my heavy boots tugging me towards the bottom.

How far have we travelled? What depth yawns beneath my feet? And where is the many-tentacled horror we saw on the screen?

My chattering teeth trap the whine in my throat, my muscles locked around it. I close my eyes instead of peering beneath the inky surface for a flash of movement. A maw of wicked teeth.

Will I feel its appendage wrap around my ankle, the gentle kiss of suckers on my skin, or will it yank me under before I can scream?

Quiet settles over the sea. No roar of engines or lovely voice calling me woman and telling me to look at him. My eyes snap open.

Where is Blake?

The calm surface reflects the stars and I float between two skies, broken only by the ripples from my shivering body.

Blake should be drifting next to me, his head bobbing above the surface, the cold making him more beautiful, not less. A god carved of ice. He'll joke about winning and ease the ache in my chest.

But I'm alone in the water.

40

The abomination got Blake. Sucked him down almost immediately and spat his bones on the sandy floor. The metallic taste in my mouth isn't the sea, it's his blood, staining my clothes and branding my skin. He—

I slap myself.

It'll be embarrassing to explain to Blake. He'll smirk at my panic, floating closer to me on a piece of flotsam.

I hear his laugh.

"Blake?" I croak, barely disturbing the quiet.

Nothing.

I spin around, battling the soaking hair tangled in my arms. Wreckage bobs in the water—blasted bits of warship and material from below-decks, exposed through the gaping hole in the boat's side. A mattress drifts by, the sheets still attached and rippling under the surface. I paddle nearer to the ship through broken pallets.

"Blake!" My strained voice echoes, mocking me with its high pitch.

His name fades.

There's no answer.

I let go of his hand. He told me not to.

More evidence of how much I don't deserve him.

I duck under the surface, dreading a ghostly shape hovering in the blackness, his eyes wide and lifeless but still lovely, his face more striking from the marbled blue of cold. I emerge, gasping and choking, my skin raw.

The pilothouse cants, its fiery glow sparkling off the sea and dazzling my stinging eyes. I flounder up the port side, too numb to benefit from the heat of the flames, and thrash around the bow to starboard.

No Blake.

A tear drops from my cheek, lost to the salty water. I find myself back at the stern.

Alone.

Screaming his name shatters the silence. I want to shout it, over and over. Worship it, whisper it.

The tightness in my chest crushes the words.

A great slurping signals the end of our warship. Water hisses, swallowing the vessel in a swirl of steam. The current tugs at my boots, daring me to follow.

He's down here, waiting. Come find him.

I stop kicking. The sea caresses my neck and licks my trembling chin. I sob and flail towards a piece of wreckage, my eyes so blurred I hit it with my face and push it out of reach.

I'll check every goddamn scrap until I have no energy left. He'd do the same for me, not whine and cry like a fucking *baby*. My strong, stubborn warrior. He'll survive without me.

But I can't picture my life without him.

Gagging on a whimper, I dig my nails into rough wood and heave. The box tips. I lose my grip and disappear under the surface. I thrash upwards, water streaming from my hair, and run my hands over every inch of the wood but, unless Blake has the power of invisibility, he's not there.

My lip wobbles. I firm it.

Next piece. *Move your ass!*

He's here, somewhere, too stunned to call out, trapped in flotsam. I just have to keep searching. He promised me. He isn't dead until I see his body.

Oh god, his body—

No. He's not dead.

I kick for the next bit of wreckage. A pallet wrapped in tarp. I fight the slopping wetness of it but my panting breath forces me to stop. I slump across the slats, shivering and weak, sodden hair clinging to my face.

I'll rest for a second. Close my eyes. Escape where the brutal, aching sorrow can't reach. Only for a moment.

A whispering rises and prickles down my spine. I turn slowly, my stiff fingers fused to the pallet.

The prow of the final warship parts the sea and slices towards me, as terrible as a shark's fin.

$$41$$

A spotlight bathes me in a circle of white colder than the sea. It refracts off the water beaded in my eyelashes and blinds me with rainbows. A dark shape looms, eclipsing the stars. Voices clamour from the deck.

I can't let them take me. I have to find Blake.

I force my clawed fingers to release their grip on the wooden pallet, the tarp wrapped around my legs like a funeral shroud. Liquid closes over my head. I flail upwards, my skin tight from the chill, and struggle to herd my limbs into coordinated movement. I break the surface in a graceless, gasping splutter. Ignoring the warship, I aim for another wooden box about ten metres away.

This is the one. Blake is underneath, disorientated in the pocket of air. Relief will fill his face, his hair plastered to his cheekbones. He'll pull me against his shivering body and kiss me until I'm warm again.

A bullet zips into the water between me and the box.

"The next one won't miss," a voice shouts from beyond the spotlight.

Do they all have a club where they share bad guy phrases? *Any sudden moves and I'll shoot. Move, and the next goes into someone's skull.* Their lines are getting a little predictable.

I giggle and choke on salt water.

Not a good sign. It isn't that funny.

My trembling hand shields my face, my legs kicking to keep me afloat despite the heaviness in my gut. The light blazes through my fingers and etches my bones in black.

"Climb up the ladder," the voice says. "You try for a weapon and we'll drill you full of holes."

Well, that's a new one.

I paddle for the ladder, my breath jittering and pained. The halo of white tracks my ungainly progress. I grab for the lowest rung, miss, swallow water and cough. My uncooperative fingers seize the metal on the third try. I hook my arm over, resting my forehead on the side of the ladder and shutting my eyes.

I am so tired.

"Move it, bitch."

I can't even muster a rousing, "Fuck you."

Blake would be disappointed.

Where is he?

I heave myself from the sea in a cascade of water. My boots squeak on the rungs, my pale hands translucent. Three faces stare down from the top of the ladder, their features blurred.

Tears, salt, shock? Who the hell knows.

I whip my head around to scan for Blake from my improved vantage point and nearly tear my grip off the rungs. The smooth surface taunts me, broken only by wreckage.

Another bullet piffs into the water. "Climb, *now*."

Maybe Blake is already on board, curled on the deck, waiting for me to get my ass out of the sea.

Don't kid yourself. He's drifting in the depths beneath your feet. The fish will nibble his perfect face until there's nothing left but bone.

I open my mouth and suck air to stop myself from vomiting and/or screaming. Hoisting my shuddering, aching body up the ladder distracts me further. Hands grab my top and yank. I splat onto the deck on my stomach, the metal warm and glorious compared to the sea. I lie still and breathe, my eyes rolling, desperate for a glimpse of Blake.

His clothes will be moulded to his slim frame, highlighting the curve of his shoulders, his flat belly, his tight bu—

A sharp kick in the ribs. "Get up."

I lurch to my feet, dripping and swaying. The grumpy voice belongs to a man with clipped brown hair and pale eyes in hooded sockets. Two other soldiers stand slightly behind him—a hunched skeleton of a man and a young boy, his hazel eyes ancient and empty. They all wear what appears to be the regulation black uniform of Unification Army's warship crew.

No Blake.

I clear my throat.

Don't you dare ask, you snivelling cow.

My lips mash together.

"Put your hands on your head," the man barks.

Is he the infamous North, disturbed from getting shit-faced on the beach? I can't blame him for being angry.

Three black and tan AK-47 rifles point at me, bayonets mounted under the barrels. I link quivering fingers on top of my salt-encrusted hair.

The man jerks his chin. "Search her."

The boy slings his rifle over his shoulder and skips forward. The final man keeps his gun level on me. The boy pats me down, water dribbling from sodden material with each slap of his hands.

Youthful face, soulless eyes. He was a baby when the war started, the fighting all he's ever known. What's worse—remembering a normal life and realising you'll never have it again or being raised a soldier? A savage, merciless killing machine crafted for the world I want to escape.

He removes my guns, knives and the holster at my waist, stripping me naked. He slots into line, his dead gaze wandering over my body, lingering on my belly instead of my chest.

Is he wondering what my insides look like? Maybe they hold the secrets of the universe. He won't know until he cradles them in his hands.

I *hate* child soldiers. The creepy, twisted little fuckers.

"What faction are you from?" the man says, dragging my attention to him.

I try to sigh but it comes out a wheeze.

I'm too cold for a sarcastic comment, too frantic to find Blake to contribute to inane chit-chat.

How long will it take to freeze to death in the sea on a mild summer night? An hour? Less? Every second that passes means more time for him in the life-sapping water.

"I have—no faction," I manage to whisper.

"You're a Borderlander?"

Is he blind? I don't have a necklace of finger bones and my clothes match.

My head twitches from side to side, my bedraggled hair bunching under my clasped hands. "Was People's Republic—and the Lost."

"A deserter," Grim Reaper sneers. "Kill her. It's all she deserves."

Sweet Jesus, does anyone still believe that shit?

The man shakes his head. "Black Agnes will want to question her. Take us back to harbour."

No! They can't leave Blake floating in the dark. I have to find him, hug him, hear him chuckle in my ear at how worried I've been.

Grim Reaper and Dead-eyes pivot towards the pilothouse, taking my weapons with them.

The man motions with the barrel of his AK-47, the bayonet flashing in the moonlight. "Walk."

I keep my hands clamped to my head and trudge where he indicates, each step sloshing in my boots. I scan the glassy sea for a heart-soaring glimpse of a pale face, the wave of a hand. The remaining warship drifts close to shore, visible only from the tongues of flame flicking through shattered windows and the smouldering red of hot metal. A smudge of fire dances forlorn on the beach.

"Looking for someone?"

I try to swallow the words but they burst free. "There was— a guy—with me. Could you find him—pull him out, too?"

"Oh, sure. We'll pull him out."

Not comforting. Two seconds are all it will take to bolt for the side and dive into the water. I won't leave until I find Blake.

Or because the man pumps my body full of bullets.

The tip of a blade pierces my lower back. "I didn't tell you to stop, bitch. One shove and I'll sever your spine."

We reach the hatch leading below-decks, acid churning in my veins at each metre away from where I last saw Blake.

"Open it and climb down."

Panic swells in my chest.

41

He's going to lock me up. I'll be a prisoner.

Powerless.

The gun aims at my leg. "Do it now or I shoot you in the kneecap and toss you below."

I descend the ladder into a corridor matching the one in our warship. Our warship that currently rests on the bottom of the sea, playhouse for fish and tentacled abominations. Grey walls and floor, white metal doors. The man's bayonet ushers me into a cabin.

I spin around and nearly gut myself. "Please. Don't go without him."

If begging can save Blake, I'll spend the rest of my life on my knees.

"Bitch, you have bigger things to worry about."

The man reverses his rifle and whacks it into my stomach. The blow lifts me off my feet, my breath exploding out. I crumple to the floor and curl around myself.

"That's for my comrades," he says.

He pivots on his heel and leaves me wheezing. The door slams. The lock clicks. My first deep breath burns through abused muscles. Another. I pull myself upright using one of the two sets of bunk-beds jammed into the narrow room.

"Hold on, Blake." My voice wobbles but I ignore it. "I'm coming for you. Please don't die."

The prayer worked before.

I stagger to the floor-to-ceiling locker at the rear. Spare bedsheets and uniforms fill the shelves. I rifle through, hoping for more. A key, a crowbar. A gun.

Nothing.

The floor vibrates under my feet.

Are we moving?

I have to get off, find Blake. Nothing matters but him. His hungry eyes, smirking mouth. I ache for him to touch me again.

Why did I curse myself for falling in love with him? Lie about how I felt? I could've had longer, knowing he loves me, too. I'll tell him everything I think without censure just to see the dazed tenderness on his face.

My fingers smooth the pain from my chest but they can't reach my heart and I force them to stop.

I ransack my prison, searching for something I can use. A mattress hits the floor, barely fitting in the space between the beds, exposing a box-spring base. I tear at the upholstered wood, ripping fingernails loose from sensitive skin.

Who cares? My fingers will match my toes.

I punch through the base and tug at the interlinked metal, a sliver twanging free in my bloodied fist.

My grin hurts my cheeks, little more than a baring of teeth.

No one keeps me from Blake. I'll destroy anyone who tries.

I whirl for the door, bracing my hand on the wall and bending to eyeball the keyhole.

One minute, tops.

Gunfire clatters from above. Everything freezes—breath, heart, blood. The spring slips from numb fingers.

Blake.

They're shooting at him.

42

Who knew listening to the slaughter of your soulmate could catapult you into an out of body experience?

Images saturate my brain—Blake circled by blazing light that highlights high cheekbones and pools shadows in the curve of his lips. Bullets zip into the water in a burst of froth and spray. He jerks as one thunks home, tearing through his slim body in a plume of blood. Another and another. The water red-tainted and thick. Violet eyes dim but filled with regret.

Regret for ever having met me.

I launch myself at the door, rebound, and hammer it with my fists.

"Stop!" My voice cracks on the scream, slicing pain into my throat. "Don't kill him! *Please!*"

The guns roar. The agony of each round tastes like copper on my tongue. The door wavers but I don't need to see it to batter it until my hands bruise and my feet throb. I shriek Blake's name, over and over, as fast as I draw breath.

The gunfire halts. My thudding heart ticks off the seconds. The silence burrows into my skin.

Footsteps in the corridor.

Are they dragging someone?

Yes, please, bring him inside, let me see him. Don't let him be hurt, shredded, dead.

I back away from the door on shaking legs, my hands raised.

"Please, please, please," I rasp, my throat raw. "Please—"

"The guy you were with," an unfamiliar voice says, sweet enough to rot my teeth, "will not be joining you. My condolences."

The boy's footsteps prance away down the corridor, his bright laughter harrowing in its mockery.

My knees hit the floor.

I've no idea how long I sit there, my mouth gaping in a voiceless howl, tears pouring unchecked. The keening in my skull makes up for the quiet. One word on repeat—no. No, no, no. As if denial can magic Blake back to life.

I'll never see him again. Never have him tremble in my arms, undone by my touch. Never listen to the stories of his brother that fill his face with delight.

Half a fucking day to be loved, that's all I get?

Rage jerks me to my feet. I destroy the room and break everything that isn't bolted to the floor so it resembles my insides. I yank at my hair to try and ease the ache in my gut. Spit, curse, sob.

I couldn't even save the man I love.

Could I be anymore worthless?

I trip over a mattress and land on top of it, too weak to move despite the puffs of material tickling my face.

I have vague memories of ripping at it with my teeth.

I curl in a ball, struggling to hold the splintering pieces of myself together. Pressure increases in my chest and forces my creaking ribs apart.

There's no space for air. No Blake to rub my back and tell

me to breathe.

I can't breathe without him.

My heels drum a staccato on the floor, a hissing static muffling my ears and shrouding my eyes. A wave of blackness follows close behind and I welcome it.

It hurts too much to stay conscious.

As I surrender to oblivion, a little voice whispers *this is what you deserve, you stupid bitch.*

* * *

I wake in the ruins of someone else's home. A heart beats under my ear, soft fingers stroking my hair. I gasp and shove at the chest beneath my head.

"Hey, did you have a bad dream?"

"Blake?"

"You expecting someone else?" His smirk punches slivers of glass into my heart.

I hug him hard. "Are you real?"

"Don't I look real?" He laughs. "That must have been some dream."

I crane my neck without loosening my hold, desperate to press myself closer to his warm, firm body. Huge mounds of rubble surround us, reaching to the sky.

"Where are we?"

"Don't you remember? I brought you to Livingston to meet my brother. Ah, here he is."

Blake pulls me to my feet. I blink in the too-bright sun. A hazy figure approaches us and kicks up dust.

"Anita, this is Dylan."

I back up so fast I land on my ass. "That's not your brother."

Weasel face, black eyes.

"What are you talking about?" Blake says. "You wanted to meet him. You could at least be polite."

I scrabble away but footsteps dog me, shivering through the shattered ground.

"Hello, girlie," Wick says. "You can't run from me this time."

"Blake, help me!" I lurch upright and spin in a circle. "Blake?"

"Just you and me forever, girlie. No escape."

Wick grips my shoulder, the points of his nails digging in. I wrench free, stumbling and steadying myself on a pile of scorched brick. A hefty chunk fits neatly into my hand. Wick's foul breath caresses my cheek. I swing and the stone thuds into his jaw. He sprawls in the dirt. My knees collapse but I crawl to his side, slamming my weapon down.

I've done this before—same place, different time and weapon.

I raise the rock above my head, my teeth gritted, hot liquid speckling my face. A pale hand flaps at my leg.

"Baby," Blake whispers, blood bubbling from the corner of his mouth, "you're killing me."

43

The echo of my scream bounces around the cabin and slaps at my weeping face. I shiver on the mattress, my wet clothes warmer than the dark, ice-filled cavity where my heart used to beat.

And I thought losing the dragon was hard.

Blake. I want Blake.

It hurts too much to cry. Swollen eyes, sore throat, scorched lungs. My brain sobs for me. I'm too hollow. Bleak and empty. *Nothing.*

Screw bargaining, I'm going straight to depression and staying there.

Cold seeps into every limb but I embrace it. It aches less than the grief. I want to be numb.

Blake promised to try his fucking hardest not to die and died anyway. That shitty world is one I want no part in. I need to be where he is, dead and gone.

Coward.

His voice forces a keen from my throat. I swallow it and it blisters all the way down.

If I had a knife, I'd carve his name into my skin, deep enough to scrape bone.

The last hopeful, living, fighting piece of me crumbles to

225

ash, my inner voice silent. She's curled in the darkness crying her heart out. I'll join her soon, leaving my body to wither and rot.

The door swings open. The man strides in—North or whatever—his AK-47 levelled at my trembling carcass. Lines of drool and snot connect me to the mattress.

I don't much care. I blink and breathe and move but I'm not here. A wall of frost protects me. I can look through the shimmering haze, if I wish. Nothing can hurt me but the cold and the cold is my friend.

"Get up," the man barks. "We're here."

Dunbar already? Christ, how much time did it take for me to collapse after Blake's death, ten minutes?

I smother the shame. It's too hot for my prison of ice. It'll melt the wall and force me to feel.

The man's pale gaze rakes my body, his lip curled.

I'm not at my best.

He crosses the cabin in one bound and kicks me. "I said get up, bitch."

I flop onto my back.

Where does the light in the room come from? There's no bulb in the ceiling, no lamps. Embedded in the edges where my tired eyes can't see?

The man pokes me with his bayonet. Warm liquid trickles from my bicep.

Not to worry. It'll cool soon.

"Fuck's wrong with you?"

Everything.

I shudder.

No. This frigid ice queen has no room for sorrow.

The man grumbles and wraps his hand around my arm,

his fingers squeezing more blood from the wound. He pulls and my unresisting body rises. Another tug. My legs obey, carrying me into the corridor and up the ladder. The soft breeze tempts my skin to notice its pleasant caress, carrying the scent of damp stone and fish. I turn my face to the chill light of the moon.

The warship bobs in an enclosed harbour, five others moored in the gentle swell, dwarfing smaller wooden vessels. Turrets guard the seaward entrance, their double-barrels pointed at the stars. Short metal posts ring the harbour wall, the shimmering of a particle beam fence lost in the darkness.

Crushing fingers steer me onto a gangway stretched between the deck and the glistening cobbles of the harbour walkway. Wood creaks under our weight, the space wide enough for two. The man herds me towards an arch blocked by two blank-faced sentries. They nod and step aside, their hands clasped on chunky fragmentation guns.

"Captain North."

Captain. Well, la-de-da.

Their gazes linger on me then return to scanning the harbour, the glare from mounted spotlights reflected in their eyes.

If I throw myself at them, will they disassociate me into a pile of molecules or just slap me around a little?

North hustles me into the orange glow of Dunbar before I can find out.

My feet shuffle on cracked mud instead of concrete, most of the buildings dilapidated. Blast marks scorch every surface. Vehicles disturb the water pooled in craters, the insignia of three black warships bearing a Saltire painted on each bonnet.

The stronghold reminds me of Lowkirk, another shithole

on the brink of collapse and the first encampment to take me prisoner but not the last. How many now, four?

And Blake.

Nausea ripples up my throat. I stumble and North's grip tightens, cutting off my circulation.

That's okay. I don't need it. I am ice. Steel. Once, I was fury.

A pain from my past. A lesser one and completely unimportant.

Soldiers stroll down avenues of dirt despite the late hour. They pause to sneer at my no doubt red eyes and snot-encrusted nose. They talk to the man latched to my arm but I have no interest in deciphering their babble. My gaze drifts, my boots walking where they're bid.

North yanks me to a halt. My chin hits my chest, my hair swinging forward and crackling with salt. A metal orb as tall as my waist trundles towards us, hardened mud snapping under its weight. A red light dazzles me from a shiny black eye in the centre. It hums deep in its core and four weaponised arms pop out, the barrels aimed at me. I sway closer.

Yes. *Kill me.*

"Stand down, 2501," North says.

The weapons retract with a clunk and a hiss. The ball rolls away, disappearing into an alley between a boarded shop and the shell of a building.

The *bastard*. North should have let it reduce me to a pile of ash to match my sunny outlook. A quick, clean death.

But it's too much effort to thaw and punch him.

The wide street culminates in a large building, the white stone blinding and pristine. A perfect tooth in a maw of decay. Columns support a triangular pediment above a massive oak door flanked by bronzed lions. North drags me up the steps into a marble hallway, the sickly-sweet smell of trumpet lilies stinging my sinuses. They spill from vases on every surface, the waxy petals stained orange with pollen.

Who the fuck still grows flowers?

I wrinkle my nose, trying not to sneeze.

Ice queens don't sneeze.

North briefly relinquishes his hold to throw open an ornate door beneath the arch of a sweeping double staircase. I shamble into a long room. There are no windows. Sconces cast a cold light on the pale walls and highlight sparkles of blue, like standing in the centre of a glacier.

I like it. It suits my mood.

The hand on my arm ushers me down an aisle between rows of chairs, our steps muffled on a strip of red carpet. Five people sit behind a table at the far end, the woman in the middle beckoning us despite our approach, her round face crumpled in a frown. North increases his pace and I stumble to keep up.

The infamous Black Agnes? Nothing black about her—grey hair, grey eyes, ridiculous velvet suit.

She clasps veined hands on the tabletop. "I hope you are here to report on the incident during your patrol this evening, Captain North."

No, he just likes to ferry grief-stricken women around for fun.

Who needs ice? Snark is a perfect shield.

"Yes, Black Agnes." North clears his throat and straightens his spine. "At 0012 hours, this woman and her companion boarded Captain Ramsay's ship undetected, slaughtering him and his crew. They destroyed Captain Harrison's ship, along with her crew, and attempted to steal the vessel they had boarded."

Not-Black Agnes leans forward, one foot tapping the marble floor. North flinches at each delicate tap. The other women at the table mirror their leader's movement, four pairs of predatory eyes fixed on us.

Soon there'll be cackling and the evil steepling of fingers.

"Undetected? And where were you during this attack?"

Getting shit-faced, the naughty boy.

North shifts, the temperature in the room dropping a few degrees. "My crew and I were patrolling the beach, Ma'am. We detected a commotion over the dunes and went to investigate."

If the commotion he's referring to is the battle Blake and I had with the snake, it happened hours earlier when the bay was empty.

Blake's name spears an icicle into my chest before I smother it.

Damn frost, not doing what it's supposed to.

Black Agnes arches an eyebrow as thin as her figure. "All of you? Despite my decree on never leaving a warship empty?"

North's throat clicks. "It—was C-Captain Harrison's orders, Ma'am."

Dead women tell no tales.

"Continue." The word cracks through the hall.

To give him credit, North doesn't jump but a quivering transfers from his fingers to my arm.

Where is the gruff, commanding captain full of justified anger?

Is there a leader alive who doesn't terrorise their minions?

I feel sorry for him.

"We called for assistance. There, um, was a glitch in our longer range weapons. They had to be rebooted. The jet sank the stolen ship as per protocol and returned to base. This woman"—he gives me a shake in case Black Agnes mistakes me for someone else—"was pulled from the water and imprisoned below-decks. Her comrade was shot attempting to board. We left his corpse in the sea."

I stagger, the sound of fracturing ice drowning everything else out.

Shot attempting to board.

My violet-eyed warrior.

He was coming to rescue me.

44

Blake, gone and barely meriting two sentences to mark his passing.

I hunch and struggle to rebuild my icy walls but the water pools, hotter than blood. I have no sarcasm to plug the flood. I'm too raw.

Why the *fuck* won't they hurry up and kill me?

Black Agnes's eyes flick to me. "Where are you from, *girl?* What faction gave you the skills to slaughter six of my people and steal one of my warships?"

I can't control the shaking.

Shit.

Tears flow freely down my cheeks.

Double shit.

I force my gaze over Black Agnes's scrawny shoulder and stare at the wall.

I am numb. I am ice.

Oh god, it hurts!

Silence stretches. The cronies shift in their chairs with a creak of wood. Spots of colour flare in Black Agnes's somehow rounded cheeks.

Seriously, the woman resembles a lollipop.

Yes, bitchiness, save me! Blake would be proud if only I

articulate it.

My knees buckle. North shakes me and I use it to disguise the movement, curling around myself, my head bowed.

"She's a deserter, Ma'am," he says after another throat-clearing. "Originally from The People's Republic then Soldiers of the Lost. I'm uncertain why or when she switched. Or how she got to be here."

I should tell Black Agnes just how easy it was to board her ship and subdue her crew. Maybe she thought no one would have the audacity to try, fear of their reputation (and hers, probably) enough to deter potential attackers.

Unlucky for her, my speciality is stealing powerful weapons from psychos and ruining their encampments.

"While I appreciate you bringing her to me for questioning, Captain North, I fail to see how I am to get valid information out of a vegetable. What's wrong with her?"

"The, ah, death of her comrade appears to have broken her, Ma'am."

The slash of her mouth lifts in a sneer. "How pathetic."

Bitch. How dare she judge my grief? I bet she's never loved anything but her own bony carcass.

Neither did I for a long, long time. How sweet and pure and goddamn fucking agonising it is. Would I have become like her if I never met Blake? Brittle and cruel and cold. It's worth it, meeting him, losing myself.

It's worth it to have loved and been loved so intensely, if only for a moment.

"No matter," Black Agnes says, straightening her suit sleeves with a snap of material. "She will be executed at daybreak, broken-minded or not. I'm sure she'll be quite forthcoming when the first stones hit her."

She grins, her teeth obscenely dainty for such a giant head. Her cronies titter. One even claps.

They're going to *stone* me to death? The savages. Can't they have a hint of compassion and put me out of my misery? Fine, they're pissed—I attacked them, led to the death of six of their comrades and wrecked some warships—but does that justify the most medieval form of torture?

I don't fucking think so.

They've punished me enough by killing Blake. There is no quicker way to break my spirit and make me want to die. But I'll choose the method, not them.

My death will not be an entertainment.

"Get her out of my sight," Black Agnes says with an officious wave of her spindly hand.

North marches me into the hallway and pushes me through a door at the base of one of the sweeping staircases. Crimson doors in a long, white corridor assault my eyeballs. Multi-paned windows offer a view between the columns onto the diseased streets of Dunbar.

North opens the third garish door, shoving me inside a cell no larger than a cupboard. I stutter to a stop at the back wall and listen to him breathe.

"I hope you wake up when the stones start to fly," he says, the scorn clear in his voice without me needing to see it. "I want to hear your screams, bitch. Like the screams of your little boyfriend."

And just like that, my pity turns to hate.

The door bangs shut. Fury and pain root my feet to the floor, North's squeaking tread retreating down the corridor. A second, quieter click signals I'm alone.

My knees collapse, my breath sobbing out. I press my

forehead to cool marble and try to emulate it.

Hard, unflinching, no pesky emotions. I can't live with the soul-sucking loss, the emptiness carving a hole in my chest.

The screams of your little boyfriend.

Liar! Blake is the strongest person I know. North should be grateful to have witnessed how a true warrior dies. Defiant and brave, attempting to save the woman he loves.

Doesn't he deserve your grief?

I swallow a cry and it becomes a painful hiccup.

No, it hurts too much.

You fucking weakling. Even in death, you don't deserve him. You sully his memory with your whining. How can—

I grind my fists into my temples. "All right, all right, shut up!"

I roll onto my back and stare at the ceiling, the room just long enough to stretch my body flat, though I can touch the walls on either side with my palms. The only adornment in my cell hovers above my head—a steel sink next to a tiny toilet.

Biting glass replaces the ice, every slice showing how much Blake means to me. I worship the pain because it's all I have left of him.

"I love you, Blake," I whisper to the unforgiving marble box, tears dribbling unchecked into my hair. "They'll regret taking you from me for as long as I live."

Okay, so I don't plan on it being particularly long but it will be spectacular. I'll not go meekly to the execution post, quivering and afraid, to be pounded into jelly.

To hell with not becoming a monster.

I'll destroy them and burn their faction to the ground.

<h1 style="text-align:center">45</h1>

I doze to the comforting image of ripping out Dead-eyes's dead little eyes and making him eat them. The dark hours of the night pass quickly while dreaming of slaughter.

Who knew?

A key rattles in the lock. My gaze drifts, my body relaxed. Dried salt powders my clothes and clumps in my hair. I let my mouth drop open and breathe noisily through it.

I am broken and weak.

Two men squeeze into the room at my feet, one the sneering North. The other man wears the same black uniform, a bayoneted AK-47 slung over his shoulder, a belt of grenades across his broad chest. He lingers on my breasts, his hazel eyes mashed into the centre of his face with the rest of his features.

"I'll get the head, you get the feet." North sidles between me and the wall, the bayonet of his rifle sticking up behind his skull, one wrong move from slicing off an ear. Two Brownings ride in a holster at his waist.

Not a bad haul of weapons for a rampage.

"What's the matter with her?"

"Bitch has been like this since we killed her boyfriend."

The red door stands ajar behind the new man, the sun barely

cresting the bottom of the windows.

"We have some time. How 'bout we ride that body before we ruin it?" The man flashes crooked teeth at North. "She's not bad looking, if you ignore the drool."

It's another thing they'll regret.

I blink and breathe, each swallow loud and wet.

North glances at his watch. "It'd be like boning a corpse. And we don't want to keep Black Agnes waiting."

Both men shudder.

Is she the female version of Wick? Fitting, then, for Dunbar to follow in Livingston's footsteps. Even without the awesome dragon machine, I'll reduce them to dust.

North plants one boot on each side of my head, leaning slightly to avoid the sink. The other man crouches at my feet, his fingers tickling my ankles. North squats and slides his hands under my shoulders. A patch of stubble bristles under his jaw. Neither man pays attention to me, treating me as though I'm already dead.

How can they not hear the furious thudding of my heart?

The morons.

I clamp my boots around the new man's neck and jerk my hips. His skull cracks into the wall, his rifle clattering at my feet. I fist my hands in North's shirt and yank him to the side, ringing his jaw off the sink. I pull him down and roll on top, his dazed eyes matching his comrade's, both of them blinking at me. I grab the dropped AK-47 and jab the bayonet into the man's throat. Blood sprays over North and me, my knees pressed to North's chest, my boots pinning his arms, his gun useless under his body. I smash the butt of my rifle into his face and his nose bursts.

"Call me bitch one more time."

North bares blood-smeared teeth. *"Bitch."*

I grin and slam the gun down. He chokes on his own enamel. I hit him until his body stops bucking. The wet *smack smack* tries to draw me into a nightmare but I shrug it off.

It's an unimportant memory from a life coming to an end.

Breathless, I sag on my heels. The butt of the rifle drips red, my hands splattered with it. Crimson daubs the walls and floor, thick enough to taste.

My monster stretches its claws and says *more. Kill.*

We all deserve to die.

I splash water on my face and clean my hands then strip the men of their weapons. The grenades jink against each other, thick, like lemons on steroids.

More of the mystery ingredient?

I can't wait to find out.

I peer through the gap in the door. No one hides in the corridor, the marble blinding white compared to the carnage in my cell.

It matches the doors, though.

To my right, the corridor bends out of sight, left heads back to the hallway where I entered the building. I sidle over to the window, my rifle steady.

The streets of Dunbar are desolate in the morning sunlight, the sky the only bright colour. A large crowd gathers at the base of the steps, their voices muffled by glass. They form a jostling semi-circle around a scarred wooden post and a pile of jagged stones—shattered bricks from crumbling buildings and sandstone from the coast. Their glittering eyes remind me of another mob in Fellhill.

I have so many memories I won't miss.

Black Agnes minces into view, flanked by her cronies. She

addresses her minions and they cheer, their mouths wide and dark. I lope down the corridor and press my ear to the door. Nothing but my roaring pulse. The babble of the crowd is loud through the closed panels of the main entrance in the hallway. I crack one open an inch and the noise pours in.

"—we will batter our enemies, as we will batter the pathetic fool who dared attack us!" Black Agnes yells. "She and her like are no match for Unification Army. We will slaughter and burn until Scotland is ours! Then we will unite the rest of the country. *Our* country."

The mob roars their approval. I roll my eyes.

This is what we've become—twisted by power, craving nothing but destruction.

Well, if they want to burn…

I unclip a grenade, my finger hooked in the firing pin. I nudge the heavy oak door wider with the toe of my boot. The crowd howls, probably anticipating the appearance of North and his comrade dragging my body between them.

Who doesn't want a little blood and guts before breakfast?

I rip the pin and lob the grenade, a second following in its wake.

46

The double explosion finds me in another corridor of crimson doors mirroring the one where I spent the night. It stretches down the other half of the building from a door opposite the entrance I used to get to the hallway. I hunch against the tinkle of glass as the windows shatter. A huge crater swallows the front steps and one bronzed lion, the other canted on the edge. The wooden pole dissolves, the pile of rocks disintegrated and blasted through the windows to scatter in the corridor around me.

Not quite the stoning Unification Army expected.

Pale faces huddle behind scorched buildings and dented vehicles, smoke curling from the limbs they've left behind. A woman sways on the lip of the crater, blinking at her severed arm. Blood pulses from her shoulder and patters on the mud of the road. She opens her mouth and wails, one long howl after another, loud in the hushed silence following the detonations. A burst from my rifle silences the shrieks. She collapses in the dust, her arm tumbling into the hole.

I want them all dead but I won't be cruel about it, even if they would've enjoyed watching my slow, tortured death. Perhaps the armless woman would've thrown a stone and laughed as my skin split.

240

I bet she didn't anticipate her pain and blood starting the day.

A furious screech erupts from beyond the ruined steps. "Get after her, you fucking cowards!"

Not so pathetic now, am I, Black Agnes?

My fierce grin hurts my face. I sprint along the corridor, crunching broken glass and kicking rocks across the once shiny floor. It turns deeper into the building past a set of white stairs. The door behind me crashes open. Bullets fracture marble walls and ricochet with a squeal. I leap up the stairs, pausing only long enough to lob another grenade. It rings off the wall and skitters into the corridor. A chorus of male curses greets it, their boots scuffling away.

I ignore the first floor, taking the steps for the second and placing a grenade half-way up as the marble shivers under my feet. The layout of the second floor seems similar to the ground level—a windowed corridor along the front looking north down the main street of Dunbar. I hide around the corner, my corridor at the top of the stairs continuing towards the back of the building past five crimson doors. Shadows pool in the windowless depths at the rear.

The grenade on the stairs explodes. Smoke and dust billow, flecks of marble peppering the walls. I bury my mouth in my sleeve and squint down. A wide gap yawns in the crumbled steps.

I try the first door towards the back of the building. A light clicks on, the yellow glow bathing metal shelves crammed with cans of food.

The bounty holds no appeal.

My last meal was dinner in the pod with Blake while we waited for night. Roasted pheasant and carrots dug straight from the ground, Blake's knowledge of wild forage far superior to mine. He listed everything he ate during his two months in no man's land, bugs and all, when we weren't distracted by tying each other up.

God, it was ridiculously difficult to concentrate, or breathe, with his warrior's body stretched out beneath mine, his hands tied above his head. His eyes wicked and dark.

Even when he was bound and helpless, I was still at his mercy.

I hunch at the pain, my hand fisted over my heart, but don't fight it. It carves me until I bleed, each cut proving how special he was.

Special enough to die for when all I wanted was to live.

I lurch into the next room and grip the metal strut of a shelf to keep myself upright. Objects clink, invisible to my blurred eyes.

The memory of his touch is strong enough to feel the ghost of him. My favourite position was cuddled into his side, my hand slipped underneath us to grip his shoulder blade, the ridge of his scars rough against my palm. My face buried in his neck, his pulse fluttering on my cheek, the steady beat of his heart.

I long to roll around in the scent of him—sunshine and earth. *Life.*

I force myself to release my hold on the shelving unit, red creases slashing my palm.

Dunbar's regret will honour his death. He deserves nothing less than the sensational destruction of the encampment that killed him.

I scrub my face and blink at my surroundings. My leaden heart jumps.

"Well, about fucking time."

Ammunition and military equipment fill the shelves of the room, the air tainted by gunpowder and metal. Chains of thickened machine gun bullets wink golden in the light, battery packs for L4s and shotgun cartridges slotted into wood. I place my guns on the floor and drop my grenade belt next to them, the single grenade dangling forlorn. I wriggle into a bulletproof vest, fighting against the stiffened nanocellulose.

It's more flexible than Kevlar, lighter, but tougher.

The longer I breathe, the more soldiers I kill.

I want to put a bullet in Black Agnes's face.

I grab two full grenade belts from a shelf, crossing them over my chest, and stuff four AK-47 magazines into the pockets of my combats. On the far wall hangs a row of ASM5 rocket launchers. They measure half a metre in their unextended position and can fire multiple shots. I sling one over my shoulder, tuck a box of rockets under my arm and reclaim my rifles from the floor.

As tempting as it is to keep piling on the weapons, any more and I won't be able to move.

I may emulate Rambo but I don't have his musculature.

I peek out of the doorway. Empty corridor, no sounds of approach. Muffled shouting comes from outside as Dunbar mobilises. I stand on the grenade belt on the floor and pull the last pin, then run like hell.

47

The force of the explosion tosses me onto metal stairs. The building groans, rent marble screaming in between the multiple pops and smaller detonations.

I'm glad of the space separating me from the storage room.

I turned towards the back and round a corner, sprinting down an uninterrupted corridor that seemed to run the length of the building, automatic lights pinging on. A stairway at the end led upwards to a metal door.

I grip the banister and drag myself to my feet, ignoring the throb of bruised shins, happy I avoided stabbing myself with a bayonet.

What an inauspicious way to go when I plan on being unforgettable.

I jog up the steps, weapons clanking, my boots ringing on metal. I slide the heavy bolt free and the door swings inward, sunlight dazzling me as it floods the corridor. Half-blind, I stagger onto the roof, rough stone crunching under my feet. There's no external lock on the door, only a curving metal handle. I tug one of the rifles off my shoulder and release the magazine. I wedge the gun as far as it will go through the handle, the barrel and bayonet sticking beyond the frame, stopping someone from pulling the door open. The strap secures it in place.

Let Dunbar's finest puzzle this one out. By the time they find another way up, blow the door or scramble an aerial assault, I hope to have ruined a sizeable portion of their encampment.

Smooth marble walls house the access door close to the south-eastern corner of the roof. It looks over an area of cracked concrete containing military vehicles and rusted cars. A dusty street stretches towards the boundary on the landward side, tunnelling under what used to be a railway embankment. Figures scurry between decayed buildings, most dressed in camouflage gear or jumpsuits but some wearing black. I skip back from the edge before they spot me.

A bulky heating and ventilation unit purrs between me and the front of the building, the rest of the roof space filled by solar panels. A clear border skirts the low parapet running around the threshold of the roof. I follow it to the triangular pediment front and centre. The other side of the building, where the storage room was, has collapsed, solar panels disappearing into the ragged hole. Smoke pours out and smudges the sky.

Soldiers and vehicles move in the street below, surrounding the building. My first crater has stopped smouldering, the limbs of the dead left where they fell. The main road extends to the harbour where six warships are still moored. Narrower streets disappear into a conglomeration of brick, concrete and chimney stacks. There are no taller buildings that could house a sniper. The sea sparkles in a line of azure on the horizon to the north and east. Tranquil but unobtainable.

That ship has sailed, so to speak.

For the place I'll die, it really isn't bad. Beautiful view

(the living, vibrant green and gentle hush of the sea beyond Dunbar, not the shithole of an encampment), warm breeze, sheltered. No fear. I've already lost everything. What more can Unification Army take from me?

I stack my assorted weapons, swiping dust and salt from my increasingly tattered combats. The bulletproof vest hides the dirt and dried blood coating my long-sleeved top. I pry the wooden lid off the box of rockets, foam packaging fluttering across the roof, and make a disappointed noise. Only two when the launcher can hold five.

Ah, well, better than none.

My smile wobbles. "Such an optimist."

I heft a rocket in my hand, sunlight glinting off the bronzed tip, the rest black. I balance it on my knees and telescope the ASM5 to its full length, the mechanical sights popping up. I slide both rockets home and place the launcher on the ground for later, scrabbling down the nearest row between the solar panels to the centre of the roof. I yank the grenades from my belts, pull the pins and throw them, one after another, in a circle around the building. Silver safety levers twirl and clatter on the solar panels. Ten grenades sail into the streets below. I imagine them thumping off broken-tiled roofs, bouncing on vehicles and scaring the crap out of a lot of soldiers as they thud at their feet.

Dunbar is about to get messier.

Explosions rock the air, columns of smoke and brick fountaining into view. Metal shrieks, glass shatters, people scream. Secondary detonations boom, quieter than the first. Probably fuel tanks.

Dunbar echoes with the same misery that waits patiently to suck me down when I'm finished wreaking havoc.

I shrug off the empty grenade belts and return to the pediment.

"Hey, Black Agnes!" I call over the moans of the injured and dying. "Not so great at defending this castle are you, you deluded cow."

A wave of sobs, groans and the crackle of fire fill the heavy pause.

Icy satisfaction sits hard in my heart like a marble.

"I want that whore as dead as her comrade!" Black Agnes howls.

I grab my remaining rifle and slap the fire selector to fully automatic, jabbing the barrel over the edge and emptying the magazine into the street.

"His name. Is. *Blake!*" The words burn my throat, the taste of his name both sweet and devastating.

Bullets ping and whine. More people scream.

I doubt I've hit Black Agnes. The bitch will be cowering somewhere relatively safe while her minions bleed.

Loud banging comes from the access door. I scoop up the ASM5 and balance it on my shoulder, my left hand under the barrel to keep it steady. My right hand curls on top of the trigger. I slide the launcher across the sloping surface of the pediment and press my eye to the sight, the graduated reticle measuring the range to my target.

I bare my teeth. "Yippee ki-yay, motherfuckers."

Blake would've appreciated the reference from my favourite classic movie, once I reminded him it wasn't just my normal swearing. He would've smiled, the amusement dancing in violet eyes, his black hair flopping across his forehead and kissing his cheekbones.

Now, his corpse floats in the sea.

I mash my brittle fingers down on the trigger.

48

The rocket whooshes from the launcher, its spring-loaded fins winking in the sunlight. It blazes down the main street and thumps into a covered pallet on the deck of the nearest warship. I hold my breath.

Surely the pallet contains something good, something combustible—

Gunfire rattles. I duck behind the pediment but no bullets patter into the marble of the building. I risk a peek as the roar and pop continues. The deck of the warship burns, small explosions issuing from the flames. The glass of the pilothouse shatters. Sparks fly from metal as it buckles. My rocket has hit a pallet of enhanced machine gun rounds, the warship quickly battle-scarred. Stray bullets gouge its neighbours, damaging their lovely black coating. A wooden vessel erupts in a cloud of splinters and begins to sink.

I couldn't have asked for a better 'fuck you' to Black Agnes.

How easily I destroy her precious warships. She must be furious.

I grin and reposition the launcher on the other side of the pediment, searching for a second target.

It won't be long before Unification Army toss every weapon they have at the roof but I'm not done yet. Not until I stop breathing.

Beyond the first row of scorched, crumbled houses hulks a blocky structure of grey stone. A chimney stack belches black smoke into the perfect blue sky.

A munitions factory. How wonderful.

The ASM5 kicks against my shoulder. Bullets crunch into the marble around me, fragments skittering onto the roof. The empty launcher drops with a clatter and I dive behind the pediment, rough stone biting my side. A faint whump signals the impact of my rocket, almost lost in the gunfire and yells and the roar of engines.

Have I missed? Surely not.

I jump at the deafening boom of an explosion, the building shivering beneath me. Loud snaps and bangs and crackles punctuate a maniacal fireworks display. Acrid smoke drifts over the rooftop and I cough, my eyes watering at the stinging cloud. Bullets stop pattering into the pediment. I scoop up my rifle and peek over the edge, scanning for soft-bodied targets in the avenues below.

The munitions factory no longer exists. Deadly white trails mark the path of heated ammunition from a pile of flaming, smoking rubble. More windows smash, more stone disintegrates.

Soon, there won't be an unmarked building in the whole of Dunbar, if there ever was such a thing.

A blackened, ruined area surrounds the factory. Corpses litter the wreckage and the streets, splashes of red on fractured brick. Closer to my building, smaller craters pock the surface of the road, twisted metal in the centre. Soldiers huddle in them or behind intact vehicles. Their bodies twitch and dance under my bullets. I slap a fresh magazine into my rifle. Return fire whines into the pediment and past my head, whipping my hair around my face. I press my back to the cold stone, and pant on dust and smoke.

My monster purrs at the carnage, a wild excitement fizzing through my veins and hammering in my heart. I want to throw back my head and howl at the sky.

How much fun I've missed being a principled little soul. I could've rampaged every day, no conscience. Nothing but death and hatred. I should have ruled The People's Republic from the beginning. Slaughtered until we were the only ones standing. No prisoners.

No Blake, either. My rampage-free life, though short and tormented, was worth it. It led me to him and he gave me everything I wanted.

God, I love him.

Grief turns the feral happiness to sludge.

An explosion cracks over by the access door. The smooth wall dissolves in a cloud of sparkling dust, stone blasting out onto the roof. A hole appears through the swirling smoke, chunks of marble raining from the top of the gap.

I scamper to the heating and ventilation unit opposite the access door, my eyes fixed on the black space for movement. My shoulder dents the metal of the unit, my pulse loud in my ears. A stone skitters. I pop up from behind my barrier, my finger hard on the trigger, screaming at the soldier hauling himself through the breach. His body flies backwards, his boots disappearing into the darkness of the exposed stairwell. I spray the marble and duck, reloading as return fire pings into the HVAC. We exchange bullets, using up two of my three remaining magazines. One round slams into the forehead of a woman who sticks her head up at the wrong moment. Her shocked eyes meet mine for a second before she slumps out of sight.

What did she see—a tumble of blonde hair, a pale face, bared teeth and green eyes empty of anything resembling human emotion?

Just another enemy soldier, then.

A stun grenade rattles on the roof beside me. I flick it back with the bayonet of my rifle and smile at the cursing and scramble of bodies. The unit protects me from the blast of noise and a flash like lightning. I stand and empty my rifle into the writhing people who didn't run fast enough.

A gathering roar tugs at my consciousness. I discard my AK-47 and press my back to the HVAC, looking north-west. A black jet rises into view, vertical thrusters powering it upwards.

What the hell is Unification Army's fascination with black?

The plane rotates gracefully towards the marble building, the bubble of the cockpit reflecting the sun like a huge, unblinking eye. The underside of the wings bristle with machine gun stations and triple ejector missile racks. The vertical thrusters swivel in a flash of blue, the horizontal engine at the rear firing with a plume of smoke. The jet glides towards me.

And so we come to the end.

49

Soldiers crawl like spiders through the breach. The deathly shadow of the jet swoops towards me. I unholster a Browning and press it to my forehead.

"Just let me kill a few more. Please."

I have no idea what bloody god I pray to.

The plane is still too far to bother taking pot shots at. I straighten and spin, slamming my elbows on the top of the heating and ventilation unit, my arms extended in a two-handed grip. Three soldiers run towards me, their faces grim. A woman hoists herself through the gap in the access stairwell, frowning in concentration. My bullets floor the men who are too slow in swinging their rifles around.

They really should have taken the time to put on bulletproof vests.

The woman snarls, my Browning pivoting towards her. The jet roars closer. I squeeze the trigger. My shot catches the woman in the throat. A hammer blow thuds into my chest, right over my heart. The impact rams me onto my back, my head connecting with rough stone in a starburst of white. I grip the Browning in my right hand, struggling to breathe past crushing pain. My heels dance a tattoo on the roof, air whining into pulverised lungs. Trembling fingertips stroke the bullet embedded in my vest.

The plane reaches the roof and eclipses the sun, surrounding itself in a halo of light. The vertical thrusters swivel to keep it hovering above where I lie gasping and relearning how to breathe. Hot air blasts my cheeks and I slit my eyes against the swirling dust.

The Browning in my hand weighs as much as the moon. I could raise it and fire at the jet. Maybe a lucky shot will explode an engine and send it screaming over the side of the building. It'll kill one pilot, maybe two, and whoever crouches in the cargo bay to storm the roof.

It seems like too much effort. I'm tired, sore, empty. I've ruined a good chunk of Dunbar in Blake's honour. Better to lie still and wait. Wait for the hatch in the belly to open and frame a serious-faced man who'll shoot me in the head. Or the soldiers from the breach will surround me, sheath their weapons and stomp me into oblivion.

I don't care. I'm ready.

Maybe I'll take a few more with my Browning, just to be a bitch.

Blake would be proud.

A tear streaks my face and dampens my tangled hair. Footsteps scrape on rubble. The plane dips, the heat from the thrusters drying the rest of my tears. With a clunk and a hiss, a missile disengages from the underside of a wing. The propulsion engine fires in a burst of dirty yellow light and smoke.

Overkill, perhaps, but the pilot must be too angry to think straight. At least when the rocket slams into me, my exploding body will further mar the roof of Black Agnes's pretentious white monument to her greatness.

The missile zips out of view.

How the fuck can they miss, I'm lying right here. Or maybe the pilot is taunting me, sending the rocket on a victory lap before he reduces me to ash.

I shut my eyes and think of Blake.

He wouldn't be happy with my surrender but he isn't here to call me woman and tell me to get up, keep fighting, keep living.

He should have known I can't live without him.

The roof shudders under my spine, the explosion blocked by the heating and ventilation unit. I cover my head, marble clattering all around me and crunching into the solar panels. The down draft of the thrusters hurls it in all directions. The hatch slides open, a black, toothless maw yawning wide.

I wait for a soldier to finish the job of the blind/drunk/inc ompetent pilot.

A rope ladder unfurls and slaps onto the roof. I blink at it.

Why are they tormenting me? Do I have a disillusioned soldier swooping to rescue me, hoping to screw over Black Agnes by ensuring my escape? Like Stig. Or maybe it's Black Agnes herself and a cruel ploy to spark hope in the silent cavity of my chest. I'll climb up the ladder to meet her sneering face.

Maybe she'll prove she is the female version of Wick.

I shiver on the roof, frozen to the stone.

Can't they just finish it quickly?

My rescuer will be disappointed when they realise they risked themselves to save someone who has no desire to live. What will they do if I ignore them—fly off cursing my stupidity, loose another missile and reduce my body to pink mist? Or I could climb inside, club the pilot and kamikaze the jet into the nearest crowd.

It will be all the sweeter if Black Agnes is on board.

My heart swells and shrivels with each agonised beat. I roll into a crouch, my shoulder pressed to the heating and ventilation unit. I peer around the edge, the Browning clasped tight in a two-handed grip. The structure housing the access door is gone, obliterated in a pile of burning stone and twisted metal. It could take hours for any surviving soldiers below to dig a path through.

Screw hanging around that long. I need it to be over and throwing myself off the building is too pathetic. My death should be in fire and smoke. So the plane is the only way to go.

My last hurrah.

I stare at the black, impassive shape hovering above me. Hot air whips my clothes and dances my hair around my face.

Stop gawping and do something, dammit.

I holster the Browning and lunge for the ladder. It swings under my weight, my fists clenched hard enough on the rope to send a twinge through the healing muscles of my left forearm. I try to climb but am shaking too much to release my hold, no matter what my inner voice growls at me.

She is a mouthy bitch, sometimes.

The whine of the thrusters increases in pitch and the jet rises smoothly. The whole of Dunbar opens before me, one good bombing away from total collapse.

Perhaps the pilot plans to shake me loose and break my body on the wreckage I've made. Or dangle me in front of the rabid survivors so they can rip me apart.

The machine guns on the underside of each wing roar to life. I jump and my boots slip, the rope in my hands keeping me airborne. Bullets pound the buildings in a deafening hail.

Bronze casings tinkle to the rapidly shrinking roof beneath my dangling feet. I grit my teeth and pull myself up, hooking my boots on the lowest rung of the ladder.

I guess I have no fucking idea what the pilot is thinking.

Missiles whoosh free in a puff of heat, the plane turning in a lazy circle. Jabbering soldiers scrabble for safety in the bricks and gore. When the nose points at the sparkle of the sea, the jet eases forward. The ladder jerks, winching itself towards the hatch and carrying my quivering body with it. I fumble for a Browning, my cheek pressed to the rope. Dunbar blurs below me, the black warships bobbing and scarred and then gone, replaced by the sea.

The hatch clicks shut and seals me in the dark.

50

Nothing attacks me from the blackness. No sneering Black Agnes, though even I can't maintain the delusion that she'd wreck her encampment just to lure me in.

But what do I know? Leaders are a special brand of crazy.

The hum of the thrusters vibrates through my boots, muted in the warm interior of the jet. My eyes adjust to the darkness, a fringe of light bordering the closed door to the cockpit. The winch system is a cylindrical hump beside me, the sealed hatch invisible.

I straighten my legs, my joints creaking and slow.

I won't cower at whomever is in the cockpit but meet them standing, my gun aimed and steady. I should rush across and throw the door open, surprise them with a smile and a bullet.

My feet stay stuck to the floor. My throat clicks, loud in the quiet. A bead of sweat trickles beneath the constricting press of my vest.

I've lost the crushed round somewhere, a ragged hole exposing pale, dented nanocellulose.

The cockpit door hisses open. I squint at the blaze of white silhouetting a single figure. My gun jerks up. The barrel jitters, any shot likely to hit the plane rather than the person in the doorway.

I've barely slept, haven't eaten and am grieving. Give me a break.

The figure raises empty hands and steps into the cargo bay. The door slides shut. My breath hitches, my eyes blind. Bulbs glow on above the seats and harness straps lining both walls, bathing the space and destroying the shadows. Static fills my skull, déjà vu confusing my brain with a jumble of images—white sand, hot sun on my shoulders mixed into the now of droning engines and golden light.

My gun clatters to the floor. I blink stupidly at my hand. Raising my head takes a ridiculous length of time. I bury my fists in my eye sockets to banish the hallucination.

"You're not here. You're not real." My voice wobbles. "Are you real?"

The figure moves closer.

"I'm real, baby," Blake says. "I'm here."

I think he manages to catch me when I faint.

* * *

"I've never had a woman swoon in my arms before."

"I find that hard to believe," I say, curled in Blake's lap on one of the padded chairs bolted to the wall.

My gaze drinks him in—the beautiful eyes, all violet and cobalt-blue, the smirking curve of his lips, the fascinating hollow of his throat.

"You're staring at me again," he says.

"Get used to it. I'm not stopping."

I haven't kissed him yet. Haven't cried. I'm too afraid to climb his body and feast on his mouth in case the sudden movement shatters the illusion. I'll wake in Dunbar, bullet-riddled, my brain easing my death with an image of me in Blake's arms, safe and loved.

I shiver and he cuddles me tighter.

"I'm still here. Still real." He strokes a bedraggled curl of hair from my cheek, his expression soft. "I'm sorry it took me so long to get to you."

His own hair has dried in clumps from the salt water, his face pale. Dark circles ring his eyes and shadow his cheekbones.

"I didn't think you were coming at all."

"Your faith in me, it's touching."

"That's not what I meant." I swallow past the sudden lump in my throat.

Fainting in his arms is embarrassing enough but how will he react when he learns how quickly I collapsed into a rampaging, suicidal lunatic? The things I did in his name, like I did in my sister's name but way more bloodthirsty.

How many more people I've killed.

"They told me you were dead," I manage to whisper.

The tears finally overflow and I hide my face in my hands.

What would've happened if he'd arrived a couple of minutes later?

Don't think about it.

"Oh, Anita, I'm sorry," he says.

"I couldn't find you in the water. They locked me in a cabin. I heard—the gunshots." I bury my face in his neck and sob. *"They told me you were dead."*

He rocks me, his warm hand rubbing circles on my back. "They missed. I saw them drag you onto the warship. I climbed up the ladder and waited until it was quiet but as soon as I looked over the edge, some creepy kid spotted me."

Dead-eyes. The lying little bastard.

"I dived as deep as I could. By the time I surfaced, the boat was too far to catch up. I had to swim for the beach."

"Why couldn't I find you?"

"I was sucked into our warship as it sank."

My heart clenches. I scrub my swollen face and raise my head.

"Jesus. Did it take you to the bottom?"

He nods. "I used to think being alone with Wick was the most terrifying thing but that tops it. I was blind, cold, drowning. I only survived because the water swept me straight into a room and left me with an air bubble."

How did the current not hammer him into objects below-decks and shatter his bones?

My hands flutter over his shoulders, his chest, his ribs.

Internal bleeding? I need to palpate his stomach.

He smiles softly and captures my fingers, kissing each one. "Calm yourself, woman, I'm fine. Bruised."

"Say it again."

"What, I'm fine?"

"No, the woman part."

"Woman," he says. "*My* woman. God, I missed you."

I whimper and shift in his lap, one knee on either side of his hips, the remaining Browning in its holster digging into my thigh. I fist my hands in Blake's hair and claim his mouth. A shockwave blasts through my body, reconnecting severed nerves in a tingling rush. It jolts my heart and sizzles my skin.

Blake is *alive*. And, Christ, I want to fuck him so badly I can't breathe.

His hands grip my waist, pressing me to him, his erection straining against his combats and reducing me to a quivering mess. He stands, his fingers cupping my ass, and lowers us to the floor. The weight of him on top of me bows my spine, my moans spilling into his mouth.

The vest is too restrictive. I can't feel him or the thunder of his heart through it. I need his skin against mine, the sleek slide of his muscles.

"Naked," I pant. "We need to be naked."

He chuckles, trailing his lips down my jaw to where my pulse throbs like the rest of me. "You wanton little hussy. Don't you want to hear the rest of my story?"

His teeth graze my skin, driving eager noises from my throat. I bunch his long-sleeved t-shirt in my hands and pull it off. His two pairs of dog-tags scrape on my vest and settle on the divot over my heart. Blake smirks, propping himself on his elbows, his hair flopping into glittering eyes.

He seems to be waiting for something.

I blink at him. "Um, what was the question?"

His eyes darken, spearing me with his need.

"Fuck it," he growls. "It can wait."

I writhe underneath him and he shudders, collapsing on top of me. His hands tear at my clothes, ripping the straps of the vest. He tugs it over my head along with my top and tosses them aside. He pauses to stroke the red mark on my chest where the bullet hit.

"Does it hurt?"

"Not anymore," I say.

He makes a small, pained sound and kisses me until I'm dizzy. Our clothes disappear. I can't stop running my fingers over every part of him just to be sure he's real. He pins my hands to the floor, his grip frantic, his body trembling above me.

"Baby," he says, his smile tender, "you're killing me."

I whisper his name, again and again, my eyes blurred, our skin tasting of salt. He uses his mouth to shut me up, thank god.

I'm two seconds away from blurting out all sorts of soppy crap.

His touch vanquishes the lingering darkness and reminds me what I live for.

Him. I live for him.

51

Our plane hasn't reached landfall yet so it doesn't take me as long as it feels to gather the scattered pieces of myself together. I return to my body curled around Blake, my face in his neck, his thudding pulse slowing against my cheek.

"I think I may have passed out for a second."

He laughs, his fingers stroking my back. "You're welcome. You're not exactly quiet during sex but I've never heard you make those sounds before."

"Oh, Jesus."

"Close but so much more *guttural*."

I don't have to see his face to know he's smirking at me. I burrow into him and breathe in the scent of his skin. His wonderful, warm, so-very-alive skin.

"What are you grinning at?"

"You're really here."

"You're only realising this now?" he says, wriggling underneath me.

"I never thought I'd see you again."

First order of business if the rest of the world is normal— find an immortality pill and shove it down his throat. There is no way I can go through this a second time. Or is it the third, fourth? The guy has to stop almost dying on me. My heart can't take it.

"I had my doubts, too. Imagining what they were doing to you in Dunbar drove me crazy."

I clear my throat. "They, ah, didn't actually hurt me. Not physically."

"I overheard someone. They said you were catatonic. Were you pretending?"

My cheeks flush. I cuddle deeper into his neck to hide but he rolls me over and pins me, propping himself up to look down at my face.

"Anita?"

"I… Not at first."

His thumb brushes away fresh tears. "Tell me."

Christ, this is worse than recounting my torture. What do I expect him to do—recoil and say he can't be with such a cold-blooded murderer?

"They said you were dead and I broke. Pretty fucking immediately. But the bastards mocked you. And it was weak of me to wall myself off from the pain. It showed how much you meant to me."

He kisses me, a delicate glide of lips that leaves me trembling. The raw emotion on his face punches into my stomach.

"Woman, you make it so easy to love you."

I shake my head, somewhat desperately. "But, I unleashed the monster."

"I saw the craters, the smoke and the bodies." He quirks his mouth. "My vengeful warrior. No one's destroyed an encampment for me before."

"I killed hundreds of them. I wanted them all to die. *I* wanted to die."

"You promised you'd try not to."

"Not if you were dead."

My stomach flips at his slow smile. "It's terrifying, isn't it?"

"What, my psychotic obsession with you?"

He chuckles, capturing my hand and pressing it to his chest over the steady, glorious beat of his heart. "No. Love."

"Fuck, yes," I sigh. "How can you be so calm? You should've seen me, I was wrecked."

"Your version of wrecked can still decimate an encampment in my honour. And you didn't see me," he says, his lovely eyes haunted.

His hand shakes in mine. I cup his face and draw him down, kissing him until the sadness melts away. A tightness in my chest eases.

God, we've both fallen hard.

He gives me another devastating smile, trailing his fingers across my cheek and showing me the tear quivering on one tip. "You're crying again."

"Goddammit. I can't seem to stop."

"You're such a girl when you're not slaughtering people."

I manage the ghost of a laugh. Blake bends closer and my hand slides into his hair.

"I love you," he whispers against my lips, "vengeful monster and all. I'd destroy anyone who hurt you. *No one* gets to hurt you."

He crushes his mouth to mine. Lips, tongue, teeth, our hands trapped between our bodies and pounded by two frantic hearts. His leg slides across my waist, his groin pressed to my thigh. I tilt my hips, little whimpering noises in my throat.

He pulls away and gives me his sexy, knowing, makes-me-want-to-bite-him smirk. "You never want to hear my story."

"You should know never to talk to me when you're naked."

"My deepest apologies. Let me just—"

"Don't you dare move."

"You want me to tell you my story all slippery and naked?"

I gulp. "Yes, please."

"And then what?"

"Then I want more of you. Always."

"You and your one track mind."

He rolls over and pulls me with him, tucking me into his side. The floor of the jet vibrates against my hip.

Shit. I haven't even thought about where we're going, too dazed by relief and joy. Are we being followed? Will enemy planes shoot us from the sky and scupper our hopes like they scuppered our warship?

Blake doesn't seem concerned and he knows more about aerial strategy than I do.

I open my mouth to ask but get distracted by the bruise on his chest where the snake's head struck. My fingers trace it, slipping lower to the bulge of his abdominal muscles. I freeze at his chuckle and drag my gaze up, my cheeks heating.

I lick my lips. "How far until we reach land? Can Dunbar catch us?"

Nice save, you nympho.

"We're at the slowest cruising speed so less than an hour. And no, they're not coming after us. If you'd stop fondling me and let me tell my story—"

"All right, smarty pants. First, tell me how you escaped the warship."

"Smarty pants? That's a new one. Are you mellowing now that you're all hot for me?"

"I swear to god, Blake, I can still punch you in the chest."

His fierce grin plays havoc with my pulse. Thankfully, he starts speaking before I do something embarrassing, like swoon on him. Again.

"I thought the warship would crush me," he says and his face sobers. "The shrieking it made when it hit the bottom. It jerked me out of my air bubble and I panicked until I found it again. Our prisoners survived the drop. They banged on the walls but… They went quiet after a minute."

I shiver and hug him tighter.

What a horrible way to die. How close Blake came to joining them.

"The bubble let me know which way was up. I forced myself to explore the room—find the door, the corridor—always going back for air. I had no idea how to get out of the ship and once I left that bubble… Taking my last breath was the hardest thing I've ever done."

Thank god it wasn't his last.

"I swam blind, every second expecting my hand to touch that tentacled horror we saw on the screen. I found the hole by luck rather than memory. And I kicked like hell for the surface. Got confused when I felt air on my face, sucked it into my lungs, but everything stayed black." His mouth curves in a lopsided smile. "Came up under a box."

My breath rushes out in sympathy. "Christ, Blake. What happened when you got to the beach? How did you get into Dunbar? What kind of superhuman are you?"

"Just a normal human. Nothing special—"

"Not true," I murmur into his neck.

He kisses my temple. "The rest is a longer story."

52

Blake

In spirit, I sprint along the shore, keeping sight of the enemy warship.

I'll swim out as soon as it gets closer to land and kill the crew for daring to touch Anita.

In reality, I stumble out of the sea and collapse to my knees beside the meagre fire dwindling on the sand.

Common sense stops me from falling face-first into the flames to warm myself up. Only part of the cold is due to the water, the rest the lingering fear of being trapped in a sunken ship, waiting to drown or be eaten by a monster.

Give me Wick and his black eyes any day.

I hunch over the fire, the heat steaming my sodden clothes but doing little for my chattering teeth. Salt water dries and itches on my skin.

Unification Army has Anita. They can't keep her.

The bay stretches silent and dark, the reflection of the moon silvering the water. The pilothouse of the destroyed warship smoulders red, the wreckage a softly smoking shape against the blackness of the sea.

Her handiwork. My beautiful warrior.

Get off your knees and go rescue her then, tough guy.

I pant and shiver, the blood returning to my hands and feet in a biting rush.

The seconds settle on my shoulders.

What are they doing to her? Every goddamn man we've met on the road has tried to rape her. The soldiers in Dunbar will be no different. She'll fight them, fury sparking in her lovely eyes. They'll hurt her and break her until there's nothing left.

Can you growl and moan at the same time? Somehow, I do.

I push myself upright with a few curses at my weak muscles and take off down the beach towards the amber glow of Dunbar, more zombie shamble than athletic sprint. My bruised ribs struggle to expand, pulverised by the solid head of the snake. The squelch of my boots seems loud in the dead of night.

Who am I kidding? If there's anyone who can destroy an encampment by herself, it's Anita. I'll meet her crunching through the vegetation of no man's land in whatever vehicle she's commandeered, Dunbar a ruin behind her. My ego will pout but I'll throw myself into her arms to stop from crumpling at her feet.

I want to protect her. Hold her. Hell, I'm man enough to admit she does more of the rescuing but I don't care as long as she's safe. Unharmed. Trembling and dazed as I lower her to the ground and bury myself inside her.

I can't lose her.

My stomach clenches and I pick up the pace. The bay extends in a long, slow arc of white, ending in blackness nearer Dunbar. A warship ghosts across the water around the last curve of land.

Oh, crap.

I scramble for the sand dunes and throw myself into the marram grass, the blades poking at my face and hands, sharp enough to pierce the material of my long-sleeved top.

Can they see me on their topography scan—a green stick figure of a man cowering in the grass?

I curl into a ball and pretend to be a rock.

The deadly shape sails closer to its stricken sister. I wait for the spotlight to turn my hiding place into a blazing circle. It flickers on, highlighting the wreckage off its bow as it drifts to a halt. It's not the same warship that took Anita—it has double-barrelled turrets on the bow and stern instead of a cannon and a machine gun.

I scuttle through the grass on hands and feet, my arse in the air, hoping I resemble a stunted abomination instead of a stupid, shivering human.

Not exactly my most dignified pose but dead won't help Anita.

The dunes peter into a jumble of rocks, their jagged edges tinted grey by the moon. My boots stutter and scrape, the stones shifting and clattering under my weight. I hold my arms out, flapping at the air, preferring barked shins to battling through the tangle of vegetation bordering the coast.

There are too many things with sharp teeth. It's easier to spot a slinking shadow on the rocks. In the bushes, I'll be half-way down a creature's gullet before I realise what's happening.

A shape rears and I flinch, dropping into an unsteady crouch, my Browning in my hand. Nothing slashes at me from the dark. Claws resolve into the ruin of a ship.

Not one of Unification Army's.

I skirt around it, the night turning the twisted skeleton into muscled limbs, the glint of metal the glitter of an eye. I totter another few metres on the slippery rocks, jumping canyons of black.

A round stone humps out of the jumble, close enough to breathe on. The naval mine nestles among the smaller stones like a cuckoo's egg, hollow spikes bristling from its curved surface. The thick steel of the mooring cable snakes into the darkness. I back away, my teeth gritted and hurting my jaw.

Since it's broken from its mooring, the deactivation mechanism should make the mine harmless but who knows the effect of years of rust. The mine could be one accidental brush from exploding.

Screw blowing up, I'll face the beasts. At least I can shoot them.

Gun in hand, I push through the bushes above the tide line. Spiky arseholes, every one.

They end in a saltmarsh, the water level low enough to avoid slopping into my boots. Every step puffs brine and decaying vegetation into my nose. Unseen creatures scurry, an uncomfortable reminder of my first two months in no man's land, listening for the rustle as abominations gathered to eat me.

Sleeping in trees offered some protection, if you could call jagged three hour bouts of shut-eye, sleep.

But I'd do it all again for Anita.

That's me, a romantic. Just took me a while to get there.

I slog closer to Dunbar, skirting the wetter areas shining under the moonlight. The ground hardens to a meadow of waist-high grass. The bushes and rocks disappear, an unmarred expanse of beach curving to the orange glow of the encampment. I ease into a jog on the firmer ground above the pure, white sand instead of hurtling through the night, blind and deaf.

Faster. They're killing her!

Grass whips my combats, the sodden material chafing my thighs. Thudding footsteps, pounding heart. The landscape blurs. My muscles scream at me to slow down, my joints overextending as I stumble on the uneven ground, each shock jolting my spine. I sprint straight into a bush—no thorns, thankfully—and rebound on my arse. I slump on my back, panting at the stars.

My ribs politely remind me I was head-butted by a snake only a few hours earlier.

I try not to whine as I force myself up. Fail. I stagger into the clump of plants, the ground soft and shifting under my boots. I push through with increasing urgency, slim fronds slapping my face but better than a thorn to the eyeball.

I have to be close. Dunbar should be beyond the bushes. An hour, two, and Anita could be safe with me again.

But what am I forgetting?

I shove through a thicket, the vegetation thinning beyond, the tantalising promise of streetlights haloing the branches.

I slam to a stop.

You can't just stroll up to their fence, you idiot.

Scrambling backwards, I end up on my arse for the second time.

Why am I always on my arse or on my knees? This is getting embarrassing.

I hug my legs to my chest and make myself sit still, frustration building in my gut.

I can't go anywhere until dawn. All my knowledge of Dunbar's legendary warships doesn't mean squat. I have no idea what they use on their boundary fence—laser-cameras, buried mines? I could've blundered between the posts of a particle beam fence and puffed into ash.

How am I going to get past? Hide on the path to their main gate and wait for a vehicle heading in, hoping it'll halt long enough for me to cling to the undercarriage? This is real life not an action movie. I'd be a smear on the road as soon as it picked up speed.

Guy from *Die Hard* I am not.

Anita's favourite movie. So ancient and outdated, I barely remember what happened in it—tall building, bad guys, Christmas—but I'll watch it, over and over, if it makes her happy. If I can hold her in my arms and see the delight on her face.

I'm going nowhere for the next few hours. I need more information. I need *light*. Which means she stays in Dunbar the whole night. What will they do to her? An enemy who almost stole one of their prized warships. Beautiful, mouthy. A pain in the arse.

"Please don't die." My voice doesn't sound like my own. The words she whispered after she said she loved me. She *loves* me. "Please don't die, please don't die."

I find myself rocking on the sand. Snarling, I leap to my feet and pace, round and around in my little prison of bushes.

She's probably dead already.

Stop it.

Who knows how many pieces they've cut off of her.

I said stop it, you moron.

I prowl. I count my heartbeats, my breaths, the stars. I crouch and fist my hands in the sand when I can't bear it anymore. The wind sighs through the fronds. I alternate between shivers as my damp clothes dry and sickening heat, picturing what Anita is going through.

She's a prisoner again for the fourth time. Fifth? Do I count? She survived Wick's torture, brutalised but still breathing. Still fighting. Is she remembering it now? What must that be doing to her? What if Unification Army torture her? She's stronger than anyone I know but Wick's torture broke her. She'll carry the scars for the rest of her life, inside and out. How can she live through more? I'll arrive too late and find the shell of her body, her lovely eyes empty, her mind gone where no one can hurt her.

No one gets to hurt her.

I complete another bout of pacing, frantic enough to sculpt the sand. A ghostly shape glides overhead, an owl on the hunt. I wish I had its wings to soar into the encampment.

I can't lose another person I love. Dylan was bad enough. My cheeky, foul-mouthed little brother. It's ironic that the thought of Anita's death already feels worse than the reality of his.

I know he'd understand.

"Dylan, what am I going to do?" Yes, he's dead. Yes, I'm talking to myself. But it comforted me through the darkness of no man's land and it comforts me now. "Where the *fuck* is the fucking sun?"

Okay, perhaps he isn't the only foul-mouthed one. I blame Anita. The woman is a terrible influence on my vocabulary. Encouraging me to swear because it turns her on. The dazed look in her eyes, her breath catching in her throat. Gets me every time.

Oh god, how much longer?

The crescent moon disappears, the stars wink out. The

endless night seems hushed, a space between heartbeats. The landscape changes in one blink, grey leaching into the black, the suggestion of light on the horizon.

A tiny shape with a stuck-up tail scolds me from the bushes, the bird version of small guy syndrome. I crawl forward and it flits away. My stiffened joints complain, my muscles rigid. I rub a fist into my gritty eye and fill it with more sand.

I'm no stranger to sleepless nights before battles, during battles. Worrying about Wick, worrying about Dylan. No man's land. And now Anita.

I peer through the shadowed fronds towards Dunbar, praying I'm out of range of the scanning field of any laser-cameras. The bushes end fifty metres from the boundary fence, separated by a lopped strip of land.

Nowhere to hide.

Posts support horizontal lines of barbed wire, marked by the white glow of ring insulators.

Who still uses electric fences?

Nothing sits atop the posts.

I lower my forehead onto my dusty arm and huff out a breath.

What would I have done if they had laser-cameras, thrown rocks at them? I lack Anita's finesse. Shoot at them and alert the encampment? At least I can approach the fence, near enough to feel the static crackling, hear the wires humming.

If only I were as amazing as she believes, I'd leap it in one bound.

I need to get in. *Have* to get in.

Don't you dare have a panic attack, you pussy.

A few deep breaths ease the tightness in my chest.

I'll find a way. I have to. Everything will be okay.

And I thought Dylan was the optimist.

While the darkness lingers, I skirt the boundary, staying next to the vegetation line and darting for cover when sentries patrol on the other side of the fence.

They seem more concerned with talking and laughing than scanning the ground beyond the perimeter. Suits me fine. All I need is a gap. Sagging wires, a breach. Somewhere an animal has dug underneath. I'm slim—as Dylan often reminded me, the douche—I can fit.

I give the main gate a wide berth. My circuit terminates at the northern boundary where the electric fence ends at a harbour wall, the top ringed by a short particle beam fence.

They protect their warships better than the rest of their encampment.

I double back, nearer to the fence. Guards pass and I throw myself flat, pretending to be a hummock. Their voices fade. The purr of vehicles and the chatter of people rise in the encampment, the residents of Dunbar stirring themselves for a new day.

Did Anita survive the night?

I force myself closer. Ten metres. Five. Two seconds from stepping on a disturbed patch of ground, I dive away and, yup, land on my arse. Three rough circles run parallel to the fence, evenly spaced.

Replaced mines.

No doubt there are more, better disguised, all around the perimeter.

The sun crests the horizon, stretching my shadow to the west while I sit on my arse and frown at the fence. No gap, no way to reach it even if there was.

No way through.

I lurch to my feet and pivot on my heel.

I'll wait for a vehicle on the road to the main gate, shoot the occupants and take it for myself. And if none comes? Walk up to the gate and ask nicely?

Head down, fists clenched, I march into the glaring sunshine. Longer shadows greet me, a messy block of conifers I noticed the two times I passed through. Faint red crosses mark each trunk, as though they've been scheduled for felling but someone forgot.

It's stupid to leave them standing so close to their boundary, especially with an electric fence. One storm could topple them and damage it, even flatten—

I slap my hand to my forehead. "You *idiot*."

A pine cants towards Dunbar in the middle of the block, held aloft by the branches of its neighbours and another pine between it and the fence. I launch myself at it, pain flaring in my shoulder.

This is where I need Dylan's humongous arse.

Cones patter on the soft carpet of brown needles. I shove again, my boots slipping. Roots hiss out of the sandy soil, branches crunching as the pine shifts. I dart around the other side and jump, wrapping my arms and legs around the trunk as if I can wrestle it to the ground with my body. My cheek presses to rough, piney bark. The tree drops. Wood cracks. Metal twangs. I lose my grip and thud onto my back, the trunk looming over me. I scrabble out from underneath it. It leans across the boundary fence, caught on the upper wire, needles raining into Dunbar. One root anchors the pine and keeps it from rolling.

Holy crap, I did it.

I place my boot on the sloping trunk and ease myself onto

it, gripping it with trembling fingers. Metal squeals.

"This is a stupid idea," I whisper, my nails digging into the bark. Hand over hand, my feet shuffling behind, I climb the trunk. "A stupid, *stupid* idea."

Is wood an insulator? Or will it burst into flames as I approach the fence?

Hello, crispy Blake.

Maybe Anita will find me after she frees herself and curse my smoking carcass for breaking my promise.

Shimmying up a tree ramp to leap electric barbed wire probably goes against the trying not to die part.

I suck at rescuing women. Suck at terrorising them, too.

The tree bounces beneath me. Wires screech, sagging under the weight, the barbs tearing chunks of bark from the pine. I move faster, air whistling through my teeth. The hairs on my arms bristle. Wires hum, separated from me by a single hunk of wood. I reach the lowest branches, fighting through the clawing needles to get a little higher, a little further from heart-exploding, spine-snapping death.

The tree sways.

"Oh, Christ, please don't roll."

It rolls. I jump, snapping through branches obscuring my view of the perimeter.

Am I clear of the wires? Will the barbs bite my skin and check my fall a second before the electricity zaps me? Sentries will find my body entangled in the fence. A blackened husk with a rictus grin.

Ugly in death.

My boots hit the dirt. I slam onto my face, too shocked to attempt a fancy flip to dissipate the impact and put me on my feet.

Just as well I'm a self-assured guy. Or an arrogant son-of-a-bitch. Anita's words. Also beautiful, awesome and nearly perfect.

Those are my favourite.

I groan and inhale a mouthful of sand, pushing onto my hands and knees, needles pattering around me. A quick scan confirms no soldiers are hustling my way.

A barren waste ground separates me from a scrubby embankment and the buildings beyond. To the east, a long structure and patches of gorse hide the main gate. The tree lies canted against a steel post, smoke curling lazily with the scent of burning pine.

Homey.

I shuffle through the dirt, destroying my boot and face prints.

Maybe they'll think the tree fell by itself.

A spark pops on the electric fence, the first lick of flame crackling on the trunk. I pull creepy Gavin's blade and sprint for the embankment on tip-toes.

I must look ridiculous.

No cries of alarm chase me to the embankment. I dart up the shallow slope covered in bushes that smell like cat pee, skip across the disintegrated remnants of a railway line and crouch on the other side, huffing on leaves. The bottom abuts the back gardens of a row of semi-detached houses curving to the east and west. Weeds and grass obscure broken plastic slides and rusted play-sets, the remnants of a time when children were innocent and playful.

Now, they'll shoot you in the gut and watch you writhe.

Most of the windows are boarded or opaque with grime. Cracks snake up the brickwork, slabs of roughcast shattered onto broken paving slabs.

It reminds me of Livingston.

Not so homey but home all the same.

I slither over a low, chain-link fence, the wooden border rotted, and sneak through the grass to the side of the house. I crab-walk up the narrow, shaded space between the buildings and hide by the corner. A similar row of dilapidated houses faces me beyond a rutted mud road. East, a junction and another dirt road heads north towards the sea. West, the street curves out of sight in a line of forgotten, broken houses. A door opens across from me. I flatten myself to the side of the building.

I am a brick. You do not see me.

Bricks don't hold whopping big blades. I punch the ground trying to hide it, and swallow a curse.

Two men emerge from the house, AK-47s slung over their shoulders, the older man an ageing image of what the younger one will be in a few years. They swagger down the driveway in their camouflage uniforms.

"How long do you think she'll last?"

Anita. She's alive.

Or they have more than one prisoner.

The older man grunts. "I'd like to think long enough for me to toss a stone this time."

"You only have yourself to blame," the son says, clapping his father on the back. "You killed that guy straight out with a blow to the head and spoiled the fun. Your aim ain't what it used to be."

"That was ages ago!"

"We don't forget." Their voices fade as they march east. "Prepare for disappointment. I heard she's practically comatose—

a real looker—shame—"

Friendly banter, horrific in content.

I sag against the wall, sweating, shaking, the knife gripped so tightly, my knuckles are a jagged mountain range of bone.

"Motherfuckers," I whisper. "Motherfuckers, mother-*fuckers.*"

Anita would be proud.

What have they done to her?

I'll kill them all.

Bile stings my throat and lies bitter on my tongue.

They've tortured her in the few hours I was shackled by the darkness. Raped her.

I stuff my fist in my mouth to silence a moan.

But she's alive. It isn't hopeless. If I have to spend the rest of my life nursing her back, I will.

I peer around the corner of the house. The men walk past the junction, continuing east, soon to be out of sight in the bend of the street. I bolt into the rear garden and leap the fence, sprinting along the bottom of the embankment.

No one shouts to ask what the hell I'm doing.

Maybe they're all gathered for their stoning spectacle, the savages.

I stop at the last house, the embankment veering south-east. I crawl to the corner, gravel biting my palm and the fingers gripping the handle of the knife. The road is empty to the west, no more soldiers skipping along, buoyed by the prospect of watching Anita be battered to death.

I manage not to growl, the rage a painful pressure trapped in my chest.

The happy father and son reach a wide junction and approach the side of a huge, white building. A crowd mills at the base of the steps at the front, a wooden pole and a pile of rocks visible between their bodies. A hubbub of excited voices echoes off the pillars supporting the roof.

The *cunts*.

"Sorry, Dylan," I mumble.

Who am I kidding? He'd pat me on the back and tell me I'm finally a real man.

Stop talking to your brother and come up with a plan, jackass.

Anita is in the white building, waiting to be dragged out and tied to the post.

Practically comatose.

I shudder.

They'll pay.

But there are too many of them. More people join the mob, filtering in from the surrounding streets.

I need a vehicle. A tank. Something with a remote-controlled machine gun or cannon to mow them down. Or a diversion—a bomb, a grenade. I'll go a few blocks away and fire my gun in the air. Anything to draw them away before they hurt her.

Hurt her worse.

There's the growling-moaning sound again. I really must stop that.

I stagger to my feet and dart towards the first junction I saw.

Screw caution. *Hurry, hurry, hurry* pounds my skull as loud and hard as my heartbeat. If I meet anyone, I'll pretend to be one of them. Or I'll rip out their throats.

And Anita worries she's the monster.

We all have that beast inside us.

I run north up the road, dried mud puffing under my boots, my fingers numb around the knife. I dread the roar of the crowd.

Will I hear an awful whack when the first stone hits? Listen to her screams as the skin I've touched and kissed, bruises and bursts?

Not strong enough or fast enough to save her.

My flailing hand slaps the side of a building and stops me from falling. I bow my head and suck in air while I convince my stomach not to vomit.

I can't wait any longer.

I fumble for the Browning with my left hand. An explosion shakes the ground beneath my feet. My head snaps up. The surrounding barracks block my view but screams come from the direction of the white building.

The screams of more than one person.

"Anita," I breathe.

Practically comatose, my arse. My warrior won't go meekly to her death.

I have to help her.

Two steps back the way I came, a metal orb trundles along the street heading east. It pauses, swivelling towards me. I throw myself down a row between two squat structures and hide behind a wooden crate. Mud cracks. Something whispers like wind through grass. I hold my breath. A burst of gunfire rattles from the white building. The whispering fades.

There's no sign of the orb, whatever it was.

I step into the street. Two more rolling balls of death amble towards the ruckus without stopping.

"Get after her, you fucking cowards!" a female voice

screeches.

The infamous Black Agnes?

My face aches. I realise I'm grinning.

My woman is wreaking havoc. *Mine.*

Dunbar won't know what hit them.

I want to run in her direction, find her, scoop her into my arms—all defiant green eyes and stubborn jaw—and kiss her until we're both breathless. She'll make an eager noise in her throat and destroy my self-control. I'll forget everything but the slide of her skin on mine and the way she moans my name.

Reverently.

Okay, maybe not in the middle of a battlezone but as soon as humanly possible.

The need to see her, confirm she's unharmed, freezes me to the ground.

The best thing I can do is get us a vehicle Unification Army can't sink. She wants to escape to the rest of the world and I'll damn well get her there.

Turning away from her is the hardest thing I've ever done.

I sprint north. The road ends in a T-junction at a high wall topped by a line of mown grass. Beads of dew glisten in the morning light. A hint of landscaping in the tangled mess of the encampment.

Footsteps scamper from around the corner.

I press my back to the last building, my knife ready.

Whoever it is, they have to die.

A slim figure scuttles through the junction. Before I can sweep her leg and send her sprawling, she jumps back, hissing and glaring up at me. Air whistles through the gap in her front teeth.

Not knocked out in a fight or rotted away.

She's lost her baby teeth.

My balls shrivel.

I *hate* child soldiers.

Her AK-47, ridiculously large in her small hands, swings towards me, the rolled sleeves of her combat jacket flapping over her skinny forearms. I lurch forward, grabbing the barrel to keep it pointed away. One slice of the strap and I rip the gun free.

"You're fucking dead, dick-face," she snarls.

I stop myself from gasping, "*Language!*" and use the rifle like a bat, cracking it into her skull as she dives for me, her tiny, pink-painted fingernails ready to claw out my eyes.

Not that she'd reach.

She crumples to the road and my temple pulses in sympathy. The end of her ponytail trails in the dust. I bind her hands behind her with the strap of the AK-47 and carry her weightless body to the crate where I hid from the mystery orb.

Muffled explosions continue from the direction of the white building.

I tuck the girl out of sight and return to the wall. I toss her rifle up and follow it, heaving myself over the top and crawling onto the short grass, soaking the knees of my combats. The mown area stretches to the white sand of the beach beyond the boundary fence. Half of a stately building has collapsed into an old crater to the west. To the east, a strip of concrete runs to a small cluster of vehicles.

Hello, sweet jets.

Now I can stop acting like a whiny little pussy and do some damage of my own.

I scoop up the rifle and bolt for the airfield. Nothing moves in the hangers or between the ten planes parked on the tarmac.

52

Biofighter P-50s. The same model we had in Nationless. One of the best, as long as the cyanobacteria in the power cells behaves itself.

Dunbar has painted theirs as black as their warships. Each jet has six engines, including double thrusters on the end of each wing for vertical take off and landing.

I slide my hands along the smooth, carbon-fibre body and push the cockpit release button. The motor whines, the glass dome winking in the sun as it rises.

I have one leg in the cockpit, the other dangling outside, when more explosions rock the encampment. Dirty columns of smoke circle the white building hulking out of the smaller surrounding structures. Metal squeals, soldiers shriek. A rocket blazes a trail to the harbour next to the airfield. It hits a warship in a burst of flame. Smaller explosions rattle from the fire. The pilothouse shatters.

"That's right, baby. Make them pay."

Fine, so we stole one of their warships. They reacted as any faction would have. As Nationless and The People's Republic would have. But they took the woman I love and planned on stoning her to death.

I shimmy into the left hand seat of the two-seater cockpit, ignoring the helmet hooked to the back of the chair.

No high G-force manoeuvres required today. The cabin can be pressurised, like a passenger plane, the rear compartment able to carry twenty soldiers plus cargo.

The ground shudders under the Biofighter's wheels. Pops and bangs echo through the encampment. I force myself to concentrate on the controls instead of craning my neck to see.

I flick a switch and the console lights up. The engines roar, the throttle unlocking on the side-stick controller. As the jet works up to idle speed, I perform my pre-flight checks and scroll through the screens on the control panel. Weapons stocked and engines at maximum capacity.

At least Unification Army take pride in their vehicles. Legendary warships, perfect planes.

I've missed the sky.

A green light flashes on the instrument panel.

Good to go. Almost.

I slither out of the cockpit. Creepy Gavin's knife dices the tyres of the other Biofighters. A clod of turf in the nitrogen filter grounds them completely.

No one is flying in to ruin our escape this time.

Back in my jet, I palm the side-stick and engage the vertical thrusters. The Biofighter eases into the air, the ground dropping away. I turn the nose from the sparkle of the sea and point it at the white building. The wheels clunk into the body. I push the side-stick forward. The thrusters swivel, the engines firing in the rear. The jet glides over Dunbar and the smoking vehicles, crumbled bricks and bodies in the street.

Closer. *Closer*.

Please, let her be okay.

My heart bounds into my mouth. A figure crouches behind a metal unit on the roof, firing at soldiers approaching from the wreckage of an access door. A wild tumble of blonde hair. Breasts.

Hello, baby. Breaking hearts and kicking ass, as usual.

God, I love her.

She sprawls backwards. I almost nose-dive the Biofighter into the front of the building, my teeth clamped on a howl of her name. I fight the harness and strain to see past the stupid blurriness in my eyes.

Moving. She's moving.

My breath whooshes out. I slump in the seat, my trembling hand guiding the jet above the roof and mantling over her like a huge bird of prey.

Mine. She is *mine*.

Three soldiers clamber through a jagged hole onto the roof. They don't even glance at me.

Their mistake.

I toggle my missiles and press a button on the side-stick. Using a screen on my console, I guide the short-range rocket at the advancing men. They disappear in a puff of fire and smoke, stones clattering across the roof and fracturing a swathe of solar panels. The breach collapses into a pile of rubble.

I slap the hatch release button and switch to my cameras. An image of the roof below me flickers on one of my screens. A rope ladder unfurls. Anita blinks at it, still on her back, a Browning in her hand. I wait for her to get up.

And wait. Wait some more.

"Come on, woman. Get off your arse."

Being this close to her but unable to touch her, talk to her, kills me.

Is she injured?

I jerk forward in my seat, the harness crushing my ribs, and press my nose to the screen.

No blood. A bulky shape on her torso. Bulletproof vest? Her face is pale and streaked with dirt, her clothes no better. Her eyes are dull, reddened, but she's in there, tired not empty. Not broken. Dried salt clumps her hair.

She's beautiful all the same.

She rolls into a crouch and peers around the metal unit. She tilts her face towards the hatch and stares at it. Air from the thrusters dances her hair around her head.

Maybe she doesn't realise it's me. Who else has the skills to swoop in and save her? Not that she needed much saving.

I swear, the woman can fight her way out of anything.

I flick through the cameras to make sure no one on the ground is aiming an anti-aircraft missile at us. Soldiers scurry in the streets, battalions forming and entering the building. Jeeps gather but no one points at my jet and shrieks, "Impostor!"

Yet.

Anita throws herself at the ladder.

Thank god I'm sitting down or I would've been on my knees with the relief. Or my arse.

Technically, I'm already on my arse.

Am I babbling?

I switch the thrusters to vertical. Machine guns and missiles ensure there won't be enough soldiers left to take pot-shots at Anita clinging to the ladder. I point the Biofighter for the blue salvation of the sea and punch the winch to bring my woman home.

<h1 style="text-align:center">53</h1>

Blake's heart beats steadily under my ear, matching mine in the hush of the jet.

This man who fought hard and risked himself to find me in an enemy encampment. The person who obliterated his home and killed his brother. He deserves to know everything. I don't need to hide or run anymore.

Not from him.

"I needed saving," I whisper to his collarbone, "from myself."

He strokes my hair, our dog-tags tangled on the smooth planes of his chest, my fingers tracing the violet bloom of his bruise.

I'll match him in a few hours, a separate pulse throbbing where the bullet struck my vest.

"Worried about your monstrous tendencies?"

I jerk my head. "I was going to let them kill me."

"Let them? Looked like you weren't quite done teaching them a lesson."

"I was almost out of ammo. The woman shot me. Getting up seemed like too much effort. If you'd taken a minute longer, you would've been too late."

The images flood my brain—the soldiers from the breach overpower me but I welcome the end of my pain. Blake swoops in to find me dying. He cradles me in his arms and whispers my name. My soulmate returned from the dead. The realisation that if I'd fought on for a heartbeat more, we would've been reunited. My bleak final moments, hearing his voice break, watching him press his shaking fingers to my wounds, trying to stem the bleeding. His anguish the final thing I see before I die, leaving him lost and alone on the roof in Dunbar.

He cuddles me closer to the frantic pounding of his heart. "Promise me you won't do that again. You can't stop fighting. I'll come for you, always."

"I thought you were dead."

"Even if I am dead, you have to keep fighting."

"I can't—"

"I'm not worth dying over."

"Don't be ridiculous."

He chuckles. "How is it ridiculous to not want you to kill yourself?"

"Because I can't live without you," I say in a rush.

It's the terrifying, unvarnished truth. All the shields I've built, the vows I made after Gizzy to protect myself, crumbled to dust the moment Blake touched me. This man I've known for mere days has the power to destroy me.

But I trust him not to.

His body stills underneath me.

Crap. Maybe it is a tad melodramatic. Or obsessive. Desperately needy. Why isn't he saying—

He rolls and pins me. I forget to breathe, as usual.

"Woman, you are the best thing that's ever happened to me." He cups my face, his thumb skimming my cheekbone. "And the worst."

53

Of course I'm the worst thing. I left a trail of ruin through his life and trapped him into loving me, my face a daily reminder of all he's lost.

A tear wells and scorches a path to my temple. "Then how—"

"You never let me finish. You're the worst thing because the thought of you hurt or dead is worse than losing Dylan. And that is very painful to admit. Please don't tell my mother."

Holy fuck. The thought of him hurt or dead is worse than losing Ailsa.

Sorry, Ailsa.

I laugh through another damn crying jag.

The guy turns me into a blubbering idiot.

I pretend I'm a confident, mouthy bitch and not a twittering female who dissolves every time he says something nice to me.

"In that case," I say, "I retract my earlier statement."

Blake cocks an eyebrow. His version of haughty. "You've decided you can live without me now?"

"No, you asshole—you *are* perfect."

"A perfect asshole? Such flattery."

I fist my hand in his hair, pulling his mouth to mine. He makes a noise low in his throat and deepens the kiss. He tilts his hips and I suddenly remember we're naked.

Wonders never cease.

I arch into him, always so eager. We probably should be steering the jet, scanning for land, discussing a plan, but it pales in importance to the weight of Blake above me, the slide of his body against mine.

And he calls *me* a wicked temptress.

He teases me, the tip of him barely inside me, the slow roll of his hips driving me gloriously insane. I writhe underneath him, swollen, aching, choking on need and the wild throb of my heart.

"Blake, *please.*"

He smirks, his arms shaking where he props himself up. "I know, baby."

I whine and try to wriggle closer. He continues his punishing rhythm, watching me while I blink and squirm and moan.

Speakers in the wall of the plane crackle. "Unidentified aircraft, you are not authorised to enter this airspace. Divert your course."

Blake jumps, losing his grip on the floor, and collapses into me, thrusting himself deep.

It's probably unintentional.

My body doesn't care.

I explode and tighten around him, dragging him with me into the most intense orgasm I've ever experienced, despite the interruption.

He pants into my neck. "Jesus Christ, that was not how I meant for it to go."

I manage a groan.

"Unknown Biofighter, you are in Danish airspace. Identify yourself." The voice circles through several different languages, each as indecipherable as the last.

I rediscover the power of speech. "Do you think they'll shoot us down if we don't respond?"

"Best not risk it."

We scramble for our clothes.

<h1 style="text-align:center">54</h1>

"Unidentified Biofighter, you have thirty seconds to respond. Interceptor jets have been dispatched." An accent mellows the voice, the words thick enough to swallow.

Blake and I stumble into the cockpit, our clothes in disarray, the sun blinding through the bubble of glass.

Little time has passed despite the weight of events. I was ready to die, a vengeful wraith, my journey ending in blood and dust instead of salvation. I'm struggling to keep up with reality, Dunbar hundreds of miles behind us, Blake alive and perfect and as crazily in love with me as I am with him. Contact from the outside world. Someone is *there*. Not a savage who immediately shoots us down without warning but a human being.

Can you go into shock from too much joy?

Blake half-falls into the seat on the left, the button of his combats undone. A control panel of levers, dials and flashing lights fills the front of the cockpit, data scrolling on multiple screens. I lift an AK-47 from the remaining seat and take its place, copying Blake as he straps himself into the harness.

"Unknown aircraft, you will be intercepted in fifteen seconds. Identify yourself and state your intent."

The blue of the sea sparkles below us, a strip of green

expanding on the horizon.

Land—foreign land.

Untouched by war or just another cesspit waiting to poison us?

I grab Blake's hand. He flashes me a smile.

How anxious do I look?

"You might need to let me go so I can answer the nice man, Anita."

"Hell no, I'm not letting go. Maybe in a few years when I know you're not going anywhere."

His smile softens. "I'm definitely not going anywhere."

An alarm bleeps on the console, a screen flashing to a radar display. Two bright blips close on our position.

Oh god, it's another awful repeat—our glorious escape thwarted by the missiles of a fighter jet. Nowhere to run, our plane a twisted fireball plummeting into the sea.

Why do I deserve a life while the rest of my country fights and dies?

What a fool.

"Ease up on the hand before you break my fingers," Blake says, grimacing.

I relax my grip, tension singing in my joints. "I'm sorry. Sorry for dragging you into this. My stupid idea is about to get you killed."

"Still no faith in me. I have feelings, you know." He leans forward, tugging on my hand clamped in his to flick a switch on the console. "Controller, this is the unidentified Biofighter. We are from Scotland and we mean you no harm. All we want is refuge. We await your instructions."

A hysterical giggle bubbles in my throat. "You make us sound like aliens. We come in peace, zoop zorp."

54

Blake chuckles and squeezes my hand. "It's an open channel. He can hear what you're saying."

"Ah, fuck. I mean, shit. I mean—" I slap a palm over my mouth.

Blake shakes in his seat, his lips pressed tight together. Laughter expands in my chest.

This seems like the wrong way to respond to the threat of two fighter jets and a distant voice that has the power to doom us. Maybe we've finally cracked under the pressure, the stakes too high.

A polite throat-clearing distracts me. "Biofighter P-50, please repeat. You are from Scotland?"

Details solidify on the approaching land-form. A beautiful white beach stretches into a flat expanse of green. Two grey shapes zoom towards us in the clear blue sky.

"That's right, controller. Two refugees from Scotland."

A pause. "Are you sure?"

Blake's eyes meet mine, his brow raised.

Has no one else made it *ever?* We can't be the only ones who decided to run for it. Maybe they washed up in a different country and communication of news is still in the dark ages following the internet collapse and whatever other catastrophe befell the rest of the world to keep them so quiet.

As long as they have hot water and comfy beds, I don't give a rat's ass.

Two jets streak past, disappearing between one blink and the next.

I jump at the blast of noise. "Holy fuck!"

"Anita, he's still listening," Blake says, his voice high. Definitely laughing at me. "Yes, controller, we're sure."

I stuff my fist in my mouth. Blake grins at me and I stop

myself from climbing into his lap.

The land blurs below, the sea whisked behind us.

Excitement curls in my stomach.

They're less likely to shoot us down and risk civilian casualties.

Unless they're at war and don't care one bit.

I scan for craters, smoke, bullet-pocked buildings but the ground zips by too fast.

"Biofighter, please proceed behind the Royal Danish Airforce F-35s. Land where they indicate. You will be met by police and the Home Guard. You must relinquish any and all weapons."

"Copy that, controller."

"Thank you, Biofighter. Controller, out."

Blake flicks the switch on the console, his hand clutched in mine, my fingers numb. He slumps in his seat, his breath whooshing out.

I gape at him. "Are we—did I—he's letting us *land?*"

"Baby, he's letting us land and rolling out a welcome party."

"They could be at war and are just more civilised than us. We'll be prisoners as soon as they take our weapons."

"Doubt it. They would've shot us down." He pulls me closer across the small gap separating our seats, his hand cupping my head. "Welcome to the free world."

He kisses me and I melt into him, straining against my harness. My mind whirls despite the tantalising press of his lips.

The free world. Are they peaceful and safe? Can we have a normal life, a normal relationship?

Jesus Christ, Blake could be my boyfriend.

Do people still have boyfriends?

His mouth curves and he eases away. "Quit thinking so hard."

Is he my boyfriend?

Don't you dare ask him that!

"What if I don't want to give up my gun?" I mumble instead.

His fingertips trace the blush on my cheeks. "The price of peace."

Engines screaming, the F-35s return to flank us, the Danish flag a splash of red and white on the tail of the jet off my wing. The pilot salutes from the bubble of his cockpit, an elephantine helmet hiding most of his face.

A dignified soldier would return the salute or respond with a sage nod of the head.

I wave so hard it hurts my wrist, grinning like an idiot.

"Making friends already?"

I turn my grin on Blake and he matches it. My heart surges.

God, he was worth it, worth everything I've suffered and lost since it brought me to him. Worth the wrenching grief and sickening fear at the thought of his death.

But death is on the distant horizon instead of chasing us through the shadows. Now, perhaps, we can really *live*.

We race over the land, the F-35s pulling ahead. Houses sprawl among the green. Blake taps at the console with his free hand and grips what looks like a computer joystick beside his seat.

"Can you fly this plane one-handed?"

He smirks. "Of course."

The jets bank and he follows, smoothly adjusting our speed and height. The residential area gives way to agricultural fields. The F-35s circle, dipping their wings over the same patch of green split by the straight line of an unfenced road.

The field is huge, and empty.

Blake tuts. "They obviously don't know I could land this thing on a roof. Time to blow their minds."

Our plane rocks, tipping its wings to the other pilots. The jets peel away and resume their circuit at a distance. We slow to a sudden, spectacular hover, the vertical thrusters swivelling to hold us aloft. A clunk signals the lowering of the landing gear. I bounce in my seat, my free hand gripping the edge. We drop steadily, the field expanding until I can see blades of grass flattened and dancing in the down-draft of the engines. A soft jolt and we settle on the ground.

My breath rushes out. "You are fucking *amazing*."

"About time you appreciated my skills. Does this mean I'm better than you?"

Blake flips switches on the console, the thrusters powering down with a whine. The dust of our landing drifts into the field.

"At flying. And maybe boats. And fine, the sex, too."

He raises my hand and kisses my knuckles. "You always sell yourself short."

The glass of the cockpit hisses open, warm air smelling of grass and burnt candles pouring in. Our escort roars overhead. Sirens wail in the distance.

Not warning sirens in the depths of an encampment but emergency vehicles speeding towards us.

I hope.

"When did you last hear a vehicle with a siren?"

I shake my head. "Years. It's not like we wanted to announce ourselves. Except for John Anders and his ludicrous WarCrier."

"I hate that guy."

"Such a dick."

More grinning stupidly at each other. My cheeks ache, giddiness fizzing through my veins.

This is true happiness, me and the love of my life in the land of the free. Or is that America? What is Denmark the land of, pastries?

It doesn't have quite the same ring to it.

"You ready to accept they're normal, yet?"

"Nope. I want to see where they live and whether they shove a gun in my face."

"I'm glad you haven't lost your optimism. They probably will point guns at us at first."

"If that's all they do then I'll accept it."

Blake stands, shaking my hand linked in his. "Let me go so I can help you out."

I pout at him.

"Only for a few seconds, I promise."

"You're lucky I trust your promises."

His expression does crazy things to my pulse. "You trust me?"

"With my life."

He grips my face and captures my mouth.

If I weren't sitting, I would've melted into the chair.

Blake vaults out of his side of the jet and leaves me dazed and blinking. His boots thud on the field. I fumble with the harness and lurch to my feet, wobbling at a wave of light-headedness.

"Easy, Anita. I'm right here."

He smiles up at me from the ground on my side of the plane, the tender smile that means I've done something endearing. Generally present when I babble about how great he is. Or panic when he's out of my sight for a millisecond.

How embarrassing.

I perch on the edge of the cockpit and roll, the metal biting into my stomach. Blake guides my boots into the footholds and catches me, swinging me around into a tight hug, his nose buried in my hair.

"Listen," he whispers. "No explosions. No gunfire."

The jets thunder across the sky. The sirens swell, a few fields distant.

We have seconds to enjoy the solitude before a swarm of humanity descends on us.

We step away from our plane and turn to face them, two soldiers—no, *survivors*—granted refuge in the dust of an unfamiliar country.

What the hell will our future look like once the initial hubbub has subsided? How will we adjust from fight or die to living? Will boring, glorious normality be the same as I remember it or something new?

"I can't believe we made it. Are you sure this is real?"

"Baby," Blake says, slinging an arm around my shoulders, "this is as real as it gets."

Let Me Know What You Think!

Thank you for reading my book! I love hearing from my readers so please leave me a review.

Can't wait to hear from you!

For a free prequel to *The Faction War Chronicles,* you can also join my mailing list at nadinelittle.com/free-prequel by scanning the QR code below:

Love Blake? Read the Novella: *Nationless Will Fall*
Discover how Blake survives the annihilation of his faction and what he really thinks when he first meets Anita.

Buy the Finale: *Homecoming*
Why did the rest of the world fall silent? And will Anita ever find her place in it?

About the Author

Nadine Little lives in Scotland and is an ecologist with an interest in botany. She writes science fiction and fantasy in her spare time when she's not reading or playing *Fortnite* on her PlayStation.

The year 2020 seemed the perfect time to publish her debut trilogy *The Faction War Chronicles* since it all went to hell. Sometimes she worries that people will look at her differently.

But not really.

You can connect with me on:
- https://nadinelittle.com
- https://twitter.com/Nadine_Little_
- https://www.facebook.com/nadinelittleauthor

Subscribe to my newsletter:
- https://nadinelittle.com/free-prequel